# HOLIDAY SPIRIT

## JOHN DEGUIRE

**Holiday Spirit**
by John DeGuire
Copyright January 13, 2023
by John DeGuire

TXu002370053

*"Sometimes standing against evil is more important than defeating it. The greatest heroes stand because it is right to do so, not because they believe they will walk away with their lives. Such selfless courage is a victory in itself."*

N.D. WILSON, DANDELION FIRE

# CHAPTER 1

Dusk crept into night as the trick-or-treaters scuttled and scampered through leaf-laden streets. Miniature zombies, pirates, witches, and ghosts, not to mention the endless parade of capes and crowns, rang and banged doors holding outstretched bags and hollow plastic pumpkins. Clamoring to get to the good houses first before they turned out the lights. Chocolate twists and turns and gummy worms. No apples nor popcorn balls lest a razor influence your taste. Never anything that wasn't wrapped and vacuum-packed in a hermetically sealed Chinese factory.

Few dared make the trip up the long walk at the end of the road which led to the old woman's house. They teased the old woman every chance they got and made it clear to anyone and everyone that she was a witch. A "bitch witch," they would say as they laughed, threw rocks, and ran away. The old woman kept quiet and chose to keep to herself in hopes of avoiding any further conflict. Children can be so cruel.

On that particular Halloween Eve, the old woman at the end of the road filled one of her grandmother's ornate serving bowls with the best Halloween candy that she could find and afford, even though she knew there wouldn't be any trick-or-treaters again this year. She left her outside lights on and had several carved pumpkins illuminating the pathway up to her doorstep. She had placed several peel-off

7

bat silhouette stickers on her window in celebration of the autumnal mood. She just wanted a small bit of social camaraderie and celebration with her neighbors on this All Hallows' Eve. It was, after all, her favorite holiday of the year.

As the sun grew dim and was mimicked by the fireplace in her hearth, the old woman finally nodded off in her recliner while reading an old tome. Finally, there was a knock at the door and a ring of the bell. Until now, she hadn't realized how old and creepy her doorbell sounded echoing through the foyer. It's no wonder the kids were skittish. She hopped up out of her chair and checked herself in the mirror on the way to answering the door.

Her costume was that of an old witch, just like last year, and the year before. She was getting too old to do anything but recycle Halloween costumes. Not a sexy witch. Nor an expensive period piece witch ensemble. Just a simple old witch costume worn over her pajamas since she planned on going to bed after the trick-or-treaters had dispersed for the evening.

She opened her door with exuberance at the sight of the children's costumes and held out the candy-filled antique container. Suddenly, from the back of the group of children, a hail of raw eggs were thrown at the poor old woman, smashing all over her face and torso.

Shocked and dismayed, the old woman dropped her grandmother's heirloom and it shattered with shards of porcelain and candy flying everywhere. She fell to the ground as the assault of eggs and now rocks continued to rain down upon the bloodied elderly woman, smashing windows and her temporary solace.

"Bitch witch! Bitch witch!" they shouted as they scooped up the candy remnants on the ground around her, ignoring her pain and needs despite her cries for help. She lay there on her front porch bruised and bloodied, listening to the laughter of children fade away down her street.

Slowly, the old woman crawled onto her feet and looked at her broken windows and the pieces of the bowl, the one memory of her grandmother she had left. She quietly moaned and groaned, which turned into a giggle. Her giggle turned into laughter, which then crescendoed into hysterical cackling. The inside joke was turning out.

"Those precious little devils don't know how right they were the first time." The old witch chuckled and spat and squealed, wiping the blood, spittle, and egg off her face, all the while planning her revenge. She was, in fact, an actual witch. An honest-to-goodness practitioner of the dark arts, a purveyor of the impure, the Wiccan custodian of evil malignant supernatural powers.

Just then another child, dressed as a ghost, appeared at the front doorstep of the witch's house and said, "Trick or treat!"

The old, haggard witch leaned in close to the tiny ghost face and whispered, "Trick."

# CHAPTER 2

The wicked witch had a name, just like everyone else. She was Bridgett Bishop, named after her great-great-great grandmother who was persecuted and hanged in 1692 for being a witch. Her ancestor was accused, tried, and found guilty of numerous instances of "sundry acts of witchcraft" as well as having a third supernumerary nipple and was hanged by the neck till dead. She was just the first to be executed during the Salem witch trials.

Of the two hundred people who were tried, nineteen were hanged and one compressed to death by rocks, a process known as *peine forte et dure*. The official legal record of this lawful process reads, "The guilty shall be remanded to the prison from whence he came and put into a low dark chamber, and be there laid on his back on the bare floor, naked, unless decency forbids; that there be placed upon his body as great a weight as he could bear, and more, that he hath no sustenance, save only on the first day, three morsels of the worst bread, and the second day three draughts of standing water, that should be alternately his daily diet till he died, or, till he answered."

It took Giles Corey three days to die. Truth be told, he probably couldn't speak even if he wanted to after having his torso crushed on the first day. To date, it is the only recorded case in American history whereby court procedures executed someone by this means.

Bridgett had heard the stories handed down in whispers from

generation to generation. She didn't need a DNA test to know that she came from a long pedigree of witches. Her mother, grandmother, and on and on as far as she knew.

Women were not allowed to own land and became wards of the town, which was not always met with good intentions. They lived modestly as best they could given the communal restraints of the time.

When Bridgett was just a small girl, she remembered being teased and bullied because she was poor and different, a doubly troubling combination. The locals had always discredited her and her mother's oddness as some form of familial mental illness. They just hoped that it wasn't contagious.

Bridgett had no real friends to speak of growing up, so she was left to form a meaningful bond with the earth itself and share in the secrets that it held. Her mother taught her their Druidic ways and heritage, as best she could. Bridgett developed the tenacity to survive, and although times were often tough, she had learned the importance of family and the loving support that came with it.

Both mother and daughter had an unspoken bond, which they shared with her grandmother as well. Bridgett also had two sisters slightly older than she whom she loved dearly. They were a coven of witches, representing several generations. They shared magics and dinners, successes and failures, and pitched spells and bewitched unruly neighbors. That was before the Dark Days.

She remembered playing as a child on the floor of their one-room abode. The windows were open on that bright, beautiful sunny day, letting in a cool breeze to combat the stifling summer heat. She played with twigs and sticks forming different shapes on the dirt floor of her house. What started off as jackstraws turned eventually into some playful Wiccan puzzle. It was just a healthy form of meditation was all.

Soon it was Halloween in the Northeast, a gorgeous fall season of shedding leaves and garnishing costumes. Bridgett shared it with the neighborhood children by bobbing for apples, singing songs, and eating delicious little cakes baked up by some of the local women. Truly it was a special time for Bridgett as she finally felt as though she belonged there, laughing with the other children happily and staying up and playing after dark. Halloween was her favorite holiday. At least it was the only one that she didn't try to forget.

It was only a few short weeks after that Thanksgiving came to town, the next day of celebratory festivities. This particular year was different, however. Bridgett was playing on the floor by the open window as usual, but outside the menfolk of town were working hard and diligently on the structure while the womenfolk watered and fed them.

Bridgett remembered hearing the solid pounding of the nails into the sweet oaken beams, the scent of which wafted through her window. Above the newly cut smell of wood arose the heavenly odor of freshly baked bread. It made her mouth water she was so hungry. Bridgett felt sorry for them working so hard in the heat of the day and hoped that they didn't get sick. They were her friends and neighbors after all.

At dawn the next morning everyone in town gathered around the scaffold to watch as Bridgett's grandmother, mother, and two young sisters were hanged while she hid under a nearby porch watching. The sun was directly in front of her so that the glare was interrupted only by the silhouette of her family's legs swaying back and forth out of sync like windchimes in a hurricane. It was Thanksgiving Day.

She started to scream but quickly compartmentalized her horror and sorrow into a tiny little box in the corner of her mind. Bridgett had narrowly escaped with her life. She was smuggled out of town in the cover of night during the darkest of days by the local vicar and his wife and four children. But she lived. The rest of her family wasn't so lucky.

Bridgett stayed with her new family in a settlement a few towns away and did her best to blend in with her unfamiliar sisters and brothers. They were Rigley, Ezra, Bocephus, and Persephone Van Helsing, and they seemed to accept their new stepsibling with open arms. Or as Ezra put it, "The Bible says that we should be nice to everyone, even people we hate." She was trying her best to adapt to her new surroundings and was grateful that she had escaped by the skin of her teeth. Or so she thought.

Christmas Eve was thirty short days after her precious loved ones had suffered the ultimate judgement by a jury of their peers and dear neighbors. Everyone knew where everyone was that night of the year: at home, with their families. It was a night when unsavory business could be conducted without interference.

Bridgett sat around the modest Christmas tree with the vicar Van Helsing and his wife and children singing carols in a language she was unfamiliar with to a barrage of innocent giggles. There came a knock on the door of the cabin that was their home. The vicar's children were shocked and looked at each other in disbelief. Surely the giver of gifts didn't come round this early in the eve, as it hadn't been dark for too long even though days and lives grew shorter that time of year.

Suddenly, the door smashed in and several men with axe handles burst into the room. They all wore gunny sack masks with eye holes cut crudely into place. Bridgett thought for a second that they had their holidays mixed up.

The first was dressed in all fur from his head to his toes, except for his sack mask with an extra hole for his nose. His eyes—how they twinkled with hate and with fury, and his protruding nose dripped snot in a hurry.

The second brute was all hunched with small hands like a troll that clenched a parchment rolled up in a scroll. "By order of the Servants of Justice, Bridgett Bishop has been found guilty of witchcraft and consorting with the devil. We hereby pronounce sentence upon you. May God have mercy upon your soul."

With that, the third and fourth vigilante grabbed Bridgett by each arm and threw her face-first into the corner Christmas tree and proceeded to cut green branches from the Noble fir. She was whipped mercilessly across her back and front, including her face.

The short troll man had broad shoulders and a round, plump, full belly that shook when he laughed as he whipped her skin into jelly. He was chubby and plump, a right jolly old elf, and Bridgett laughed when she saw him and then shit herself. Then they switched to the axe handles and beat her even worse.

The vicar's children laughed gleefully at the evening's entertainment, which was Bridgett's pain. She just lay there bleeding, fading in and out of consciousness, looking up at the tree with the shiny homemade star atop.

The leader whistled to gather the men. The frenzy subsided and that was when, with a wink of his eye and a twist of his head, they gathered their things leaving Bridgette for dead. As they exited the room, justice served with a might, one yelled, "Happy Christmas y'all, and have a good night."

The vicar Van Helsing's family went about celebrating their Christmas around Bridgett's almost lifeless body as if nothing had happened. Business as usual. Why should they sacrifice their fun just because they had befriended the wrong person? And a witch no less.

But Bridgett had survived yet again. The bad penny that wouldn't go away.

After everyone went to bed, Bridgett snuck out of the cabin, bloodied and beaten, and made her way into the forest which became her new home. She eventually matured into the witch of the woods. The sylvan she-devil. The evil enchantress that fireside stories were made of to dissuade bad children from bad behavior.

Really just a rumor more than anything. A hushed whisper lest she hear you.

The now grown witch Bishop noticed that she was getting so worked up that the vein in her forehead was ready to pop, so she tried to calm herself. Deep breaths. Let it out slowly. Her head and heart were about to explode with dread and death wish. No more.

Bridgett thought back throughout history and was reminded of all the practitioners of witchcraft who were tortured and murdered just for being themselves, as well as those who were simply accused of said practices. Dorothy Good was only four years old in 1692 when she was found guilty of practicing witchcraft by a court of law and sent to prison. From the Greek Circes to the biblical witch of Endor to the Salem witch trials, Wiccans had always been persecuted and killed for their beliefs. Even in Vermont. Killington, Vermont. Her chosen home away from.

She'd fallen in love with the Northeastern seaboard and Vermont in particular. Killington was an outdoor paradise nestled in the lap of the Green Mountains. It possessed a charming natural beauty with colonial architecture and bucolic farm-to-table restaurants. It was also home to folklore and legends. And monsters.

Its population of fourteen hundred was just right for a small-town girl like Bridgett. Summer trails and winter walks lent their ears to the earth's voice. The Wiccan was mistress to the land as soon as she stepped foot, or rather jumped in feet first. But Vermont still had a rich history of misgivings and injustice toward her fellow worshippers of Mother Nature. Sink or float.

Even a century past the end of the Salem witch trials, her brethren had been legally put to death. This made Bridgett all the more furious and vengeful. For the most part, she had tried to stay low-key and blend in undetected with her community, but everyone has a breaking point. Today, the people of Killington were enjoying another spectacular fall foliage concerto on a beautiful autumnal day. *I'll fix that*, she thought.

She had simply had enough. They caused her loneliness. She tried to be good. They broke the dam, now they get the flood. And it was long overdue. It was time for some payback, and she swore with absolute resolve to indulge in this monstrous undertaking.

She would need some help, though, given the magnitude of the task at hand, and she knew just where to look. Her intentions were no minor feat. The witch aimed to kidnap all of the children in this small town so as never again to be bothered by the likes of the little tykes. She would spread dread and foreboding amongst the parents of their close-knit community. Holidays were indeed intended for children, and she would make it her mission in life to make sure that there was never a celebration of one again.

# CHAPTER 3

Sitting on a bench outside of St. Mary's Hospital, the two shadowy figures watched the midnight shift come and go as the early sun perched itself on the horizon and looked in on the new day. Waiting—it's like cancer or the death penalty. Waiting for time to pass. The two of them watched the ambulances and staff frantically transferring patients of every kind of trauma and tragedy into the ER.

In the cold air, some of those on stretchers exhaled visible life for the very last time. Cheyne-Stokes irregular breathing was a frequent precursor to their final death rattle. The man wondered what it was like for them. Knowing and waiting for the end. A clock running down. An hourglass half past, half forgotten. Is it better to know or not know when you're going to die? What if the answer were never?

He was bundled up with scarf and overcoat and turned up collar cloaking and keeping his neck from the wind. The wide-brimmed hat and wraparound polarized sunglasses seemed slightly out of place given the time of day, but they weren't worn for style—rather, protection. Sitting beside the cloaked man was his ever-present wife and aide-de-camp named Aoife. She tried to keep the night chill away with her long alpaca suman coat, wool fota skirt, and traditional batik headscarf. Aoife was his consummate lifelong friend, who happened to be a female werewolf. A wolfwoman, or werewoman? Whatever she wanted or chose.

Aoife gazed at her partner. "Mo gradh." *My love.*

He replied, "Mo chridhe"—*my heart*—as the next ambulance pulled in to transfer its patient occupant. The lower loading dock door swung open, leading to the sub-basement morgue of the hospital. The desperate couple had recently fled their burning home from which they'd been driven. They sought refuge in this most unusual shelter with the help of one of the local EMT's who also had immigrated from a similar part of Eastern Europe.

Under the strobe effect of the loose, blinking fluorescent light above the doorway, Krystiyan the EMT ambulance driver greeted the two dark figures as usual and invited them in from the night air. He was accompanied by an assistant who would join in helping the unusual couple with their task at hand: seeking shelter and respite from the new day. "This is Maria Claudia Luminita, our new night shift aide. She will serve you well, mine shah."

They had both grown up hearing stories of the Count. To Romania and the surrounding countries, he was a hero. The king who kept his country from being invaded and pillaged by attacking hordes and enemy kingdoms. There were statues of him in town squares all over Eastern Europe, and people prayed for his wellbeing. To this day, he was remembered in history books as their greatest king who would do anything to protect his subjects. *Anything.* To Maria Claudia, it was a great honor to meet this larger-than-life historical figure, let alone serve him.

The black and white square tiles that lined the hallway floor smelled of bleach and sterility and resembled a *shatranj*, or a board for an ancient Persian form of chess, a game the man had played many a time eons ago. It was more specifically derived from the expression *shah mat*, "the king is dead," or the modern parlance "checkmate."

Looking at her feet on that floor, avoiding eye contact, Maria Claudia Luminita committed her allegiance and services. "Is there any way that I may be of more assistance, your lordship?"

The shadowy figure replied, "Call me Count. Count Dracula."

The king is dead. Long live the king.

# CHAPTER 4

After welcoming the unusual guests, Krystiyan apologized and excused himself to go on another emergency call. It seemed to be a busy night for trauma and he assured the Count and Contessa that Maria Claudia was more than up to the task of assisting them with their endeavors. Both Krystiyan and Maria Claudia emigrated from a similar Eastern European homeland as the vampire and werewolf. Ukraine was but a stone's throw from Transylvania and Romania. The old country. A place of myth and mystery where legends were as old as the generations of families who settled there.

Aoife walked arm in arm with the Count to the morgue's cold locker, which contained the numerous postmortem cadavers—their nocturnal neighbors for the evening. They walked along a series of pull-out wall slabs which led to the oversized one on the end which was to be their shelter. She nestled into her true love's arms as the drawer was closed to all light. Aoife looked forward to drifting off toward some much-needed REM time. Her mind recollected the complex circumstances and situations that had led the two of them to this steel-encased boudoir together.

She remembered being at home in Romania with her family, seemingly forever ago. How could she forget her abusive father's drunken tirades, which went ignored by an enabling, non-nurturing mother? Many an evening spanning years had led to her hiding in any crawlspace, nook, or cranny, like a bug escaping a boot. On one such night when Aoife was in her mid-twenties, she retreated from the unprovoked physical abuse by running haphazardly into the nearby forest. It was there that she was bitten by the wild wolf that walked on two legs.

The French Canadians had called them *loup-garou*, or *rougarou* in Cajun folklore, and in Norman France they were called *garwulf*. In ancient Roman writings, werewolves were called *versipellis*, or "turned skin." The earliest record of human-to-wolf transformation was from 2100 B.C. in the *Epic of Gilgamesh*.

Aoife had run out into the darkest forest without any hesitation or fear. The only fear that she knew came from inside her own home. The deep forest was full of life but absent of light. So she hid in the dark foliage and settled upon a soft, mossy patch under an underutilized shade tree. She sat very still listening for her father's apoplectic voice but heard nothing.

As she let out a sigh, Aoife noticed that her tongue was tingly and numb and she became acutely nauseous. The full moon cast its spell and shone through the leaves. She looked around in the dim light and saw that she was lying in a patch next to some purple monkshood. Aoife recognized instantly the extremely poisonous plant whose toxins could be absorbed through the skin. She remembered her elderly gypsy grandmother warning her, "When the wolfsbane blooms in the full moonlight, human becomes beast throughout the night. When the sunlight clears the night mist away, beast becomes human, until the end of day."

She jumped up and screamed out, frantically scratching her skin. Her cries and the open scent of wild wolfsbane drew the attention of the beast. The giant wolf stood on two legs and towered above the young woman. Its eyes were wild from the wolfsbane, and it grabbed Aoife by the ankle and held her up as if to size the trophy, then took a nasty bite out of her shoulder as she shrieked wildly. But then some-thing stirred inside the beast. Almost like fear as it sniffed the air curi-ously. It just tossed her aside and left. As she lay there bleeding, she thought that her pain was finally over. She closed her eyes, just for a moment, only to awaken the next dawn.

Having survived the attack, she was well aware of the consequences and knew her fate when next the moon showed its face. It had to do with the changing magnetic fields, not unlike the tides. They came and went every day. Likewise, Aoife would be able to turn into a wolf every day, as long as the moon was out. The tides were larger during the fullest moon, so her transformation into beast would be quicker and more vigorous and painful.

The very next day, she confided this predicament to her mother and her father, who became enraged. His toxic hate and bigotry at such a lowly life form as the wolf beast knew no bounds. He would not allow such a disgrace to be in his home, let alone be permitted to live at all. He grabbed the large, silver Romanian kilij sword from the mantle; a similar sword was used by Vlad Tepes, "the Impaler," in past times to torture and fight the Ottomans.

As he raised the huge sword above his head with drunken, mead-filled red eyes, the door flew open and in walked a strange man who had apparently been passing by and heard the escalating ruckus. The stranger lifted Aoife's father with one hand and fiercely sunk his sharp teeth into his neck, severing head from body. Her mother was aghast as he then fell upon her, sheltering Aoife from the horror by shield-ing the feeding with his cape.

Aoife shuddered in the fetal position in the corner of the room staring at the events unfolding before her. The creature had been lurk-ing in the shadows nearby and heard the commotion and cries for help. Speak of the devil. It was he. Vlad the Impaler himself. Only now cursed to live as *nosferatu* and wander the earth forever.

She then saw the creature in his true visage. His sorrowful gaze was filled with tears at her unfortunate situation, as fresh maternal blood dripped from his cheek and lips. That moment in time was forever frozen in her memory. Her moment of freedom. And a chance at a new life bereft of physical, mental, and emotional abuse at the hands of those who should love and protect her the most.

A tearful Count recited, "Death be not relevant of the morrow. Today's sadness becomes nigh. The next moment you choose will stand before the test of time and behind the veil of life, revealing answers only to those who dare to seek." The vampire then picked her up in his arms, cradling and rocking her, and they cried together as the moon retreated across the Romanian sky.

"There are darknesses in life and there are lights, and you are one of the lights, the light of all lights," Dracula said, gently. "The stars leave no shadow, nor does the light within you. Though sympathy can't alter facts, it can help to make them more bearable. I am longing to be with you, and by the sea, where we can talk together freely and build our castles in the air."

Vlad confessed that it was he who had saved her life from the wolf in the forest that fateful night prior, no less than the present eve from her dreadful loving patriarch. Himself transformed, Vlad had hunted the area and heard her cries for help. The lycanthrope that had bitten the girl had no prior exposure to vampyr, but it could sense danger, so it left Aoife for more fertile hunting grounds. The next day, Vlad the Dracul wandered the forest about her abode concerned for her safety. Alas, now they were both creatures of the night.

As Aoife tried to come to terms with her new situation, Dracula recounted the chrysalis of his genesis into vampyr. Ironically, he had been bitten by one of the invading Turks, his sworn enemy. Little did they realize the monster they had created. Of course, they had intended to kill him. However, the Turkish soldier vampyr who had bitten the Count was so euphoric in glory that he didn't notice the half-dead Vlad pick up his sword emboldened with his family crest.

A weakened Dracula took up blade and lopped off the vampire's head and regained his throne once more, as fates would decree. The count Vlad Dracul. Savior of his people. Forever cursed with the blessing of immortality. But that had been a lifetime ago.

That night with Aoife was the beginning of their love, which only grew into more and more new beginnings. Aoife had always been disappointed by her previous suitors, who never lived up to her dreams nor her standards. Aoife always hoped to meet someone better. Someone she could truly share life with.

Dawn broke like silence. The two lovers had fallen asleep in each other's arms outside under the awning of forthcoming daylight. Aoife grabbed Vlad's hand violently and they rushed for cover exuberantly like their younger versions that never were. They embraced the morning with a kiss hidden from the sun by their newfound den. Somewhere between iniquity and a humble abode, it was shelter from what the new day might bring. A cobblestone cottage with a partially thatched roof yet still giving protection from the storm of sunbeams. It was empty, but full of warmth and comfort. Not long abandoned, the once a home was now their temporary shelter and shade from without. They both realized that they were together. For the first and last time. Because tomorrow was forever.

Dracula was impressive in every way. She found him charming, knowledgeable, and quite attractive. He looked like a gorgeous man in his midlife, which he was, sort of. They traveled and scoured the countryside together, learning, teaching, and soon loving each other as only one who knows the same could understand. Adapting and surviving the different places and prejudices thrust upon them along their way.

They even found a place and parson to perform their wedding.

The working preacher discussed the trials and commitment involved with marriage, unconventional or not, and did his best to counsel their marital needs. For as he put it, "Everyone deserves to love and be loved with whomever they want, especially you two. I've seen that your tribulations have only strengthened your love and devotion to each other, the likes of which many can only dream of."

The Count pledged himself to Aoife and offered his hand in marriage. In a whispered howl, she said yes and, on that very night, she became the bride of Dracula. And they both couldn't have been happier. *Everything's in the timing*, he thought. The stars were aligned above on that moonstruck night when the heavens kissed the earth.

Many plan for their special wedding day with multitudes carrying on into the night. However, the intimate wedding ceremony between the Count and Contessa was private. Their hearts filled the room, matching the sweet scent of lilies in the vase on the corner table. Resplendent splendor without exception.

Dracula placed the three-carat Alexandrite custom ring on Aoife's fourth finger of the hand closest to her heart and they kissed. The color-changing gemstone was discovered in 1830 Russia and appeared to be an emerald by day and a ruby by night, especially that night. The gem was named after Emperor Alexander III, the czar of Russia. The Count had acquired the jewel not long after and had secretly saved it hidden away for just such an occasion.

They spent the rest of their wedding night alone together dancing, loving, laughing, crying, and finally falling asleep holding each other. It was a beautiful night and beginning to the next chapter of their sweet saga together.

The two lovers met a variety of people along their travels, some human, some not, and not everyone supported their mixed marriage, but most did. So they went about their way as husband and wife, dedicating themselves to each other's happiness and survival, until they finally made their way to America. Land of the free. At least for some. They eventually found themselves in the small, picturesque Northeastern town of Killington, Vermont. The fact that they now slumbered on a morgue slab meant little by comparison as long as they were together.

In the basement tomb of St. Mary's mortuary, Aoife exhaled a mumble as sleep descended upon her conscious mind. She drifted off like a sailboat between oceans of reverie and nightmare. Dreams overtook Aoife and her breathing grew slow, full, and deep, knowing that they would awaken in each other's arms to whatever fates a new day and night would bring.

# CHAPTER 5

I t seemed like yesterday, because it was, that they had finally found a place where they could live just as they were, in the peaceful privacy of themselves.

Dracula and Aoife tried their best to maintain a low profile as much as possible wherever they went. Not everyone in the town of Killington even believed in their existence, and some of the ones who did weren't exactly happy that they inhabited the same town, or state, or, for that matter, planet. Some of the elders especially preferred not to believe in certain things the closer that death approached them. "If seeing is believing, then these old folks are blind to anything past the 5 p.m. dinner rush at Crapper's Buffet," their friend Connor would say.

Connor and Noah owned and ran the local rare bookstore and were not themselves strangers to unwarranted prejudice. The Count and Aoife had befriended them and enlisted their help in purchasing a small house on the outskirts of the county. The Count and Aoife had a standing invitation to enter their bookstore anytime, but they did it infrequently, taking care not to bring unwanted attention to their new friends.

Noah and Connor had purchased the home in their name. They themselves lived in town above their bookstore, but the way the Count saw it was that it was the two gentlemen's property. Someday, maybe, they could use it to get away. He just happened to buy it for them and they, in turn, allowed Dracula and his bride to stay. Until it was time to move on, which was inevitable.

The colonial home sat on a private property of ten acres surrounded by forest. Dracula and Aoife both enjoyed the night sky and cool breezes that inhabited the woods that they shared with their woodland neighbors. They would often end their night together on the veranda discussing issues of the day and watching the night sky turn slowly into dawn's pre-light.

On one such unassuming morning a few days prior, they had retreated indoors to their bedroom for a welcomed rest. Aoife sat up in bed, still excited as the falling moon shared the sky with the rising sun, while Dracula fought to keep his eyes open.

"We should think about moving into a retirement home," said Aoife.

"Do I really look that old?" asked Dracula.

"No, silly. Their residents' circadian rhythms are the opposite of ours."

"They slumber as we rise," said Dracula.

"And bingo won't be crowded at all."

"I never did like that game. There's no such word. It's made-up."

"Yeah, but... never mind. Listen, I'm gonna run out and get a few things while you rest. And don't worry, I'll stay below the radar," said Aoife.

"Be careful, please," said the Count with care.

"I will, my sweet. Lock the door." She exited through the back entrance. Dracula gave her a thumbs-up and lay down just for a second, then promptly fell asleep.

As he dozed peacefully, an angry mob was forming outside getting worked up. "He's a monster," whispered one of the masked group.

"She is, too," whispered another.

"We don't know what they're capable of," said a third.

"We can't let these creatures roam around free doing god knows what."

Even though Covid was well on its way down, this motley group kept their masks on at all times to obscure the truth of their identities. The only thing they didn't bring were pointy white hats.

The group of masked vigilantes passed around a bottle of brown courage followed by a bucket full of wooden stakes and mallets. They snuck up the steps onto the front porch, trying not to cause the old wooden deck to creak. The door was ajar and the front intruder gave a toothless smile from under his mask and a thumbs-up as he entered without invitation.

Fortunately, some of the locals knew of the formation of the posse not endorsed by law enforcement. As the intruders entered the front door, Connor, Noah, and Dracula were quickly exiting the back. Connor and Noah had arrived just in time to awaken the weary-eyed vampire from his slumber. As they made their way through the darkened backyard to the tree line, Dracula asked, "How did you know they were coming for us?"

"They asked us to join them! Can you imagine? I'm just lucky I didn't bust out laughing," said Connor.

"Connor asked them what the dress code was. Seriously. They said business casual and to act nonchalant," said Noah.

"I said, 'Like *Freaky Friday?*,' and Noah kicked me. They were oblivious." Connor laughed.

"Or just thought we were weird," said Noah. The three of them snickered as they went in search of Aoife. They had to intercept her before she made it home or these masked idiots were in for a rude awakening.

The enraged bloodlust of the angry mob continued uninterrupted as they openly destroyed and disregarded these innocent strangers' sanctuary. They set fire to the house, turning the home to ash.

Dracula held Aoife in his arms as they watched their dying domicile burn from a forested hill not far from. Noah and Connor did the same, sharing the moment with their friends, saddened by the total nonsense of such misguided hate. *Why? And for what?*

The Count remembered and repeated the exact words in his mind yet again. *Why? And for what? Ignorance is wanton bliss for the weak. We shall seek solace elsewhere, my love.* And so began their sojourn to a deathbed slumber, hidden in the bowels of St. Mary's. What safer place to hide, than amongst the dead.

# CHAPTER 6

## OCTOBER 31, 1993

Once upon a time, in a land of wonder, there were three mice. They were captured by the mean old wicked witch and forced to work very hard. They scrubbed floors until there was nothing left to scrub. They dusted dust until no mote was left. They fetched water and lugged logs. By the end of the day, they were so tired. Too tired to run away," said Rachel.

With sleepy eyes, Connor asked his mom, "So what happened?"

"They all got together to form a plan. One of the mice distracted the old hag by knocking over a wooden jar from the shelf, while the second mousey ran up her back and neck to startle her, which it most certainly did. The third mouse unlatched the window so that all three could flee to safety across the sill, which they did hastily as the witch bent over to pick up the old jar that had once been her grandmother's. You see, it contained her remains. This made the old woman cry. The three mice felt bad about this and went back to apologize to the pitiful old woman. The witch was so taken aback that she wiped away her tears and invited the mice in for tea...."

"What happens next?" asked Connor.

"Uh, nothing, sweetheart, that's it. The end," said Connor's mom, who always knew how to tell a good story and tuck him in for the night. She made him feel safe and secure, and he couldn't wait to start another brand new day with her.

"Goodnight, little moonbeam," she whispered as she gently kissed his forehead.

# CHAPTER 7

Connor and Noah had always wanted to run a bookstore together, and Killington was perfect. Occupying a corner location in the town square, the bookstore itself had a modest but substantial collection of written lore. "All the good writers are drunks," Connor would note.

"So are all the bad ones," replied Noah, his partner in crime, and business, and life for that matter. From the front of the front room to the back of the back, the bookstore held a musky charm. At midday, the light shone through the storefront window, taking just a bit of chill out of the fall air. It was the perfect time of year. Transition. Leaves started to tremble, hanging on for dear life while some blackbirds wondered if they should follow the flock. Peer pressure.

Connor walked through the door rubbing his shoulders as if to shrug off remnants of the chilly air. Noah was on the library ladder in the back of the room, either repositing or retrieving something from the section on magic. Words can be powerful. Wars had been fought over mismanagement of the written word. "Hey, c'mere. You gotta see this," said Noah.

"What? What's so special?"

"Check this out. I got this from that estate sale on the way to Pownal," Noah said as he climbed down off the ladder and walked over to place the heavy object on the main desk.

"Some old hag was already in here today wanting to buy the book but I told her it wasn't inventoried yet, but she could try back later. Gawd, did she give me the evil eye. She actually had only one good eye. The other was all whitish and opaque."

"Gross," said Connor.

The book itself was rather old, with worn-off gold etched bindings and an odd leather cover. There were no writings on either, front or back. The spine of the book looked as if it had some form of congenital deformity. It even carried an odd smell with it that followed the pages across the room.

"Creepy," said Connor.

They both looked on as Noah opened the book to a certain passage that he had identified earlier, taking care not to damage this piece of history. Or folklore. There were spells and diagrams spewed all over the pages in some Gaelic language understood by neither of them. It was a book of the mystic black arts and sinister machinations. The inner cover page revealed the book's title. *The Book of Shadows*, first edition.

"This can't be good."

"Are you kidding me?" Noah replied. "This is awesome. Just look at the artwork. I'm pretty sure it's hand-drawn. This has to be worth a small fortune."

"Just sell it," said Connor.

"Why? Why not just—"

"Please just sell it quickly? For me?" Connor felt like a kid all over again.

"Sure," Noah said. "No big deal. I'm sure I can get rid of it, I just thought . . . I mean, I'll take care of it."

"I love you," said Connor.

"Love you too," Noah said as they held each other. One frightened, one confused. No matter. Everyone needs a hug sometimes. Even porcupines.

# CHAPTER 8

After a proper time of rest on the slide-out slab bed in the morgue's cold locker, Maria slid open the chamber which held the two lovers, still nestled in each other's arms. She'd have hesitated to wake them if not for the Count's previous instructions. Besides, they were stirring awake already, wiping the sleep from their eyes. Maria Claudia greeted them into the start of a new night. "Good evening."

They both arose from the drawer, stretching and yawning as slumber had only just left. Dracula asked, "Do you mind if I feed, my dear?" Without hesitation, Maria Claudia removed the decorative cross necklace that her mother had given her from around her neck.

The Count's countenance was as hypnotizing as it was enchanting. For Maria, time slowed like a bradycardic heartbeat that was still capable of pumping the necessary blood. She asked if it would hurt. The Count replied, "You tell me. You gave me sustenance and generosity when I needed it most. You barely noticed, but I truly appreciate the gift of life that you bestowed upon me."

Maria Claudia palpated her neck for wounds, and only then did she become aware of the slightest of puncture marks made with surgical precision. Barely noticeable except for a mild lightheadedness and the warm flush spreading about her cheek and palms. A bite is just a bloody kiss. The Count knew not to drink enough to kill Maria

Claudia, nor to change her into vampyr without her wish or consent, lest she drink of his blood. The blood is the life.

He truly appreciated her sacrifice and support as one in genuine need and desperation would. As she sat, the Count fanned her face and concentrated his efforts on her comfort and wished her a peaceful slumber. She smiled as she fell into his arms while a blissful sigh escaped her lips and she drifted off to the security of sleep.

# CHAPTER 9

I t had been a week since the first child had gone missing. His name was Billy Gunther. Local law enforcement assumed Billy's parents were somehow responsible, as quite often was the case. After all, Billy's father had a rap sheet long enough to wallpaper a room with, including a record of domestic violence. But it seemed that the little boy in the ghost costume had just vanished into thin air, and not into the robust and hearty stew that he had actually become.

Bridgett had been busy making some simple DIY home renovations and redecorating. She had replaced the hearth rug and mismatched candlesticks which once occupied her oversized fireplace with a rather large cauldron over a roaring fire.

In her left eye, the old witch had a dense white traumatic cataract. Many moons ago, her first cat had freaked out in fear during an incantation and penetrated her eyeball with her claw. Bridgett's pupil was permanently dilated and her lens had become completely dense white. She had wrung the cat's neck, then sent its corpse as a wrapped present to the grade school anonymously.

When Bridgett spoke to you, she always led with the other side of her face and then slowly turned her traumatic side into yours, closer than you were comfortable with. Close enough to touch. Or kiss. Or bite. She never had her eye repaired because she liked the way she could freak the hell out of people. Especially the kiddies. She called it her evil eye, though every part of her body was as well.

Even though she lived alone, Bridgett still took pride in the culinary arts, albeit dark. She had recently become active on social media and infrequently took a foodie photo of her dinner plate, if it looked exceptionally good, and posted it on Facebook and Instagram. She tried YouTube and TikTok but there were always some disturbing cries for help audible in the background. *#discomfortfood*. Tonight's dinner plate was titled "Bridgett's Old-Fashioned Braciole," served along with "freshly baked brioche and pain au lait," but she didn't reveal the secret ingredient. Beat that, Bobby Flay.

She fumbled and thumbed her way through her collection of very old books, all the while clanging to herself, "Peter, Peter, pumpkin-eater, had a wife but couldn't keep her. He put her in a pumpkin shell, and there he kept her very well."

The old woman had consulted her old texts, including *The Grimoire Journal of Witchcraft*, *The Book of Forbidden Knowledge, Curses, Potions, and Maledictions*, and even *Witchcraft for Beginners*, with wolf-leather binding, from her earlier days. Bridgett absolutely loved her books and the knowledge and secrets that they held within.

She even had a small but substantial collection of classic cookbooks, including *Larousse Gastronomique*, *The Escoffier*, and *Mastering the Art of French Cooking* by Julia Child. Not to be confused with *Aunt Julia's Joys of Hoodoo Bayou Curses*, which she also had a first edition of. There were incantations for everything from necromancy and goety to simple mischievous diablerie and yes, even love, although how true a love one could only guess.

She was only missing one or two classic but hard-to-find occult books to complete her collection, and always kept her one eye looking out for them. Especially *The Book of Shadows*, first edition. For some it was considered the witch's bible, or the occult gold standard.

Bridgett recalled her grandmother had a first edition that she handed down to her mother, which would then be handed down to Bridgett, until the Dark Days took everything from her. Bridgett sat at her kitchen table and took paper to pen. She wondered if eye of newt was on sale or even in season. *Cooking really is both art and science*, she thought. "Sometimes it's even like performance art," said the wily witch with a snicker. "Boy, are they in for a show."

She went about making a shopping list for ingredients to help carry out her nefarious plans. Many of the items needed were quite rare and hard to come by, but she was determined to check the boxes off her list. Oh, and she was out of milk. A girl has to eat.

# CHAPTER 10

Have you seen the kitties?" asked Noah.

"No. But listen. I never told anyone about this and I'm not sure I wanna relive it now. My mother's soul was condemned," said Connor.

"What?" said Noah. They sat on the bed facing each other.

"I think I want to tell you something, maybe," said Connor.

"What? What? You're freaking me out."

"You know that I had a fucked up childhood, right?"

"I'm so sorry. I love you," said Noah.

Connor replied, "I know. I love you too, but I need you to listen. So, when we were kids, there was a lot of alcoholism in our family on every side but up. Mostly good, decent people."

"Racists," said Noah.

"Yes."

"Homophobes," said Noah.

"Yes."

"Batshit crazy," said Noah.

"Yes, yes, but shut up," Connor said. "I'm sorry ... Anyway, my mom was seriously mentally ill. I guess it got worse as she got older. No joking. But I was just a kid, so I didn't know anything, let alone what a normal adult should be like. My mother grew to be abusive to my father and me. She installed spy cameras to stalk my dad, she was so paranoid. She'd pop up out of nowhere to check up on him. She'd pretend to leave and just watch the hidden cameras to see if he was cheating on her. He never did. But she would never in a million years believe it. She was obsessed.

"One early evening at dusk, he told me he was tired and gonna lay down for a bit. He looked so haggard, but he smiled anyway 'cause I knew he didn't want me to see him cry. Or crawl under the covers for being a poor father, which he wasn't. As he lay down on the bed, I said, 'Are you okay?'

"He said, 'I'm fine, honey. Just working too hard. We'll be just fine. Getting through a rough patch is all.'

"I kissed his forehead and he smiled and closed his eyes. As I was walking out of the doorway, I looked back to smile at my dad, and there was my mom. Hiding under the bed with a butcher knife. She smiled back at me and put her index finger to her lips to shush me. I screamed and jumped onto the bed onto my dad's chest and he jumped up and I haven't stopped being afraid since."

Noah didn't know what to say, so they sat there in silence.

The wind was blowing up outside, and there came the strangest of howling shrieks. They looked at each other then out into the yard, and there were their two Persian cats with their tails tied together, slung over the clothesline, swinging and fighting, making a god-awful noise.

Just then the lights went out, and as they sat in the dark, they heard the most sinister giggle coming from under the bed. The voice said, "Goodnight, little moonbeam. You should've sold me the book!"

The lightning struck outside and the thunder grumbled as if it were feeding time and the night screamed on and on.

# CHAPTER 11

The gray clouds morphed slowly across the sky, changing from wispy feathery cotton balls into crystals, from the outline of a snowman to the face of Lucifer himself. The pareidolia lent itself to the accumulating fear and disdain among the townsfolk below. Looks like rain. Or much worse. Bridgett Bishop donned her fur-lined forest green velvet witch's cape and shawl and hit the bricks, heading toward the town square. Her hood tapered down her back into a point. Certainly fall fashionable, it was warm, practical, and still in line with her Druid heritage.

Although she possessed the necessary skills and primal knowledge of the earth to perform her magic, she still needed some essential supplies from her shopping list, and she knew just where to find them: Henry and Edward's Apothecary and Compounding Pharmacy. It was a staple of the local business district and chamber of commerce, as they worked closely and adjunctively with the town's hospitals and medical community.

It was run by two brothers, Dr. Henry Jekyll and Mr. Edward Hyde. Bridgett opened the door to their emporium and was announced by an old-fashioned shopkeeper's brass hanging bell that rang as the front door opened and closed. She was greeted by a well-groomed, professional-looking young man wearing a spotless white lab coat and horn-rimmed spectacles. It was Dr. Jekyll, who reacted immediately to her presence with a concerned and frantic look.

"Good day, Miss Bishop. I hope the season has been good to y—"

"Cram it. You know why I'm here," she said in a rather terse manner. "Now go fetch your partner posthaste."

With that, Henry Jekyll disappeared into the back room of his store behind a long beige curtain. After some audible arguing and exchange of different ideas and approaches, Mr. Hyde emerged in a well-worn smock carrying some half-filled vials and mumbling curses to himself under his breath.

Unlike Jekyll, the consummate polished professional, Hyde was overtly grotesque in appearance and manner. His hair, unkempt and wild, was a fitting match for his true nature and toothy, deviant smile. Spittle ran down the corner of his lips while he greeted his customer in a most unflattering way.

"Back again, are we? Can't get enough of a bad thing, eh?" His words were spoken loudly, hurled like sarcastic insults. "I told you before, we don't carry eye of newt or bat's blood, but if you're not picky, there's still plenty of blood to go around. Yes, yes, a sticky red pleasure, I say, to spatter and pool the night away!"

"Calm yourself, Mr. Hyde; just my usual order will suffice," the witch replied. "And be quick about it!"

"My time is mine own!" Hyde screamed. "Do not dare to hasten me, woman, or the blood that I fetch will come from your throat! I'll prepare your order personally before that milquetoast goody-two-shoes Jekyll returns. I'm afraid that the fool's demise is soon to come, and none too soon for my taste."

Bridgett, assuaging, said, "Be that as it may, I'll pay double for your efforts and privacy."

Mr. Hyde spit on the floor and retreated behind the curtain with a scowl that would frighten most. After several minutes of clanking and cussing, he returned to the counter and rang up the witch's requested compounds and sundries.

Bridgett paid and left promptly with her prescriptions, backing out the front door. She knew enough never to turn her back on Hyde, lest she herself become victim to some form of acute blunt force trauma.

The door chime again resounded heralding her exit, and she could hear Hyde smashing Pyrex glassware and ranting from behind the counter. "Every time a bell rings, another neck that I shall wring. Yes. The more callous torture that I shall bring. Yes indeed."

# CHAPTER 12

The old witch consulted her books of spells and the dark arts. They were a tome template for terror and transmutation. Especially her newfound favorite, *The Book of Shadows*, first edition. As far as she could recall, it looked almost identical to her mother's copy, and even held the same vague scent of brimstone and wormwood. It had been a while since she had performed these ghastly rituals with their prescribed concoctions.

Little by little it all came back to her. Like riding a bike or shanghaiing the child who owned it. But most of all, she was interested in the enchantments for summoning the soulless creatures of chaos to do her bidding.

Bridgett cast her enchantments and decreed her wicked portent over a bubbling cauldron filled with charms and curses and blackened entrails. "Charon the ferryman steers the shades of the dead across Styx and Acheron for coin from a head. A scythe he does yield to those who did fall. The Angel of Death makes fools of us all."

Unleashing the evil which lived within her heart, the old witch delivered her magic spell to the skies above and hell below. "With a hate-filled heart I must implore that the joy of holidays will be no more!"

And just for an instant, time stood still. The old witch knew that her malevolent intentions had fired the first volley and that the calendar pages would fall to her folly as her revenge grew to fruition.

Outside, the murmuration of thousands of starlings danced and twisted, performing like aerial ballerinas. The immense flock of birds formed beautiful and dazzling patterns in the sky created from thousands of wingbeats, hesitating just a second between rotations. The swooping mass of swarming birds morphed into graceful shapes at first, but then the images became more sinister and familiar. A hideous skeletal face, a jack-o-lantern, and a ghoul that would give Edvard Munch pause. Finally, in a macabre twirling fashion like an oil well gushing, the birds formed an upside down cross, held for a moment, then exploded. Thousands of dead sparrows rained down upon the earth.

Bridgett snickered and laughed in the dark as day became night, just watching the nightmare begin. She gathered her things and thoughts and once again went out into the dead of night on her mission of carnage, determined to eradicate any semblance of holiday spirit among those who would defy her.

# CHAPTER 13

Twenty-six hundred BCE Fourth Egyptian Dynasty. Or so the sign said in the east wing of the Natural History Museum. It also said that the wing was closed to the public for renovation. The wing was as dark and quiet as a tomb, literally, since it contained the Egyptian tombs of several mummies.

It had been a while since Bridgett had been to the museum. *It isn't the Smithsonian*, she thought, *but it does have some interesting pieces. Three of particular interest. And it always makes for a lovely field trip for the kiddies to learn about death.*

The modest exhibit was sponsored by the University of Vermont archeology department. Like so many artifacts and grave exchanges, items got moved around like currency. Some even got lost in the hustle and bustle of an oversized customs storage facility. Bridgett did her research and was pretty sure that these were no run-of-the-mill mummies, but rather something special.

At the entrance to the Egyptian exhibit was an example of one of the first known scarecrows. Three thousand years ago, ancient Egyptians hung tunics and nets on reeds and wooden frames to scare the quail away from their wheat crops along the Nile River. Bridgett appreciated the fact that the pharaohs and gods of the time used fear as a tool of force.

The witch continued on her tour until she came across the glass, walled-off enclosure that separated the mummy exhibit from her greedy hands. The showcase held three open sarcophagi with their respective residents. The ornate lids were off so that passersby could sneak a peek at the dead people. The witch tapped the glass with her broomstick handle, just to make sure they didn't move. *You never know*, she thought. *This is gonna be fun.*

The first sarcophagus in the exhibit just so happened to contain her first prize, the god ruler Anubis. Anubis wore a jackal-head mask and was well known as the protector of tombs and the god of mummification and death. Many hieroglyphics depicted Anubis opening the mouth of the dead so that they could breathe in the afterlife. Right next to him was his personal attaché and servant, Manu Rajeev, who was buried alive with him to serve his every need in the afterlife.

Seventy days. That's how long the process of mummification took. The preservation required in anticipation of the afterlife was extensive. First, a hook was inserted through the nostrils to take out part of the brain. Then, the belly was cut open to remove any potentially decaying organs and the abdominal cavity was wiped with palm wine and spices. Embalmed and wrapped, desiccated and taxidermized, Anubis went through a series of rituals and religious processions awaiting the time that he would live again. A waking curse upon anyone who dared to disturb him.

The last sarcophagus contained the mummy of the Egyptian goddess of death and the night, Nephthys, who seduced her twin sister Isis's husband Osiris to conceive her demigod son Anubis. Nephthys was married to the usurper god of disorder, Seth. Her name meant "mistress of the house." She possessed the knowledge of certain sacred words and magical spells capable of raising the inanimate.

The exhibit placard displayed the translated ancient curse that supposedly accompanied the dig site. Little did the museum curator know that it professed an actual mortal warning from the god of the dead, and his mom. And Manu. "Those who would dare desecrate these graves shall become beetle dung compost for the scarab and worm. Death will be welcomed as a longing friend." With the witch's help, their vengeance would be properly displaced in the right direction. The residents of Killington.

Anubis the god of death and Nephthys the god of death and rebirth, along with the manservant Manu Rajeev, would live again.

It is estimated that seventy million mummies were made in Egypt over the three thousand years of their ancient civilization. "Surely no one would miss a few," the witch said to herself.

Bridgett had prepared diligently for this moment. "If only these idle fools knew what was in their possession, they would have protected it better," she muttered. "One man's misfortune is another woman's joy." The witch twirled around as if performing some strange incantation or abstract street dance, but then just turned and grabbed her broomstick with her grubby hands.

She impulsively smashed the wall of glass separating her from her unholy cohorts. The witch then used her broom to sweep a clear path free of shards to her final reward. Through a series of complex incantations and necromancy, she addressed the three mummy corpses before her.

"Oh, great King Anubis and Queen Nephthys, and accompanied servant to the great life beyond, I do command thee. Egyptian gods that you were, you will now serve me. Awaken thou dead! Awaken thee thrice! Three shall come forth, no less will suffice. Walk the earth again, for trouble is nigh. Bring parents to weep and children to cry. Come forth, my mummy servants, and live once more!"

Grizzled hair stirred faintly within the open sarcophagi while dust and decay fell from every part of the mummies' joints and movements. Jaws stretched back and forth, shaking cells and tissue from the mouths of the reanimated corpses. They slowly crept out of their ancient ornate coffins, gathering their bearings and balance. Death shrouds fell away as the mummies took their first steps in over two thousand years.

Bridgett Bishop introduced herself to the reanimated mummies. "Welcome back to the land of the living, my noble friends. We have much to do together. Come with me, my malevolent monstrosities, and we will rule the night together!" The witch then escorted her new extended family back to her house undetected. She welcomed the three long-dead dignitaries of death into her home as they settled in, out of sight, out of their minds.

The very next night, the old witch began her premeditated plan of vengeance with the mummy manservant Manu Rajeev. Step by step, the shadow of the mummy led the way through the aged cobblestone streets in the older part of town. The obsequious mummy was under her spell and forced to comply with her discordant cacophonous chants and bidding. Bridgett thought, *First stop, the mayor's house.*

# CHAPTER 14

Gretchen Dorschel, just six, would soon lay herself down to sleep, but first she knelt at her bedside to perform her daily ritual of nighttime prayer. Her flannel pajamas kept her warm on this most intemperate of fall nights. "…and bless Hank and Mommy and Daddy."

Outside her bedroom window stared the soulless orbits of the undead mummy Manu Rajeev. The lack of breath did not fog the pane of glass nor obscure the hideous grimace peering in on this chilly eve.

Gretchen climbed up under the covers and settled in. Her comforter had glow-in-the-dark butterflies seemingly in search of a home. She wasn't afraid of the dark. She just liked glow-in-the-dark butterflies. Her ceiling was likewise adorned with glow-in-the-dark heavens. Her parents even splurged for the oversized Saturn.

As she lay there surrounded by pillows, the princess surveyed her kingdom. "Pretty cool," she said to herself. Her eyelids started to droop and she could almost imagine floating weightless in space. In-between blinks, she thought, *Why is there a mummy in outer space?*

Manu the mummy quickly grabbed Gretchen and muffled her screams. He had crept and crawled quiet as the undead through the open window in the next room and silently made his way to the sleepy child. With the child in his arms, he slunk down the long hallway to her brother's room to snatch the boy as well. It would appear that the witch was preparing for a mighty feast, or potluck.

The mummy secured the children by wrapping them in their favorite security blankets, which were handmade and given to them by their nana. The security offered by the weathered blankets was no match for the death-wrappings of the mummy.

Though painstakingly methodical in his movements, the mummy nonetheless knocked over a burning scented candle at Hank's bedside. The babysitter and her boyfriend had left scented candles in key locations to disguise the scent of vaping and herb. The fire crawled up the wall, setting the linens afire, and the room burst into flame. The fire found its way and quickly spread throughout the house.

Hank and Gretchen's parents were out for the evening at a mayoral holiday work party. They'd left the care of their precious loved ones to the teenage babysitter, who now fled from the fire with her boyfriend, panicked and unthinking.

The entire house was engulfed by the fiery fury. Smoke alarms chirped like tweets throughout the house until they melted into the night. The bewildered mummy was now flagrantly afire and dropped his youthful cargo as his feet became embers, and he collapsed upon himself into the burn pit. Ashes to ashes.

It grew as quiet as a church mouse, until the air filled with distant distress signals and alarm bells from the town's fire station, providing an airy hope that help would soon be there.

Mayor Dorschel and his wife were just arriving home and were aghast with horror to discover that it was their address that was supplying the billowing black smoke that filled the air. The babysitter and her boyfriend were standing outside crying and explaining the situation when the first EMT vehicle arrived at the scene. Luckily, it was the EMS captain. The fire truck sirens were still off in the distance when the EMS driver was confronted by the frantic, desperate parents.

"Our two children are inside! Please, please help us!"

They were still hollering gibberish when the paramedic donned a mask with self-contained breathing apparatus and personal alert safety system device and ran into the blaze to search for and rescue the two children. The captain manually activated the PASS Personal Alert Safety System just as he entered the front door to the blaze. It emitted a strobe and audible, ninety-five-decibel alert in order for incoming firefighters to be able to locate him, as well as to notify potential victims of his presence.

The paramedic heard screams and rushed into one of the back bedrooms, where he found both children crying, still wrapped in Nana's blankets surrounded by a room filled with smoke and fire. The children were untouched by flame so far. The EMS paramedic thought that their covers must have been made of nylon and polyester, fire-resistant materials. *Must be their security blankets*, he thought.

His knees were shot. Bone on bone. *I know, first thing to go. I probably walk like a monst*er.

As the building succumbed to its burning destruction, it appeared that there was no way out. He grabbed the two bundles and ran like hell through the flames. The outside onlookers were shocked to see this large creature of a man carrying two children suddenly burst through the burning wall as the building collapsed. The mother shed thankful, joyous tears while she grabbed her intact children to look them over.

Mayor Dorschel grabbed the big man's hand, which overshadowed his own greatly, and shook it profusely. He then went in to hug the wheezing and coughing paramedic when he noticed that his back was still on fire and patted it out. The mayor hugged him some more and said, "I can't thank you enough. I'm in your debt."

The EMS hero removed his mask and replied, "No problem, Mr. Mayor. Just doin' my job."

By now the fire trucks had arrived and were in full action as snakes of hoses spewed foam and water to the dying home. Once the other newly arrived hospital personnel had arrived to take over the children's continued care, the oversized EMS paramedic retreated to the emergency ambulance and lay down on the front seat, huffing oxygen.

His firefighter partners asked him if he was okay, obviously quite worried about their friend and cohort. "Man, that was close. Are you okay? How do you feel?"

With his clothes still smoking and his calves and feet hanging out of the front seat cab, he responded, "Fire…" He coughed. "…no good!" They all laughed together. He then noticed his hands shaking and rubbed them together, thinking about his near miss with death and how lucky he was to be alive.

More importantly, Gretchen and Hank were safe and unharmed. *Cute kids*, the EMS captain thought. Hank was named after his father. He even looked like a junior version of Mayor Hank Dorschel.

*Well, I'm not a junior by any stretch of the imagination, but I still have my father's last name*, thought the big man. Frankenstein.

They called him Frankenstein after his father. With his mask removed, one could see the countless facial and neck scars that many had attributed to occupational hazards.

Frankenstein resembled a homunculus homo sapien with hands and feet that were disproportionate at the very least. He was a formidable figure no matter how hard he tried to fit in. His thick-soled, hot asphalt boots were fireproof and made Saul appear even larger. Those who worked with him knew and respected him for exactly who he was: hard-working, smart, and dependable. A better captain you couldn't find. The people under his command would follow him into fire, but the hierarchy of work also kept potential friends at a subordinate distance.

Many of the townspeople collectively feared him, though he hadn't given them any cause. They said that he wasn't human, that his kind wasn't welcome. His kind? Somehow, he always did feel different, but didn't everyone sometimes?

From what he'd seen of mankind through his work, people often seemed neither man nor kind. But he tried not to judge anyone by anything other than the merits of their actions, since those spoke for themselves. Knowing that everyone was unique together was what united them all.

He whispered to himself, "Father, I miss you. I hope that I make you as proud as I am of you. Well, Captain Frankenstein, best get moving. We're burning daylight. Just hope that's all."

The oversized creature was made from human scraps and brought to life by the so-called "mad" doctor himself. At least that's what many of the townspeople said. Images of droopy eyelids, flat-top haircuts, and neck bolts in flesh flashed before their eyes, while the truth held less mystery and more blunt use of sutures and stem cells. And, yes, electricity. We are, after all, life-sized batteries, from cell to sapien.

He was somehow outcast among outcasts. Sometimes lonely and wrapped in self-loathing, especially around the holidays, his body-dysmorphic reflection stared at him through a mirror full of cracks and scars. Born alone. Like everyone else. Death, however, sometimes brings company.

# CHAPTER 15

Those who knew him very little called him monster. Truth be told, he was a son and a friend to Dr. Victor Frankenstein, whom he lovingly referred to as Dad, or Father if he wanted something frivolous growing up. Dr. Frankenstein likewise loved him and treated him as such. Perhaps in his quest for answers to life's questions, he found the answer to loneliness, which was the love of a son.

As the good doctor became the good old doctor, then just old, his self-made son took care of him as the son himself had been taken care of by the father. The cycle of life. The creature looked after his father's every want and need until the old Dr. Frankenstein succumbed to his frailties.

People would often ask, "So why didn't he give him a name?" Well, of course he did. His name was Saul. And yes, they were Jewish, big deal. But it was their choice to maintain their privacy so their sentiment could not be sullied nor misrepresented by a bigoted and less than amicable population.

They held and portrayed a deep sense of love between them as father toward son and son toward dad. Saul's own idiosyncrasies and insecurities were reminiscent of his. He thought of his father fondly. Dr. Frankenstein was smart and kind and compassionate. He was always as good as his word, whether well-received or not. He had said that he only wanted for his son's happiness and wellbeing and Saul believed him. His father had always impressed upon Saul to believe in himself, no matter what. He'd say, "Shoot for the stars. There's so many, you're bound to hit one."

Because of his experiments with electricity, Benjamin Franklin was called the modern Prometheus. Saul thought of his father that way. The Titan Prometheus stole fire from the gods and gave it to humanity. Victor Frankenstein's scientific foresight and noble quest for knowledge allowed him to leap farther than anyone previously could understand. But then again, it didn't end well for Prometheus. He was chained to a rock while birds ate out his liver daily. He was punished for stealing a gift from the gods that he couldn't control. Like nukes, viruses, or AI. Or Saul. Whatever the case, the Swiss scientist would describe his son as "the Adam of his labors," and they both loved each other dearly.

Saul hated the bigoted rumors and defamation upon his father's character by the unjust hands and voices of his fellow man and neighbors just for being different. Just like they treated him. It was strange to be hated by someone that you've never met.

His father devoted his life to medical research that would hopefully benefit all people everywhere. He worked incessantly and held a deep passion for his work and the contributions that he made to medical science. Some of the medical community and his professional associates believed in Dr. Frankenstein and his work but feared reprisals should they publicly voice their supporting opinions.

Alas, Dr. Frankenstein bore his burdens alone, though he did not lose his resolve or determination. He had hoped that his work someday would contribute toward the treatment of a variety of diseases and maladies. He was simply before his time. After the fact. Saul was reminded of one of his father's favorite sayings: "Life is full of surprises. Living isn't."

It's odd how one day you're the good guy but history remembers you as the bad. Saul remembered him simply as the kind and gentle man who was his dad. When it was time, Saul mourned for his loss like all others did for their own and struggled on in memory of all that he was taught.

Some of the townsfolk brought by food and condolences while others could not get past their preconceived prejudice against his kind. Of which, apparently, he was the only one. Saul Frankenstein was a genetic mixture of numerous individuals and phenotypical traits from a variety of cultures and peoples. With a little help from his dad along the way.

A man constructed in his father's image. A chip off the old block. Saul knew that his unnatural size and scarred asymmetry made him look more golem than human in some people's eyes and hate-filled hearts. So it went on, with slurs and slashes more venomous than an adder.

Saul had studied and worked as a volunteer firefighter to overcome his phobia of fire. Aversion therapy. The gradual progressive exposure to fire was exposure therapy, and used in conjunction with psychotherapy to treat his pyrophobia. Studies on identical twins indicated a genetic factor related to the development of pyrophobia. He thought about the many different organ donors that contributed to his body. Which of the many men and women of varied ethnicities had he inherited this trait from?

He eventually graduated and rose through the ranks from EMT to paramedic to EMS captain, whereby he evaluated EMT and paramedic skills, identified system-wide training needs, oversaw field personnel, and worked closely with hospitals and providers.

Saul celebrated the holidays, including Christmas with his small circle of friends and coworkers, but he also celebrated Hanukkah. His true beliefs were in Judaism, which was how he was raised and what he had fondly celebrated with his father.

He enjoyed the holiday spirit in general, sharing the same sentiment with strangers as well as his true friends—speaking of which, he wondered how the Count and his wife Aoife were doing.

Frankenstein spoke into his watch and made the call. It went straight to voicemail, so he left a message and realized how excited he was at the prospect of reuniting with his old friends. He looked forward to a relaxing time with good company.

He heard ambulance sirens off in the distance and remembered those free, friend-filled days from the past, forever lost to present responsibilities. No rest for the wicked. Even less for those choosing to help them.

# CHAPTER 16

Another day had passed as the weeping willows shed their leaves like tears in remembrance of a fallen day. Winter slowly began to reveal itself, with its wispy tendrils stealing out to touch the transmutation of the seasonal cycle and solstice. Outside the hospital, the moon was disguised by the clouds and it was pitch black. Nine o'clock at night: time to rise and shine, the start of a new day again.

Once more, Maria Claudia Luminita slid back the morgue slab, allowing the vampire and werewolf slowly to gather their bearings. She brought them some hot fresh coffee, for which they were immensely thankful. "Good evening, my count. My contessa. Please forgive the mess," Maria said apologetically, "but it's been a rather unusually hectic day and evening. Must be a full moon." As soon as she said it she realized who she was speaking to. "I'm so sorry ... I didn't mean—"

"Please, please, my dear," Aoife said. "We can't begin to thank you enough for all that you do for us. You honor us as well as your patients by the sacrifices you make every day and night, full moon or not ... but yeah, I get it."

A local mortician and his diener were working in the morgue at the time, making funeral preparations for a recently expired patient. The decedent was scheduled to have a viewing and a small ceremony in the hospital chapel upstairs, as per family request. The mortician's assistant was aiding in the postmortem exam process, making embalming preparations while the mortician himself was busy preparing to wire the jaws shut so as not to drop open at an inopportune time, scaring the hell out of any funeral attendees.

The Count, the Contessa, and Maria looked on with a quiet, grim fascination. The morgue slab revealed a hideous corpse with a shrieking face, obviously some victim of an unfortunate, grisly tragedy. The deceased had terrified eyes bulging out of their sockets and mouth wide open agape with rigor, as if frozen while screaming. The dead, dry tongue dangled off to the side like a toad seeking a nonexistent fly. Decorticate posturing revealed stiffened arms and hands reaching up as if to defend against its soon to be last makeover.

All three were gazing at the ghastly corpse when Aoife said, "He looks so peaceful. I wonder how they do it."

The mortician, the diener, Maria, and the Count all stared at the deadpan werewolf.

Dracula snickered and replied, "Behave, my dear," as everyone resumed their present duties.

Aoife noticed that Maria Claudia looked exhausted and somewhat haggard. She hoped that the young nursing assistant wasn't being worked too hard. Ever since Covid, these were tough, demanding times for medical personnel. Maria seemed quite dependable, if not passionate when tasked with her extensive range of duties.

The Certified Nursing Assistant pulled Dracula and Aoife aside in order to speak more privately and address the local news and rumors that had been windmilling around her new friends.

"Apparently there has been a rash of child abductions around town. Children are going missing at an alarming rate, and everyone is afraid. Some locals have even insinuated that it's the doing of monsters. They have specifically mentioned you two by name. Please forgive me, for I know that not to be true, but once the rumor mill starts it's hard to stop."

"That's horrible, Maria. How can we be of assistance?" said Aoife.

"I'm not sure. I just wanted you to know so as to be careful. I'm sorry about your recent home invasion and arson, I don't know what I'd do. You both know well that angry vigilante mobs aren't necessarily a thing of the past. Why, they're even arranging for a town meeting to address everyone's concerns and develop a plan of action. Law enforcement's assurances that *everything will be taken care of* isn't appeasing them anymore," said Maria Claudia.

"Panic produces dangerous people. Fear and hatred are its byproducts," Dracula said. "We'll look into it, and thank you, Maria. We don't know what we'd do without you."

"It's my pleasure, Count. I have two children of my own whom I would do anything to protect."

Aoife looked at the Count intently and said, "Perhaps it's time that we looked up some old friends." Dracula nodded, and off they went into the night, heading in the right direction. Aoife suggested that they meet their old friend in person, so they made their way across town toward the castle on the hill. Castle Frankenstein.

# CHAPTER 17

The Count had kept his cell phone turned off while they were in the hospital so as not to disturb anyone, including themselves. As fate would have it, he saw just as they were leaving that he had a voicemail from their old friend Captain Frankenstein. He wished the two of them well and asked them to call or stop by for the holidays. *Fortuna fortes adiuvat.*

Dracula and Aoife were walking past the local comic book and collectible card store on the corner of Deacon and Lafayette with its two owners, Finley and Seamus O'Sullivan, hanging out front. Finley said, "Excuse me, Mr. and Mrs. Maybe you shouldn't go that way just right now."

An emporium of comic book delight, Finley and Seamus's store stocked new as well as back issues with a couple dozen decent slabs on the wall. They also carried all variety of card realms and wanderings and gatherings.

The two ginger brothers had always imagined having a comic book and collectibles store as an excuse to hang out with likeminded fangirls and fanboys. Talking about the important things in life. They kept a pretty good turnover of decent-plus inventory and occasionally were graced with rare gifts from the gods like a pre-murder O. J. card or the first appearance of Doom.

"There's some pretty salty-AF mean drunks in Corey's Bar up the street," said Finley to Dracula and Aoife, "and well, you can hear it from here."

"I don't care if he thinks he's somebody special, this is 'Merica! Not 'Sylvania," yelled Tad Hafstaff, owner of Hafstaff Automotive, Inc. The successful auto dealership had been founded by his father, Eli Hafstaff, who handed it down to his oldest son, along with his racist bigotry and intolerance of others.

"That was an old TV brand, douchebag," said his wife, Katy.

"No, you shut up! I'm stakin' him," said Tad.

"I'm with you, boss," said one of his employees, his brother Ricky.

"Goddammit! You morons," said Ricky's wife Carol.

Dracula shook Finley's hand with a firm grip and said, "Thank you."

Finley exclaimed, "Damn, you HAM!" as he pulled his hand free and wrung it in his other. "We gotchoo," he said.

As they turned around the corner and walked away, Seamus was watching Aoife from behind and said softly, "Choice. That some snack."

From the dark beyond the lamp post, they heard Dracula say, "I can hear you," and they both fell and climbed over each other trying to get back into the store hurriedly.

So the Count and Contessa moved down the alleys, taking the long way to Castle Frankenstein. Soon they were in awe of the landscape as they made their way up a long, private driveway. A sculptural jacaranda bordered by hedging guided their path to the private entrance guarded by a wrought iron gate.

The stone castle itself was built into the mountainside, leaving only the front undefended against intruders and interlopers. Perhaps that is partly why it wasn't destroyed in the past by angry mobs and townsfolk wishing to do harm to the dwelling and its residents.

Castle Frankenstein. The exterior structure of the castle itself was made up of a menagerie of mismatched gray stones that shouldn't fit together but did, not unlike the master of the house himself. The roof's edge all along the outside walls were adorned with several grinning gargoyles standing guard, never leaving their posts. Their protruding tongues gave raspberries to unwanted visitors, warning off door-to-door panhandlers and Johos. These Gothic creatures otherwise performed their main duty as waterspouts, conveying the roof water away from the castle, thereby preventing the erosion of mortar in the masonry walls.

The French legend of the Gargouille describes an event whereby Saint Romanus subdued a fire-breathing dragon with bat wings by capturing it with a crucifix and the help of a condemned man. They took it to Rouen and burned it. However, the monster's head and neck didn't combust because of its naturally fire-retardant tissue. The head was then mounted on the church wall to protect against evil spirits. In commemoration of Saint Romanus, the archbishops of Rouen were annually to set a prisoner free allowed on the day that the reliquary of the saint was carried in procession.

Somewhat lost to keep, the impressive architectural design of Castle Frankenstein was still foreboding to those unfamiliar with the home's long heritage. The property had been paid for long ago and housing prices had skyrocketed inexorably. The land itself was likely worth a small fortune. Saul kept it simply because it was his childhood home, holding countless fond memories of him and his father.

Just prior to reaching the wrought iron gate, Dracula and Aoife were suddenly confronted by a figure from the shadows: none other than Dr. Henry Jekyll, one of the owners of the local apothecary. He looked about, then voiced his concerns fervently with a hushed hesitance:

"Pardon the intrusion, dear Count and Contessa, but I really didn't know who else to trust with the information that I possess. It is of the utmost importance that you hear me. Heed my warnings, please.

I've tried to hide in the quiet of alone, but there is evil afoot in this town, the likes of which it has never seen. It has come to my attention that certain local individuals are to release a scourge upon our holiday season that will leave only heartache and pain in its wake."

His sheepish heart bleated like goat speak as if innocent bleeding were draining the moment. The vampire and his wolf partner listened on in earnest to the skittish stranger, who then skulked off into the night, leaving them to wonder whatever had they walked into.

# CHAPTER 18

The old Druid heard a noise just outside in her backyard. To the window she flew like a flash. She tore open the shutters and threw out the sash. Then what to her wondering eyes should appear? Why, none other than the disheveled Mr. Hyde himself. His eyes looked mad as he stuck his head through her window and announced, "I told you, witchiepoo, that Jekyll was not to be trusted! At this moment, the fool is revealing your plans to the Count and that werewolf wife of his! He'll be the downfall of us all! Kill him you must, I say, lest your wretched soul be consumed. I live to love to hate, and his very being lies at the apex of my hateful discontent."

"Do tell," said the witch. "Do tell."

Hyde continued his unsavory rant. "It was that piecemeal monster Frankenstein that foiled your retribution against the mayor's inbred pups. And by the way, you've one less mummy to feed. Ha ha ha haw."

The witch Bridgett was outraged. "How dare that oversized sewing kit interfere with my plans! I'll deconstruct him like a gastronomical delicacy. Tell me, Hyde, how do you feel about revenge?"

The scowling, drooling creep exclaimed, "Now you're talkin', toots! I thought you'd never ask."

"Methinks it's time to up the ante. Come, my wicked fiend." Bridgett led the exuberant Hyde to the door and inside, to the massive cauldron on the open fire within her hearth. Her chanting and obscene castigations competed with the juvenile cries for help which droned on from the damp, dark cellar below.

# CHAPTER 19

The creature lived in the deep, murky depths of the bottomless lagoon. Black water matching the darkness in the monster's uncaring heart. It was an animal composed only of id. A creature of habit. As bad as habits get. It wanted only to feed. A gillman whose mouth gaped for air and malice. An evolutionary freak of nature. A throwback to when swimming led to walking and gills led to lungs. The amphibious man had both. He was a protohuman whose gills extracted oxygen from water to excrete carbon dioxide, just as his lungs did with air. However, he had not yet developed the capability of human speech, not unlike so many humans.

Still, an omnivorous machine that was never quite satiated. Webbed palms and feet to assist in underwater locomotion and a vestigial tail harkened to some reptilian offshoot or mutation. The monster resembled some deep-sea relative like the angler fish and had a similar glowing lure on a stalk emanating from its forehead. The distracting light was used to draw curious prey into the kill zone. This modified luminescent fin ray contained bacteria capable of producing light. Using a muscular skin flap, the monster could either hide or reveal its lighted lure. How many such piscine humanoid creatures existed and survived into the present, no one knew for sure. Maybe it just got lost from the rest of its collective school, or knot, or army, or maelstrom. Probably maelstrom.

Its diet consisted mainly of plants, fish, and the occasional red-blooded mammal. Born out of hell's dark night, it lived beneath the waves. Lurking, searching, stalking its next prey to feast upon. Its appetite for consumption knew no bounds. Whereas others strived and struggled to survive, the beast from the depths sought only to kill. Again and again.

The old witch knew that she could dispatch the creature and its unholy terror upon whomever she so desired. Controlling its murderous instinct and intent was accomplished through a series of ancient runes and invocations. Yes, he would do nicely in carrying out her villainous revenge.

Bridgett Bishop flayed her hands, wrists, and arms in a cantankerous, crippling manner, swiping ghostly fumes from the surface of the cauldron. Just a pinch more of turmeric and superstition. Yes, that's it. A sprinkle of wanton desire and rage and her curse would lend caution to the devil himself. Giddy as a schoolgirl, the witch flew about the room in exuberant, mad delight.

With that, the witch and Mr. Hyde made their way from the devious domicile, journeying down to the lagoon water's edge. Bridgett fell into a depraved meditative state as her eyes rolled back into her head and her lips commanded the dark forces to unleash their blasphemous maelstrom. "*Vloecur kanika trembla exones curatos.* I summon thee, creature from the deep, to come forth from the liquid in which you sleep."

Reveling in revulsion and revenge, the old witch continued her irreverent incantations. "Give rise to thee, my iniquitous fiend. Death to those whose mine curse has gleaned. Attack and consume what beholds my spell. Cast away, cast away to the darkness of hell."

Arising from the watershed edge, it was drenched and dripping with the stench of the swamp and rotted flesh from its last course. The night water did little to disguise the veracious nature of its being, adorned in kelp and seaweed. It truly was a creature from the depths of hell through and through.

The monster clamored forth from a watery grave that always held room for one more. Its bloody claws tore, ripped, and shredded flesh as if it were butter. An unquenchable appetite hungry for destruction and chaos. Its numbing callousness was at the beck and call of the cursed witch who controlled the watery demon with her cruel enchantments.

"Demon, demon, rise up from the abyss. Come forth to taste with your mangled kiss. Feast, my beast, my slave, my friend. Together our vengeance will have no end."

*Creature* was such a brash and tawdry moniker for this exquisite gill-man. *Beastie* sounded like some form of food predated upon by unscrupulous hunters in celebration of some autumnal harvest.

"Drink deep, my earthly monster. Eat fully, my unholy servant. Eat to fill, more to kill. Go forth, serpent, and claim my reward. Bring forth unto me the children of Killington, lest you suffer my wrath. Go now and dispatch my retribution!"

And with that the creature from the black lagoon, still wet with sweat and the stink of decaying vegetation, disappeared into the deep, dark forest shadows between streetlights meant to illuminate the unsuspecting suburbs. The glowing lure on its grotesque head blinked and faded into oblivion, not unlike the future of its next victim.

# CHAPTER 20

The mist rolled in softly as if it were a dream coming to fruition. One couldn't see the forest through the trees while the giggles and playfulness of children seemed ever more distant. As the number of missing younglings escalated, the villains conspired and strove to make sure that familial holiday wishes never came true.

A family not far from the lagoon had reunited for the seasonal holidays in their annual Airbnb waterfront cabin rental. As they did every year, they drove in from out of state to celebrate the leaf-colored fall in the arresting landscape.

Occasional splotches of snow overlapped the dying green as they ascended in elevation. November would soon fall away, surrendering to the coming onslaught of winter and her barren womb.

All of them looked forward to an evening of hot chocolate, s'mores, and glasses of Macallan fifty-two-year-old single-malt Scotch whisky around the fire. One of the couples, newly engaged, had planned finally to end the night with a relaxing hot tub soak and a bottle of 2000 Royal DeMaria Chardonnay ice wine, a favorite of the recently deceased Queen Elizabeth.

The creature from the black lagoon was just becoming acquainted with the glow of lights coming from around the house and the lights inside revealing moving things. The monster was attracted to the light much in the same way as its own prey to the blinking light hanging from its head. A faint scratch at the dining room window glass aroused unwanted feline curiosity which was bound to kill the cat.

Craig had decided to Jacuzzi it sooner than later and now sat back while the water jets and lights massaged his muscles and ego. He wasn't sure what he had done to make his fiancée mad, but he assumed that he was probably guilty. So he inhaled deeply the rising bath salts, hoping for a high. His hot tub timing was due for a rude awakening.

He laid his head back onto the cushioned headrest to look at the starry sky, free of city light pollution, and thought, *What a life.* He casually closed his eyes and smiled. A few drops of moisture dripped gently onto his face and lips. The taste was terrible and foul. He opened his eyelids and saw the glowing light above him. For a second he thought it was a star in the sky until he was greeted by the scaly, glass-eyed face of the hideous creature from the lagoon.

It snarled and ensnared Craig's head with its claws and forcefully yanked him out of the soporific tub and dragged him into the nearby tree line. Craig screamed quietly when his vocal cords were severed, as well as all ties to life.

Pretty soon his fiancée Desiree walked out of the back door in her Dolce & Gabbana one-piece swimsuit, carrying a chilled bottle of the ice wine to offset the hot tub steam.

Juggling bottle and two crystal flutes while balancing in her heels, she was nonetheless adeptly texting while walking the snowy path. She had just noticed the silhouette of a head sinking down below water level when she realized that she had broken one of her recently manicured fingernails.

"Dammit! I just had them done. I knew I shouldn't have come here. Trapped all weekend with Elmer party. Broke nail. FML," she texted.

Her friend responded, "459 ily," to which Desiree typed, "tyty. I'm crunk."

The last text simply said, "Be careful."

She set everything down on the hot tub side table and eased herself into the 101degree relaxing soak. While she was attempting to pour two glasses of wine, the underwater figure swam through the jet bubbles toward her.

Desiree reached out to hand her submerged boyfriend a glass of the frosty sweet concoction when the creature rose up to stand before her. She had absolutely no reaction beyond shock and surprise as the gill-man monster took her under and the hot tub jets bubbled up blood, adding to the chromotherapy mood. The monster's red, dirty slush and snow prints left a trail that led to the back of the glamping cabin.

The rest of the family and their spouses were inside, including Craig's two brothers and sister who were watching some old black and white movie and arguing as usual.

"So who's the guy with the hat?" asked Todd.

"It's Todd," replied Brad.

"What?"

"Nothing."

"Is he a bad guy?" said Todd.

"Who?" said Brad.

"The guy with the hat?"

"What about him?"

"Who the fuck is the guy in the goddamn hat?" asked Todd.

"I said Todd, you asshole!" replied Brad.

"I'm gonna kill you!"

"You don't listen!"

"Who?"

"Shut the hell up!" said Brad.

Just then Joan walked into the room and asked, "What are you idiots watching?"

"Don't ask," they answered simultaneously.

The rest of the clan was in the living room, playing cribbage on a coffee table. Somehow the game had gotten distorted into a drinking game and everyone was skunked and pegged..

There was a partially eaten double devil's chocolate birthday cake with smoldering candles off to the side. Someone had blown out their last candle. No need to make another wish. It blended in with the smoke from a finely rolled Cuban, giving the room an earthy forest fire stank.

Suddenly the back door shattered and the creature made his entrance into the home and hearth. The fireside coziness was diluted with the late fall chill like a celebratory toast watered down with fear and desperation.

Dreams of winning the pot were replaced with decomposition and maggots crawling over carcasses. He sees you when you're sleeping. He knows when you're awake, by the sound of your shrieking in disbelief and terror.

Their blood loss reciprocated their demeanor. Bone and sinew were torn asunder in a bloodbath spatter of hellish delight. The ruddy scarlet garnish sat in contrast to the creature's green gills, making for a holiday color scheme like no other.

The Airbnb welcome book was covered in blood splatter, anticipating a less-than-five-star review. The creature left the same way he came in, leaving behind a scene of mayhem and a bloody webbed-foot imprint on the sign that had fallen from the back of the front door. It read, "Thanks for choosing us. Come back again soon!" Thankfully, the creature couldn't read.

# CHAPTER 21

Saul finally made it home and threw his keys into the Chihuly glass bowl that resembled a vaginal sea form. He was ascending the stairs to take a shower when there was a loud knock on his large, oaken front door. As he peeked through the tiny mail slot into the chilly evening, he saw the familiar outlines of husband and wife. His old friend Count Dracula and Aoife, his lovely werewolf bride.

Frankenstein opened the heavy wooden doors and officially invited them both inside. The unnecessary formality being one of respect for the Count's particular etiquette. The three of them took turns hugging and looking each other over. Time always seems to age everyone except oneself. They were all a little bit older and grayer. A bit more mature. But more than anything, they were animated to be together again. A motley crew of monsters.

Aoife was indeed the alpha of the group, and always had been. She was smart, fast, quick on her feet, and always reliable. Anyone with half a brain knew that it was better to have her as friend rather than foe. Still, she possessed a disarming animal magnetism and appealing quality about her always. Sometimes it was impossible to tell if she was becoming part wolf or part human. Even as she entered the castle foyer, it appeared that her hair structure was moving dynamically ever so subtly.

"You two are a sight for sore eyes," Saul exclaimed. "Seriously, my eyes are still burning from the smoke. I was on fire not too long ago. I must smell like a dumpster."

Aoife frowned and said, "Dear lord! Are you all right? Do you need to go to the hospital?"

"Been there. Done that. I'm okay. I just came from a house fire. The mayor's, actually. His two kids were in shock and going on about a monster. The babysitter confessed, however, that she may have left some scented candles burning to cover up the smell of her and her boyfriend smoking. Looked like every other accident we see all the time."

"No offense, but I thought I smelled something burning," the Count said. "Looks like the aversion therapy is working?"

The residual smoke rose above his work clothes and dissipated as Saul replied, "You know, yeah, I think so. I'm so focused on doing my job and completing the work at hand, and not getting myself or anyone else killed, I usually forget to have a panic attack."

Aoife smiled. "We're proud of you, Saul. You inspire us."

"I can say the same about you two," Captain Frankenstein said. "Especially you, Aoife. Sorry, Count."

Dracula reinforced the sentiment. "I couldn't agree more. She's saved my life too. More than once. I'm so glad we could get together before the holidays."

"Me too. Hey, the guest room is the same as when you were here last. After I left the voicemail, I made sure the shutters were boarded shut and the light-blocking drapes were drawn. I'll get some clean sheets and towels. *Mi casa su casa*, always."

"A shower sounds wonderful! I could use it," Aoife exclaimed. "Don't look at me like that, my dear count. Wolves like to be clean too. Saul, has it really been a year since we last saw each other?"

"The holidays, yeah. We should keep in touch better," said Saul.

"Agreed. Time seems to catch up with us sometimes. The older you get and all that," said Aoife.

"You're not kidding," Dracula said. "However, you're never too old to have the best time of your life."

"Church," said Saul. All three friends and monsters smiled and settled into the comfort of their camaraderie.

They felt at ease in their own skins as they sat in the study by the fire, getting reacquainted. Saul retrieved some tea and water from the kitchen and poured everyone a snifter of Rémy Martin Louis XIII Grande Champagne cognac.

Aoife looked around the room at the impressive collection of rare first-edition books that lined all the shelves from ceiling to floor and said, "I'm always impressed by the magnificence of your castle every time we visit. It seems to live and grow along with you in a way."

"The ivy at least. It's home. A lot of memories, good and bad, mostly good," said Saul. They continued conversing and laughing as if they had just seen each other yesterday. "So, would you two like some dinner or nosh or whatever?"

Dracula said, "No, no. None for me."

"And you, my dear?" asked Saul.

"I'm good. I've been snacking on cashews and macadamia nuts," Aoife said as she grabbed a handful from the crystal bowl on the fireside cocktail table. As Saul went to fill the almost empty bowl, he offered it to the Count.

Aoife said, "He won't eat them."

"Why not?"

"I don't know if I have a nut allergy or not," Dracula said.

"Wait. Are you kidding? How old are you?" Saul said.

"I'm not sure, but I was born before the Ottoman Wars."

"And you don't know if you have a peanut allergy?"

"I could for all I know," said Dracula. Aoife and Saul burst out laughing. Dracula continued, "Yeah, yeah. I don't think I'd like them anyway."

All three continued chuckling as old friends reunited.

"So, I didn't know that I was allergic to shellfish," Saul said. "I went with our EMS crew one time for lunch to an all-you-can-eat seafood buffet. We received a call as I was stuffing my face, and by the time we got there, I was swollen even more grotesque than normal."

"Please don't say that," Aoife said.

Saul continued, "Seriously, I looked like some hideous Franken-blob or something. Anyway, I was giving mouth to mouth to our victim when she woke up and saw me and screamed to high heaven, so I screamed to high heaven, and then she fainted."

They all sat silent for a moment. Then all three echoed with boisterous laughter.

They all embraced each other's company. They had an unspoken bond and trust for good reason. The fact that they were all outcasts simply for being different united them in a monstrous way. Plus, they loved and respected each other as living creatures. Human or not, humanity bound them together: their belief in it and the parts they played within it. Which led them to the reason at hand: the missing children. Probably rumors of nothing. They all agreed that it wouldn't hurt to find out. Or so they thought.

Little could they imagine the pain that was headed their way.

# CHAPTER 22

Law enforcement wasn't saying a lot, perhaps so as not to cause a panic or interfere with an ongoing active investigation. However, it appeared that Maria Claudia and Jekyll were on to something. Frankenstein had heard the same. Rumors abounded all around the little hamlet concerning the disappearance of the children. The Count discussed the situation with Aoife and Saul, and they decided to call their friend at the university for help getting to the bottom of this cryptic conundrum. In the morning. Which was quickly gaining on them.

"Dr. Ralph Ellison is the smartest person that I know," Dracula said. "Surely he can help. He's quite busy in his research lab and teaching at the university, though. Let's try to FaceTime him this morning, for all the good that will do."

His wife Aoife got the inside joke. How do you FaceTime the invisible man? Of course, he wasn't invisible unless he made it so, and only for reasonably short periods of time.

Dr. Ralph Ellison was one of the first black men to head and oversee the entire science department at the university. His titles did little to address his accolades, since there was no one better suited nor anyone who even came close to matching his dedication, commitment, and educational pedigree in the field of quantum stealth physics and perceptual psychology. When it came to the study of light science, he could have taught anywhere on earth, but he chose here because of family ties, the ability of the university to accommodate his research needs, and the simple elegance and beauty of the natural surroundings. He also liked the change of seasons and the iambic poetry of the ever-shifting backdrop. Who better to help solve this mystery?

Frankenstein yawned and said, reluctantly, "I don't know about you guys, but I'm exhausted and smell like a dumpster fire. You know where your room is. I had to have some repairs made so I upgraded the bathrooms. Goodnight."

Dracula bid Saul good morning at the same time Aoife said goodnight, and all three giggled, giddy with friendship.

"Thanks for being here," Saul said, reminding them all how thankful that they were to be with friends during the holidays.

Frankenstein retired to the master bedroom, as he was master of his domain and castle. Like his father before him. He only wished that he had someone to share it with. *A ruler without a queen measures only discontent*, he thought as he threw his smoky work clothes in the dumbwaiter and slowly stepped into his oversized walk-in shower. The water heater ramped up the temperature rather quickly, but Saul took little notice of the varying heat exchange as his nerve endings didn't always connect or register reality.

He bent to sniff his pits and grimaced. "Gross, you stink, Saul," he mumbled to himself as he was prone to do at times. *I so much needed this shower. I swear this scent of burning death almost makes me feel alive. The fear of fire. But no fear for Gretchen and Hank anyway. Not today.* He shuddered to think as the drops sprinkled across his heavily scarred body, never truly cleansing yet reminding him of his disfigured loneliness. He hoped someday to find someone who he could relax and shower with, safe from repulsive repercussions and salacious intentions. Someone to help wash each other's scars. Like Drac and Aoife. *Does that make me jealous, or just human? Or something else?*

He pressed the memory preset number one on the shower console, which was also Alexa voice-activated, though he never used it. *Why talk to something that doesn't understand? Okay, sometimes I do talk to her. Big deal.*

The sound and chromatic lights came on, activated by his motions, not feelings. "Clair de Lune." One of his father's favorites, and his as well when trying to throttle down his emotions, which were always geared up lately, it seemed.

The soothing chromotherapy lights that accompanied "Clair de Lune" glistened off his scarred body from head to massive scarred toe. He preferred the relaxing calmness of blue in particular, which gave his skin an almost green to gray tone as he washed himself from the hands-free dispensers mounted on the shower wall. He wished that he could smell the lilac-scented body wash that foamed up around him like rabies. For some reason, when the contractors had performed the renovations and remodel, they switched the hot and cold plumbing valves or whatnot so he didn't know which was which, but he couldn't really tell anyway. Only to a degree.

The blue light reminded him of the holidays. It was touted to promote a healing aura around one's person, reducing inflammation and swelling through the psychological benefits of positive energy. Mind over matter. Saul remembered reading an article in the *New England Journal of Medicine* which essentially concluded that placebo thinking and belief studies still led to a positive 33 percent benefit in whatever ails ya.

Saul cupped his hands together and looked at the pool of water, which resembled a chalice holding rain. The shower drops were a welcome storm to quell the fires below and around. He washed the stench of burning death upon him.

*I take a shower to try and hide the fact that I'm crying. No one could tell, even if they cared to look, but no one does. Only if I fell to my knees to the floor at the bottom of my ashamed sadness that speaks of tragedy would anyone notice. If I crashed and burned.*

His shampoo tears washed away like bubbles from wet kisses while he suffocated on the words and water that tried to cleanse his soul. But just for a moment. Till it was time to dry off. And out.

*I like the rain disguising my languish and longing. To be loved another moment. By sharing in the loss of another's pain upon my heart and superstitious hope for a healing tomorrow. For myself as much as them. To be saved or healed somehow.*

Frankenstein's monster. When he heard that some of the townspeople called him that, he was inspired instantly to think of a bad joke. It reminded him of how little they knew who he was. But did he? His parts were his own, a mosaic of modern genotypical geography. Male, female … an amalgam of unique ethnicities and backgrounds sometimes cast to the forefront despite his willingness and attempts toward neutrality and friendship. He dried off with the extra large plush towels and gave a passing glance at the mirror that was too fogged to see though clearly. *No true reflection at all.*

* * *

Husband and wife found their way to the familiar guest room in Castle Frankenstein. Aoife jumped onto the oversized bed from across the room and purred at the ceiling. "OMG! This is so much better than the morgue. No offense," she said as she made a snow angel in the silky sheets.

Dracula was opening the wardrobe to hang up his cape. "Look at this! It's full of new clothes. Our sizes. He's so thoughtful, I swear."

Aoife leapt out of bed and grabbed the woman's pink soft silk pj's out of Dracula's hand and headed for the shower. "Zoinks!"

Dracula's eyes and voice followed her as she tore off her clothes and strolled into the walk-in shower. There was no shower curtain nor steamy doors of any kind, and he just watched her as the overhead rain shower cascaded and rinsed the prior days and nights from her body.

He said, "I'd offer to wash your back, but I'm exhausted."

She looked at him and smiled. "Your loss."

If he could have flown, he would have. Instead, he unbuttoned his top collar button and said, "If you insist," and looked over as she beckoned him toward her into the hot, clean water's relief.

# CHAPTER 23

Professor Ellison addressed his postgraduate class on the mathematics of light theory, a passion project of his. "As you know, we can see objects because light reflects off their surfaces and onto the photoreceptors of the human eye. We have discovered a unique light wave that, when passed through a solid object, projects onto the surface of the background behind it, essentially rendering the foreground invisible. Each of these light wave patterns is changed and directed in a very particular way when it is sent through a distorted medium. We beam a specific light wave at an opaque layer of randomly arranged zinc oxide nanoparticles. We then calculate how the light is scattered by the zinc oxide particles and then extrapolate the pattern without the zinc oxide powder present.

"These unique light waves seem to defy our present knowledge of light reflection, proving yet again Isaac Asimov's quote, 'Today's science-fiction is tomorrow's science fact.' The practical applications of invisibility hold great promise in medical imaging and biomedical research. Time's up for today, team. Don't forget your assignments that are due, please."

Just then, the professor's phone vibrated, reinforcing his scientific belief in serendipity. He recognized the number immediately. It was his friend Count Dracula. "Count, my dear friend, it's been too long. How have you and your lovely wife Aoife been? In good tidings, I hope."

"Hey Ralph, it's Saul here too," said Frankenstein on speaker.

"Oh wow, you've got the whole gang there. We should get together for the holidays, my friends," replied the invisible man, visibly excited to hear their voices.

"Well, that's kinda why we called. We could use your help also," said the werewolf contessa.

Once pleasantries were exchanged, they got down to business. They described their unusual concern about the goings-on around the town and the perverse fear that had settled in amongst the townspeople.

"Interesting. Hopefully it's just some mass hysteria and paranoia surrounding the holidays, but I have to admit, it does seem strange. Occam's razor would indicate a nominalist and reductionist explanation. Removing unnecessary information and data is the fastest way to the truth. Chemophobia is the fear of synthetic substances arising out of 'scare stories' and exaggerated claims of danger in the media, something we've seen a lot of lately. The amygdala controls the fear response by stimulating the hypothalamus, which activates your fight or flight response. Your palms sweat, heart rate quickens, muscles tense, skin prickles, and stomach churns."

The Count, Aoife, and Saul briefly forgot that he liked to do that. All the time. Aoife giggled and asked if Dr. Ellison could meet with them to discuss the situation. He obliged. "To test our theory, we must first gather data. I'll take off tomorrow and meet you guys at Castle Frankenstein, if that's okay with Saul."

"I wouldn't have it any other way. Drive safe, bud. See you soon," said Saul.

And with that, Dracula, Aoife, and Saul hung up and adjourned to the fireside for an in-depth chat. Outside, a storm was brewing. The tempest and the teapot were about to boil over.

# CHAPTER 24

There was a small daycare not far from the old witch's house. She figured that was as good a place to hunt as any. She went about her magics and mastery of the macabre and summoned Anubis, the god of death, to pay them a little visit. He was instructed not to come back alone, lest he himself again know death's embrace, and with that the mummy willingly complied.

The daycare was half full as the children emptied out into the playground. Because of the seasonal rotavirus, many of the kiddies were at home while their parents took time off from work. Anubis shuffled his way along the perimeter of the playground. The owner of the daycare, Mrs. Hope Gibbons, saw the wrapped figure and thought it strange that Halloween hadn't yet ended for everyone and decided to confront him. As soon as she came face to face with the undead walking corpse with hollowed-out eyes, Hope knew that all was lost.

Anubis held a rather large antique axe that didn't come from a Halloween superstore. He swung the heavy blade in a full circle with almost no effort at all and bisected the daycare provider on the playground next to the slide. The top half of Hope fell onto the slide and rolled down onto the ground, greasing the aluminum chute like a slaughterhouse sluice trough. The lower half fell to the ground and, with the bloody torso still spurting, watered the grass like a blood sprinkler. The children bellowed and bawled, several falling to the ground and hiding their eyes. It was these three that Anubis snatched up and placed into a large gunny sack, which he threw over his shoulder like a big bag of russet potatoes.

As he made his exit from the crimson-stained playground, he turned his centuries-old neck to stare with empty orbits at the remaining children frozen in terror. He smiled and the cold embrace of death ran through their tiny little veins. An owl called out in the distance, inquiring to know the persons responsible for this atrocity. It was the mummy Anubis and the evil witch who lives down at the end of the lane, of course. Now, though, he too wishes he were none the wiser.

# CHAPTER 25

D r. Ellison got up, grabbed some coffee and his go bag, threw it in the car, and got an early start to meet his friends. Time had passed quickly since he last spoke with them yesterday. There was only so much one could do in a twenty-four-hour time period. His brain outpaced his motor skills such that he couldn't keep up with himself. He hoped that some new AI programs would help source this and thought, *They should have named it artificial human intelligence, since that's the definition of intelligence that it's based on. An oxymoron.*

When he was younger, Dr. Ellison had trained himself to sleep fifteen minutes less every third night in order to have more waking hours to pursue his studies and work. Eventually he got down to four hours a night. However, after a week of sleep deprivation he started seeing things, so he ended his experimental trial of one.

On his way out of town, he first had to stop by the university to tie up some loose ends and gather some research material that might come in handy. Dr. Ellison was a full-time staff member at the University of Vermont in Burlington, which had been founded in 1791. He was also an associate professor at St. Michael's College and Bennington College. In Latin, the university's initials UVM means *Universitas Viridis Montis*, which translates to *University of the Green Mountains*.

The 460-acre tree-covered campus was an eclectic mix of eras and architectural styles dating back to the seventeen hundreds. Vermont is known for its forested natural beauty, majestic green mountains, scenic hiking trails, destination-worthy skiing, and charming wooden covered bridges, which were not wasted on Professor Ellison during his road trip. It's also praised for its air quality, healthcare, and access to childcare, which made the present claims all the more troubling.

Dr. Ellison held degrees in biomedical sciences, neurosciences, medicine, and philosophy. He was comforted in knowing that he obviously did not have scolionophobia which is the overwhelming fear of school; didaskaleinophobia, the fear of going to school; logizo-mechanophobia, the fear of computers; nor dendrophobia, the fear of trees. He noted that he definitely had brumotactillophobia, or fear of his food touching, a mild form of obsessive-compulsive disorder, and diagraphephobia, or excessive fear of losing one's data or deleting files.

He drove through the White Mountain National Forest in his rental alone in his thoughts, enjoying the sounds of the wind and changing leafy landscape. Dayglow pumpkin patches and large round golden hay bales lit the path along the autumnal roadway. An eerie sense of foreboding hid beneath the pastoral landscape just out of sight. But not mind.

The crisp decay of the falling leaves led one to believe that a change in season or temperature was on its way and that winter was soon to follow. The misty-eyed Green Mountains lay down for an evening's nap without yielding their secrets. Midday had lapsed into dusk as the occasional deer had traversed the highway looking for a place to bed down for the night, not unlike Ralph himself sojourning onward toward Castle Frankenstein.

Mother Nature's handiwork was abundantly present in late September through October, and beyond if Jack Frost took a November sabbatical. A leaf storm washed across his windshield as the vehicle's auto lights came on to guide him to his destination. Killington, Vermont. *Seriously. Killington?* he thought.

Killington's Peak was Vermont's second-largest mountain at 4,241 feet and a great place to see the fall foliage hues spread across five New England states. He thought about the tales of strange occurrences supposedly happening in the area. His expectations were low—just like his gas tank, since no hybrids or electrics had been available at the car rental lot. *C'est la vie.*

Rampant conspiracy theories weren't really part of his wheelhouse, and unfortunately, missing kids weren't usually headline-worthy either. How odd that it was so commonplace as to be misconstrued as normal. Whether or not the long history of legends that thrived throughout the area had brainwashed the locals into believing in some imaginary tall tale or ghost story, or that leftover remnants of the Salem witch trials were resurfacing from bygone days, had yet to be ascertained. His money was on fear and prejudice leading to folklore as the root problem, as always.

As he drove, he noticed that the hair on his arm was standing at attention, trying to cover up the goose bumps that were not at ease. *A sudden chill in the air, that's all,* he thought, and he turned up the heat in his rental just a bit.

As far as he could remember, Vermont has been rich in folklore as thick as the trees in the Greem Mountain Forest itself. Since its earliest days of colonization and before, legends and tall tales had been handed down in Vermont from fireside chats to table talk amongst family and friends. Stories abounded regarding hauntings, witchcraft, Bigfoot, you name it. Vermont was the second-most likely state in which to encounter a UFO, with sightings occurring in eighty-eight per one hundred thousand residents according to the National UFO Reporting Center.

Ralph recalled reading some book in the university library about some unusual Vermont history. During the eighteen hundreds, the state of Vermont had a horrible outbreak of tuberculosis or consumption.

Little was known of the disease at the time, so many believed that the dead returned to "drain the life" from their loved ones, resulting in the vampire panic. In 1813, a man named Corwin died of consumption, only to be joined by his brother, who met the same fate six months later. Two reputable physicians at the time diagnosed that the first brother had become vampyr and fed on his brother. He was exhumed and his heart removed and publicly burned in the town square. It was claimed that his six-month dead heart looked fresh and was engorged with blood without any sign of decomposition.

Frederick Ransom was a twenty-year-old Dartmouth student who died unexpectedly on February 14, 1817. His father was convinced that his son was a vampire, so he had the body exhumed and the heart removed and burned.

Ralph made a mental note to tell the Count about this. Perhaps what was happening now was along a similar delusional vein.

Twilight overlapped with night and the stars were clearly visible in the sky as daylight bid farewell. He was driving over the hill when he saw it in relief against the postmodern sky. Castle Frankenstein.

The gate was left open in anticipation of his arrival and he drove onward along the scenic driveway leading to the large entranceway. The home itself was beautifully constructed into the wraparound mountain that seemed to cradle it in its arms.

Years and age had left its mark and imprint on the castle, just like it did on Ralph's face. His salt-and-pepper five o'clock shadow was spreading to all the hands on the clock. It was time to see his friends and he wondered if the years had left them also looking like an age-progression app—apart from the Count, of course.

Tossing his backpack and man-purse over his shoulder, he strolled to the oversized oaken door and easily visible security cameras and doorbell. He stopped for a moment and noticed the peculiar absence of people or sound. Or any life at all, for that matter. The absolute silence was noticeable as the faint whoosh and whisper of a light wind tried to foretell what was yet to come. Later, he only wished he listened harder.

# CHAPTER 26

Ralph rang the security camera doorbell. "What's the secret password?" the doorbell voice said.

Ralph responded, "Castlephobia, the insufferable fear of castles."

"Yeah, that's him. *Entrez s'il vous plait.*"

The lock clicked and Dr. Ellison pushed open the heavy wooden door. He passed through the entryway with thirty-foot high arched ceilings, rustic antler chandelier, and handcrafted woodwork embellishments that would have made Frank Lloyd Wright proud. There were ornate mahogany carvings in the finishing woodwork and brass highlights throughout. There was even a castle keep or donjon to be used as a refuge of last resort should the castle be attacked.

"We're in here," he heard Saul say, and he followed the voices into the large sitting room. The castle certainly had maintained its quintessential charm, with its huge walk-in fireplace ablaze with the comfort and scent of forest pine. The wooden beams served to protect against the ravages of time and angry mobs while wallpapered walls were adorned with the spoils of deer and elk hunts long ago.

"Come in, dear friend, we're all by the fire. How was your drive in? Can I get you something to drink or eat perhaps?" said Frankenstein.

"Fine, thank you. A bottle of water would be great," Dr. Ellison replied. Hugs and heartfelt handshakes and smiles were given all around the room and a kiss on the cheek went to and from Aoife.

"You look as lovely as ever, my dear," said Ralph.

"A little older and grayer, just like you. Definitely slower," said Aoife.

"Gerascophobia is the fear of aging, as you may know. One can deal with it by maintaining a positive outlook about elderhood and embracing your fears by creating cheerful daily habits. Also, be conscious of your values and treat your problems as an adventure, which leads us to the point of being here today."

Aoife responded, with a chuckle, "We missed you." They all sat around the fire catching up, reminiscing, and warming themselves inside and out with each other's company.

Aoife was quite a handsome woman with an almost Mediterranean look about her. Her olive skin was *la peau* and she displayed a full, dark-haired brow and flowing black hair that nested along her neckline. She was a *beaute naturelle*. Her eyes were heterochromatic, with one light jade and the other husky blue, which seemed to betray her heart. Her subtle dimples and slightly upturned nose gave off a youthful appeal that was noticeable from across the room. She never flaunted her *exceptionnelle* comeliness, but rather hid from it perhaps because of past fears and paternal reprisals. The Count loved her for who and everything that she was, and she as well for him.

"So how is your research going, my dear professor?" asked Dracula.

"Better than expected, I must say, but there's always room for improvement." Ralph continued, "I've realized that I don't cast a reflection in the mirror when invisible."

"I know how you feel," said the Count.

Saul asked them both, "So do you ever feel as if you don't exist at all?"

Dracula looked at Ralph for his affirmation and said, "No less than anyone, I guess. Does a blind person feel less than real? Probably the opposite sometimes. Validating one's own existence comes from within, not without."

"So the townspeople of this charming hamlet are concerned about monsters?" said Aoife passionately. "People have persecuted others for being different since the dawn of man. They fear anything that might somehow interrupt their complacency. After the Salem witch trials, this area and many others still legally prosecuted those accused of witchcraft. I could go on and on. Two hundred years before the Salem trials, there were werewolf trials in parts of Europe. People believed that those who consorted with the devil could transform into werewolves and would eat their children. Just for the record... not true. Not me at least."

"I believe it was in the late fifteen hundreds that Peter Stumpp was found guilty in a court of law of lycanthropy and consorting with Satan. They tied him to a wagon wheel and flayed his skin off with hot pincers. Then they chopped off his head and burnt the rest at the stake. Someone carved a wooden pole to resemble a wolf and they stuck Stumpp's head on top as a warning to the public. The secular parliament at the time recommended that the citizens form groups armed with clubs, pikes, halberds, and cudgels to hunt down and kill any named or presumed werewolves. Occasionally, some trials would include expert testimony from physicians. However, the generally accepted medical belief at the time was that consorting with Satan could absolutely lead to physical ailments and altered body humors," she said.

"Charming," said Saul.

Aoife continued, "People will judge us on our actions or not. I think that we should be true to ourselves and accept that for what it is. If you're true of heart, the rest will follow. In body and mind and sometimes much-needed restraint. Forgive my rant."

"I love you," said the Count.

"I love you too," Aoife said. "I love all of you monsters. Just exactly for who you are. As friends go, we could do a lot worse."

"Amen," said Saul.

The four of them lounged around the informal front parlor in oversized comfy chairs and a loveseat for the Count and his bride. The fire crackled and popped while they shared stories over glasses of mulled wine.

"Time passes. Yet it seems that some things stay the same. What with global pandemics, wars and conflicts, the human race seems chaotic now more than ever.," said Saul. "We've never seen anything like it. How 'bout you, Count?"

"Throughout the centuries," Dracula replied, "I thought that I'd seen the worst. However, that rarely ever seems to be the case, especially since populations continue to expand over time and many countries' aptitude for accurate reporting is in question. I remember being in London during the Great Plague of 1665 which killed over one hundred thousand residents. Fifteen percent of England's population died during that plague. Hence the rhyme, 'Ring around the rosie, a pocket full of posies. Ashes! Ashes! We all fall down.' It obviously refers to all the people who fell down dead from the bubonic plague. We carried posies or other fragrant flowers in sachets to mask the ever-present smell of death. It was horrible."

Dracula continued, "'Bring out your dead!' was heard often outside your front doors as wooden carts would roll down the cobblestone streets collecting the inordinate number of dead bodies during the time of the Black Death in Eurasia and North Africa. During the fourteenth century, one of the worst pandemics in human history occurred, killing upwards of seventy-five to two hundred million people."

"The Pestilence, the Plague, the Great Mortality. Death was in the air. They put X's on houses that were quarantined, as if to ward off the flea-ridden and aerosolized bubonic spores. 'Quarantine' derives from the Italian word for forty days. All ships and persons entering the Croatian city of Dubrovnik during the Black Death were isolated for forty days. The Great Plague killed half of Europe. Lepers, astrological alignments, volcanic eruptions, and Jews were all accused and blamed for the spread of the pestilence. Black cats were thought to be witches transformed and were burned alive, along with thousands of Jews. Those were grave times. Grave times to be sure."

They all sat solemn and silent for a while thinking of all that had recently come to pass, looking into the fire for answers amongst the burnt embers. Eventually they progressed their discussions to the unsettling business at hand. The Count and Aoife described their unusual concern about the goings-on around the town and the perverse fear that had settled in amongst the townspeople. So far, law enforcement had seemed befuddled and ill-equipped to handle whatever strangeness was happening. So it was brought to the attention of this ragtag improv group of monster friends that something needed to be done. That something wicked may be the root cause. Something wicked indeed.

# CHAPTER 27

Ivy Luminita sat at her desk in front of her class, typing her name onto the virtual blackboard that she shared with her students. The twenty one year old immigrant was thankful to land the job of substitute teacher for the seventh-grade class at Killington Public Grade School. Today, however, she was covering grades five through seven for some state-mandated social studies. By the book, if you wanted the funding to continue. Crossing the T's and dotting the I's. No child left behind. Some of the parents, on the other hand, should have been left out on a deserted island.

"Good morning, everyone," said Ivy.

"Good morning," the class resounded.

"I am Miss Ivanna Luminita. I'll be substituting until Mrs. Baldwin gets back."

"Is she okay? When is she coming back?" asked Tina.

"I hear she's doing well and will be back soon. I'll tell her you were thinking about her, Tina, is it?" asked Ivy.

"Yes, ma'am. Thanks," said the young girl.

"So, has everyone had the chance to complete their favorite holiday essay assignment in your workbooks?" asked Ivy.

An unenthusiastic "yes" regurgitated from the mouths of lambs, including from Ivy's younger brother Dorian. He had promised her at home that he would behave while she taught he and his fellow seventh graders, even though he had his fingers crossed at the time.

Pete Gunther was deeply involved in doodling a spaceship firing rockets when Tim Wilson snuck up behind him and grabbed him by his collar, screaming in his ear, "Piss pants!"

As often was the case, Pete was so startled and terrified that he dribbled a little. A lot. He was already high strung but the constant scare tactics were wearing thin.

"Look out! He's pissing his pants!" yelled Tim.

"Leave him alone!" Kwamee yelled back.

"He should just wear a diaper," said Tim to some audible chuckles.

"That will be enough, children!" shouted Ivy.

Pete sat silent, and you could see the red heat in his face burning through the unbearable truth of tears.

Annie Hawthorne was in seventh grade, but today shared class with her fifth-grade sister. *What could be worse?* she thought.

She looked at Kwamee at the desk next to her and smiled and nodded in support of his solidarity with Pete. He did the same and was just happy he lucked out and was sitting where he was.

*I'm just happy I lucked out and am sitting where I am*, thought Annie.

And so it went. Until the bell rang, signaling the end of another productive day. The children swarmed out of the front doors to freedom in the Vermont fall landscape. The brownish orange leaves fell upon them and were crushed beneath their feet as if none of them had a care in the world. Not yet at least.

# CHAPTER 28

The Boy and Girl Scout Camp was located on private property with access to a pristine lake and campground. It had hookups for electric, a potable water source, and outdoor shower and toilet, which was just a fiberglass box over a hole in the ground. Not far from the shore of the campground lagoon existed an old-timey wishing well with a rope and bucket on a crank. It had a small, refurbished roof above the original circular stone structure that led deep into the earth.

The plaque in front of the historic structure read: "Colonel Wilson's Well. This historic landmark dates back to the Civil War when resources such as fresh water were often in short supply in rural areas. The well is over 300 feet deep and connects with the water table and lake supplying most of the irrigation and drinking water to the surrounding areas. Colonel Wilson had survived the war without a scratch, which he attributed to his family's lucky well water. Over time, many came to believe that the well possessed magical powers and that anyone who willfully throws a coin into its mouth may be granted one wish. Be careful what you wish for."

The co-ed camp counselors were busy getting all of the new weekend arrivals settled into their respective cabins. Meal plans with dietary restrictions were being sorted and refrigerated. It was a good counselor to camper ratio, and the activities schedule was full.

While everyone else was scurrying around, vying for top bunk, Timothy Wilson read the warning on the well's plaque but paid it no attention. Tim had gotten into trouble for hitting his sister after she called him a booger-eater in front of everyone and they all laughed at him. She actually did see him eat a booger, but she didn't have to announce it to the world.

The boy tossed his quarter into the well and bent over the edge to listen for the plop. He closed his eyes and made a wish. "I hope my mean sister gets what's coming."

He listened on with a curious expression, not understanding why the coin didn't splash. *Maybe the well's run dry,* he thought. He looked down into the hole, into the abyss, and thought he saw the faintest light wiggling slowly closer and closer. The bioluminescent lure dangled temptation, so the boy reached down into the well to grab the firefly.

The creature lurched forward, grabbing the boy as he crapped his pants and dragging him back down into the deep dark hole. The boy's cries echoed hollow up through the well until he could be heard no more.

As Tim fell into infinite darkness, it crossed his mind briefly that he should have wished for something else.

Hundreds of water moccasins erupted from the mouth of the well as if fleeing from some terrible monstrosity. Several dozen of the male snakes formed a gregarious snake ball around the lucky female who welcomed the orgy of writhing slender bodies. In an act of sexual cannibalism, she then ate the lucky male nearest to her as another male took his spot. The snakes then slithered and scattered into the nearby woods and lake in search of an after-party, or at least a child's warm sleeping bag to bed down in for the night.

# CHAPTER 29

The moonlight glistened on the water's surface in the background, making for a perfect s'mores moment while listening to ghost stories around the campfire with friends old and new.

*These are the memories that I'll never forget,* thought Kevin. And he was right. His annual attendance at these fall scout outings made him a sort of pro. He figured it was up to him to show the newbies the ropes. After all, he was seventh grade and they were fifth and sixth, so dodgeball would be fun this year. He'd worked hard to earn his Boy Scout badge and 101 of the possible 138 merit badges, including the ever-difficult Inventing badge only ten scouts had ever received.

Kevin noticed one of the younger kids mumbling to himself alone and said, "Hey, my man. Could you give me a hand with some of this kindling? Preesh it." So they both walked over to the fire and threw the gathered wood onto the woodpile and took a seat with the rest of the troop.

The boy and girl scouts of Troop 414 huddled close together around the campfire, not because of the temperature at the deep forest hike-in campsite, but rather the intemperate ghost stories that seemed to flow freely from Scoutmaster Gary Larson's tall telling. He seemed to quite enjoy scaring the children with the well-known folklore that was passed on enough times to become local legend.

This particular yarn was about a ferocious water creature that dwelled within the nearby lagoon, steeped so long in fertile minds as to become lore. When the kettle whistled over, Gary clutched the mug of a dark, bitter Earl Grey left too long in the hot seat. *Something to warm your bones*, he thought, *take the chill out of the air.* He'd done this many a time, this scary rite of passage, and he didn't mind it at all. Kind of like payback for all the times he was bullied and scared as a kid. Being a scoutmaster was the perfect façade for a previous sex offender to blend into the community at large. If they only knew.

The firelight glow reflected off his face and eyes in a way that lent a certain credibility to this bedtime story more suited to daylight hours. He continued his fervent narration: "The water baptism was going well and traditionally in every way expected by the Southern Baptist Church of Vermont. But not far from this very spot was where that horrible tragedy had occurred. It was just when the preacher had dunked the first child that the creature emerged, bursting through the water's surface. With no afterthought, it snatched the child and preacher as well and dragged them to the godforsaken bottom of the muddy, silty lagoon. The two never surfaced again, and those present wondered if the ceremony had gone far enough to grant the child admittance into heaven. Shocked in disbelief, no one stayed around to find out, and they never spoke of it again for fear that the blasphemous creature would return for their souls as well."

Kevin stretched out as he listened and looked out to the lake beyond the fire. He noticed that between the lake and Scoutmaster Dingus was Old Colonel Wilson's wishing well. *That's odd*, he thought. The flickering shimmer of light dancing reflectively off the surface ripples was trippy. It almost looked like a flickering light was coming from inside the well.

The gill man's light lure rose up out of the hole as its dark claws crept up onto the wishing well's rim. It crawled up and out of hell's wishing hole and started toward the kiddie campers.

Gary the scoutmaster saw the horrified looks on the children's faces and smiled at his obvious gift for fearful storytelling when he noticed that they weren't looking directly at him at all, but rather the space just behind him. He winced and turned to come face to face with the creature. Now standing full upright, dripping wet with black slime and decayed flora, it mouthed movements as if trying to speak.

In a nonchalant way, the creature picked the scoutmaster up off his log perch and slowly but methodically removed his arms. The blood spatter extended to the nearby scouts when suddenly the disturbing person of Mr. Hyde appeared next to the aqua-monstrosity. He interrupted the broken shrieks and screams as he said, "Now, who wants to go for a drive?"

# CHAPTER 30

Officers Dailey and Holt were assigned the scout camp case. They did a background check on Scoutmaster Gary Larson.

"Alias Gary Linkletter, a.k.a. Jerry Lancombe. Red flags were everywhere," said Officer Holt.

"You gotta be kidding," said Officer Dailey.

"Get this. He had a history of third-degree rape and child endangerment and was not allowed to be within five hundred feet of a school. As a registered sex offender, he should have notified the appropriate authorities. His case file should have been transferred to his local parole officer, which he should be following up with. He was also court-ordered to continue his outpatient care through a mental health facility with random urine testing. Gary did none of that," she said.

"He was hoping that no one would notice. He'd slipped through the cracks before, why not try again?"

"What the hell was he doing as a scoutmaster? Isn't that kinda cliché?"

"Maybe for good reason. So, sex offender escalates into mass kidnapping?" asked Dailey.

"Who knows with these nutjobs. Let's put an APB out on the son of a bitch. And no one's gonna look twice if he gets shot resisting arrest," Holt said.

"Copy that."

# CHAPTER 31

Dracula's name was Vlad Tepes or Vlad Draculea the III or Vlad the Impaler, born 1431. He was Voivode of Wallachia three times starting in 1448 and a national hero in Romania. When he was a boy, he and his father Vlad II and his seven-year-old brother Radu were captured by Ottoman Empire diplomats. He and Radu were held hostage for five years in a citadel atop a rocky precipice in Turkey. It was there that he learned the arts of war, science, and philosophy.

Later, his father was killed in a coup by the local warlords known as the boyar, and his oldest brother was tortured, blinded, and buried alive. As a ruler, Vlad threw banquets for hundreds of invited members of rival families just to have them killed before dessert was served.

Often outnumbered, he resorted to torturing, poisoning wells, burning crops, and infecting his enemies with diseases. He had a penchant for disembowelment, beheading, skinning, boiling alive, and impalement, and would even dine in a forest of impaled bodies. Vlad dipped his bread in his enemies' blood and literally consumed it.

Some have even claimed that the Romanian prince was the creator and record-holder of impalement. He was believed to have impaled over twenty thousand people on pikes as a warning to those would-be conquerors who dared to attempt an invasion of his beloved nation. Stick-figure scarecrows drawing the lines in battle, pointing toward merciless torture of thine enemy. On one occasion he met with

Ottoman envoys who refused to take off their turbans for religious reasons, so he nailed their turbans to their heads with three spikes each.

To the people of Romania, Vlad brought justice and civilization. He fought for their freedom from tyranny by their fifteenth century enemies the Turks and Bulgarians. At the time, the dynamic world was a daily struggle for survival with everchanging landscape and borders. The authoritarian ruler fought against local crime and was highly revered.

The Romanian military forces later even named the AH-1RO Dracula helicopter after him. King Charles III of England, the current monarch formerly known as Charles, the prince of Wales, actually owns several properties in Transylvania and is heir to Vlad the Impaler's bloodline.

Dracula always hated that moniker, but he *had* been prone to outbursts of anger and violence since his youth. He was initially infected by the vampire's bite during the Ottoman War and went on to rule as vampyr. A strigoi who walked among the living. He performed his diligent duties by doing whatever it took to defend his realm and landholdings. To be sure, there was no shortage of other very bad people back then engaging in very bad behaviors as well.

At the time, Vlad thought that the only way to defend against these overpowering forces was fear, and the beheadings and impalements that decorated the entrance to his castle proved fruitful. Even in death, the skin retraction around hair and fingernails appeared to grow as if undead, terrifying their enemies further. It certainly was a deterrent to Sultan Mehmed II, who retreated back to Constantinople after witnessing the horrors of the countless number of his soldiers' heads on pikes that lined the three-mile long road toward Dracula's castle.

Over the centuries, though, Dracula came to grow weary of war and man's aptitude for violence. He eventually became an outspoken conscientious objector against wars of all kinds. *Why choose war when you can have peace?* he thought. Dumb question. He grew to abhor violence, even the petty nature of vampiric feeding. However, he was restricted from being totally vegan by his bodily needs. He did his best to turn the other cheek even when their full juicy jugular vein was presented.

Dracula *did* use his mental powers of persuasion, but as far as he knew, he hadn't killed anyone for a hundred years ... maybe, with few exceptions. He was just getting too old for that shit. Maturing with age like fine wine, not blood. He'd seen enough horror and gore and blood to make even a vampire sick to his stomach. He had his fill. Literally. He just wanted some semblance of peace. He longed for the imperfect kiss that would sway his imperfect heart, and would no longer delay him the satisfaction of being worthy of love. The moment of truth whereby love either defines or destroys itself. No looking back but just forward to just rewards.

Dracula had truly risen from the grave. Falling in love was the best thing that ever happened to him. It was his best friend and true love, his wife, Aoife. He didn't care if she was lycanthropic, or anything else. He loved her exactly as she was. Maybe this in part helped to mellow and mature him. Conquering and conquesting just didn't seem important anymore. So, there they were. A pacifist vampire husband and powerful werewolf wife just living the dream. The Count and Aoife had found the love of a lifetime. For Dracula, it just so happened to be literally forever.

# CHAPTER 32

Come in, come in from the ghastly cold, dear friends. You poor things must be freezing. Please warm yourselves by the fire while I fetch you something hot for your bellies," said the old witch. The two uniformed law enforcement officers entered the witch's home and removed their hats.

"We don't mean to be a bother, ma'am. We'll just take a minute of your time, if that's okay," said one of the officers. "This is Officer Dailey and I'm Officer Holt. We've been canvassing the neighborhoods looking into the disappearance of some of the local children and were wondering if you've seen or heard anything?"

"Oh dear, that's terrible! My word, I've never heard of such a thing," said the sly old witch. "Please have a seat, officers, my legs aren't what they used to be."

"So you don't know anything about it? Maybe seen anything suspicious around the neighborhood?" said Officer Holt.

"My dear, no, I haven't. When did you say this happened?" said Bridgett, listening carefully for any noises coming from the captured boy and girl scouts locked in the basement below.

The officers sat on the old antique loveseat near the fire while Bridgett served hot coffee with sugar and milk and placed the tray on the coffee table nearest them. She purposely stumbled slightly as if her body were frail and feeble. When Officer Holt stood to ensure her safety, Bridget exclaimed, "Fiddlesticks! I'm fine. I'm fine. Slow, but sure. I'll get there, by golly." She took a seat across from them.

Officer Dailey held out a photo of one of the missing children and handed it to Bridgett. "Have you perhaps seen this little girl by chance?"

The witch took it, frowned, and put on her reading glasses to examine the picture. "I'm afraid my eyes are failing me as well. The golden years, you know. Let's see," she said as she pretended carefully to inspect the photo. It was a five-year-old girl who just happened to match identically the photo on the side of the milk carton on the coffee table before them. She was three foot seven inches tall and weighed thirty-six pounds with red hair and dimples to die for.

Bridgett casually refilled their mugs while rotating the milk carton forty-five degrees so that the "Have you seen me?" photo was no longer facing the cops. "I'm afraid not, officers. I'll certainly contact you if I think of anything. I'm just so thankful having you trained people to look out for an old biddy like me. Please at least try one of my homemade gingerbread cookies. I insist, it'll be Thanksgiving soon after all."

"Well, thank you, ma'am. Sorry to bother you," Holt said as they both took a cookie and a bite. "These are delicious," said Officer Holt genuinely.

To which the witch responded, "I'll let you in on a little something. The secret ingredient is cinnamon."

"Well, thanks again, and Happy Thanksgiving," said Dailey as they left.

"The same to you, officers. I'll pray for you and the family, that they find their little one." With that the old witch closed the door behind them and sat back down to look more closely at the black and white photo of the missing girl on the milk box. Her name was Cinnamon. The haggard old witch cackled in laughter.

# CHAPTER 33

For some of the townsfolk, Thanksgiving season would come and go without a huff. For the families of the missing children, the horn of plenty blew an empty, hollow sound. No turkey or stuffing. No pinecone-crafted centerpieces, no pumpkins, no naps, not even a day off work for grieving. No Black Friday, no Cyber Monday, and before they knew it, Hanukkah and Christmas season would begin. Normally there was a sense of fellowship and holiday spirit that permeated the air and attitude of the local populace. None of it was happening. No one knew who they could trust. Were their very own neighbors cleverly disguised fiends hiding in plain sight?

The people of Killington were on edge. Tensions were high and there was strange talk about the town in quiet gossip and muted innuendoes. The locals had arranged for a town hall meeting at the auditorium at Killington High School to discuss everyone's concerns. Many of them thought of Dracula and his werewolf wife Aoife, as well as Frankenstein, as monsters, plain and simple. Not to mention mummies and lagoon creatures and the like.

In their eyes, their bigoted biases and prejudices justified their hate and fear, not unlike the way many of today's immigrants were treated. They had been worked up into a mad, frenzied fervor such that their judgment and common sense had grown impaired. Good taste disappeared like ice cream at a child's birthday party on a warm afternoon.

Angry shouts reverberated throughout the auditorium. "Go back to where you came from!"

"Those monsters hide who they are and where they are so they don't have'ta pay taxes."

"Criminals."

"Abominations."

"Witches and warlocks."

"Foreign freaks!"

"Do you really want your children mixing with them?"

"What happened to those missing children?"

"I am a repeat offender."

"Those monsters pose an existential threat to our democracy."

"Destroy all monsters!"

Slants and slurs reminiscent of the Salem witch trials echoed yet again. They confabulated controversy, which deflected truth and manpower away from the actual perpetrators. Law enforcement was neither friends with nor fond of the monster community at large. Some didn't even think that this group of people, who were a little different, had any rights under the Constitution.

All four friends had previously and unanimously agreed on a plan of action. Dr. Ellison had volunteered to attend the town assembly inconspicuously using his particular optical expertise. That evening, Ralph made his way to Killington High School and became a fly on the wall.

Mumblings and whispers of torches, stake burnings, and tar and feathers slowly died down as the town meeting was about to start. The back doors of the auditorium blew open and closed as if the wind had gathered strength outside. There was a definite storm coming. One could feel it in the air as the barometric pressure dropped and numerous ears popped.

A distinctive "ahhchoo!" rung out from the back of the auditorium and a polite spectator said "god bless you" to apparently no one in particular. Ralph hated the fact that he had to be nude to perform his bit of scientific magic. He was always cold, especially as the season was about to change. He made a mental note on problem-solving theories that might address these shivering events.

Sitting next to Ralph in the nosebleeds were three young redneck men. Jeb and Kaleb from Jeb and Kaleb's Airboat Tours and their childhood friend Mac. Many of the mentally less-than-well-endowed attendees still believed in boogens and Brzoski.

"You know goddamn well that that fang-toothed mother-blood-sucker and his wolf wife are no good. They're animals," said Jeb.

"Like primates?" said Mac.

"Kiss mine. It's about time for a Drac attack. He's guilty of somethun', one ways er anothu."

"All right, settle down."

"I'll settle fer his ass, hers too."

Mac pretended to draw back his fist to shut up his friend with a lip-smacker but the meeting was getting started.

"You're an idiot," said Mac.

"You shut up. You're just like those Muslim snake charmers we saw."

"Those were bagpipes, and they were Irish, dumbass."

"People! Calm down, people! Take your seats, please," said the local bishop hosting the meeting.

"You all know me. And you know that I want a peaceful resolution to this situation and for every child to be brought home safely as quickly as possible. I want to know as badly as you who is behind these atrocities, but we must not make haste. It's easy to blame monsters and such, but let's not rush to judgment until all of the facts are in. Please."

For the next two hours, a wide assortment of grievances and possible solutions were addressed in some nonsensical order including wooden stakes, silver nitrate, exorcisms, and even posses and vigilante mobs. Ralph listened patiently and silently to their misinformation and crazy conspiracy theories. The hate-mongers were more transparent than he was.

When the meeting ended, the redneck weirdos sitting next to him approached the bishop to voice their grievances and put in their two cents and asked for change. They were having a heated exchange, yelling at the man of the cloth who just stared at his feet, listening politely.

"Buncha bullies," mumbled no one. Ralph hated bullies, so as he was quietly exiting, he tripped Jeb, who fell on his ass and blamed Kaleb.

"Goddammit, you asshole!" yelled Jeb.

"You're the drunk gibroni. You can't even walk straight," said Kaleb.

"I'll straighten you out, boy," sneered Jeb as he tackled Kaleb to the ground.

"Will you dumbfuckcicle idiots please get up? My wife's gonna be pissed," said Mac.

"Poor baby. Is it time for your diaper change?" said Jeb.

Ralph had heard enough. When falsehood can so look like the truth, who can assure themselves of certain happiness? He couldn't understand why men and women who knew all about good and evil could hate and kill each other. He shuddered to think of what these people, his neighbors, would do to him if they were aware of his presence.

Common sense and peaceful coexistence were anathema to them. There was no reasoning with abject hate and misguided information when doomscrolling was the order of the day. Dr. Ellison quietly and cautiously left the same way that he came in, taking extra care not to make a sound.

# CHAPTER 34

To protect and to serve. Not so sure about either one. Law enforcement was doing their best, but pentagrams and cobra blood were a little out of their jurisdiction. Demonology wasn't a subspecialty in the forensics curriculum either. The group of four monster friends reconvened back at Castle Frankenstein where Ralph updated the group about the town meeting.

Dracula, Aoife, Saul, and Ralph all agreed on a game plan to investigate, gather evidence, identify any detected culprits, and deliver them to law enforcement so that justice could be done. Above all else, return any abducted children to their families safely. The strength of their resolve would determine their success where others could not or were not able.

Aoife reminded everyone that they each had choices. "Apathy is a choice. The belief that you can't change anything or even yourself is a symptom of apathy. Or you just don't give a shit."

They all agreed and brainstormed a game plan.

Being invisible offered many opportunities for discreet information-gathering and subterfuge, so Ralph would pursue his mission of data analytics. He thought out loud, "The pieces don't all quite fit together yet. Something isn't right. Are there any true villains at all, and if so, how many monsters do we have to contend with?"

On the back of page six in the local newspaper, there was a small article about a break-in and unusual theft at the local museum. Aoife volunteered to track down this less than promising lead. Dracula would seek out Dr. Jekyll for a more thorough interview and interrogation using his powers of persuasion and attempt to ascertain whether he was a reliable informant or not.

That left Saul to pay a house call to the old woman who was rumored to dabble in the black arts, although he found this somewhat offensive given the history of the Salem witch trials. He certainly did not want to contribute in any way to the local prejudices and unwarranted folklore. He'd experienced that himself firsthand.

One way or another, they'd get to the bottom of the conspiracy and separate fact from fiction. Little did they know how strange the truth actually was.

# CHAPTER 35

The cerulean sky wept profusely, giving rise to a dewy petrichor. Aoife loved the rain on a sunny day. It was a trigger for her ASMR, sending a tingle down her neck and spine. Her animal hair would fluctuate from human to other, giving her a frisson of pleasure. Though the sun was out, it was still late in the day, enough such that the half-moon stood attention in the sky against the blue background. A true pluviophile at heart, her favorite scent was just before and after the rain.

Her senses were already heightened by her lycanthropy and the air was so fresh and sweet she could almost taste it. She was enjoying the synesthesia when suddenly she was presented with an intense anachronistic smell of ancient decay and decomposition amid the new fallen rain. It was complex, with hints of incense, perfumes, and spices like cinnamon. And dust. The musty characteristics were familiar to the ancient Egyptian exhibit in the Natural History Museum. More specifically, a mummy.

The werewolf was on the prowl. Her innate hunting instincts had risen to the level of being preternatural. She was the alpha female and no man, woman, or beast would or should challenge her dominance if they had any survival instincts at all. Her very acute sense of smell was a hundred times greater than a human's and she could smell danger a mile away. Aoife's hearing was equally impressive.

Despite the rain and other interference, she vaguely picked up the familiar foul scent. She could almost taste the musk and ions from eons ago. By now she was on all fours, crisscrossing the trail and reestablishing the signs and smells as they grew slightly stronger, then stronger still. It led her through the forest, across rugged terrain, and down to some farm roads on the outskirts of town.

Distinctive peculiar pheromones mixed with petrol became apparent as she hastened her pace. The source of this puzzling paradox became readily apparent. It was one of the local school buses full of children returning to their country homes.

To her surprise and horror, the bus windows displayed tiny, frightened faces scrolling by like some time-lapse photo collage, crying and gaping out with palms splayed in surrender against the glass. One of the youthful faces tried frantically to open the safety window, which was designed for safety reasons not to open. It was Annie Hawthorne, and she was sitting next to Piss Pants Pete, or Pete as she liked to call him. The front of the bus revealed the driver to be the infamous Mr. Hyde with the gruesome mummy Anubis standing guard by his side.

The school bus barreled down the unpaved road, gathering speed and momentum. Hyde floored the gas pedal and the engine burped and belched, releasing its black smoke into the sky. The front engine was overheating and billowing gray smoke, which blended into the exhaust and occasional motor backfire. Hyde was laughing so hard that he was drooling and swerving like a madman.

Suddenly he heard an unwelcome thud on the roof of the bus. It was the werewolf Aoife. She had leapt from a nearby, overhanging shale precipice. The mummy Anubis made his way to the rear of the bus and crawled atop from the rear emergency door.

As he crept behind Aoife, he brandished the ancient Egyptian weapon of death, the mace-ax. The ancient Egyptian military was one of the world's greatest fighting forces during the New Kingdom period, and the mace-ax played its role. It was as disturbing as it sounded. It consisted of a heavy, bludgeoning brass club on one end with a razor-sharp, curved blade embedded in its center. It could easily break enemy swords and bash through even the strongest bronze armor.

The smoke cleared slightly just in time to reveal Anubis raising his mace-ax above Aoife's head, about to strike her down. She dodged and rolled at the last second. She parlayed her riposte with a kick to the mummy's dusty groin, to no effect. He swung again and she fell to the roof of the bus in time to sweep the mummy's legs out from under him. The werewolf pounced and was swiftly atop Anubis, striking him down, tearing his decayed torso to shreds. She bisected his body, but was left with the animated top half still fighting and struggling.

Hyde chortled with glee and drove the bus filled with children full speed off the embankment and into the air, leaving Aoife and what was left of Anubis on the cliff edge behind. Aoife clawed and pulled Anubis's head adorned with his regal crown off his torso and tossed it over the cliff as she peered over the edge. The god of the dead was sent to meet his ardent admirers in the afterlife.

The school bus too had crashed into the lagoon below and, now, bobbed like a cork on the water's surface, attached to a fishing line that teased a bite. The children were bruised and battered but alive.

Their cries for help suddenly stopped as a presumed rescuer smashed open the back door to the bus. Annie and Pete and the rest of the kiddies saw the rescuer waving his flashlight in front of him, showing the way—but then they froze in abject horror as they realized who their savior actually was. It was the shrieking, clawing, dripping water creature from the black lagoon come to embrace them. Its gangly, blinking luminescent forehead bait lured in the prey. A sea beast that walked on two legs with talons as sharp as needles. Annie felt the water next to her get warm.

To her dismay, Aoife looked down and saw Hyde and the creature taking the children to a nearby, oversized utility van waiting nearby on the water's embankment. The two fiends and their kidnapped cargo of tykes sped away abruptly into the maze of unpaved roads dispersed throughout the forest canopy below.

# CHAPTER 36

The old witch was just finishing putting the final touches onto her basement cellar prison for the children. A soundproof door and paneling was installed, leading to the creaky wooden stairs that betrayed the witch's careful approach. She had contracted a handyman from the local Home Depot to perform the work and told him her grandson's band would practice down there at all hours.

"They're all dears, but I don't understand it and it's too loud for me. But I'm just an old biddy," she said with an innocent puppy dog smile.

Row after row of metal cages were stacked like cordwood in anticipation of the day's catch, which was just arriving. Each cage was equipped with an automatic pet feeder and water dispenser so that the captured children would stay alive and, hopefully, plump up, not unlike ducks destined to be foie gras. She salivated at the thought.

Mr. Hyde burst through the lower cellar door while the creature from the black lagoon opened what once was a coal chute and started sliding the screaming children down the sloping trough into the awaiting cages. Pets or poultry, no longer free range.

Mr. Hyde then began lapping his lips and aggressively shaking one of the cages, much to the dismay of the kid inside, who scurried to the rear of the enclosure like a fleeing hamster. It was Piss Pants Pete. The scared boy frantically crawled and clawed at the back of the cage and tried to scream and cry at the same time, but got all choked up and just gurgled. This time, he was doing more than pissing.

Bridgett reached out and struck Hyde on his hands with her broom handle and scowled. "Don't play with your food!"

Hyde retreated with a grimace. A black cat hissed and ran across the floor to hide from this obscenity beyond even her capacity to watch.

"There was old woman who lived in a shoe. She had so many children, she didn't know what to do. She gave them some broth without any bread; she whipped all their bums and sent them to bed," clanged the old witch. "I surely would've known what to do. That old bitch didn't know how good she had it." She licked her greasy fingers.

# CHAPTER 37

One of the reasons that Professor Ellison wanted to stop by his lab at the university before he left on his journey to Killington was that he wanted to pick up a few things that he had been working on recently—more specifically, a new trial of nanotech injectable serum that would give the user an alternate transient window, per se, into invisibility.

It still needed further randomized trials, and the statistical data was raw, but he was chomping at the proverbial bit to try it. He was still somewhat unsure of its duration of effect on an average seventy kilogram man, but he believed it to be 126 minutes. He was 74 percent sure, with a standard deviation of plus or minus 2 percent. He loaded up the essentials just in case he found a suitable environment for an in vivo trial, and went on his way.

Still, Ralph decided to perform his part of the reconnaissance *au naturelle*, and without the aid of Professor Invisible, or Dr. Invisible, or whatever moniker made the most sense. His tailored gray fall flannel suit cast little doubt or shadow upon his station in life as he made his way through streets and cross-streets. He chose to start with some of the local grade schools, since children were involved and they weren't as easily prone to outright lying like many adults. He welcomed the innocence and truthfulness that was embedded in youthful minds.

It was recess when he approached the schoolyard and, as fate would have it, a misdirected soccer ball bounced off his feet. While Dr. Ellison bent over to retrieve the ball, a young black seventh-grader ran up to him and held out his palms to receive it. The professor tossed the ball back. "Excuse me, young man, but I'm Professor Ellison from the University of Vermont, and I was wondering if I might ask a few brief questions."

The child responded by holding out his hand and gave a firm handshake, all the while looking Ellison in the eyes and up and down, checking him out for stranger danger. "Hey, I'm Kwamee, seventh-grade class president. How can I help you, sir?"

Dr. Ellison took the opportunity to break the ice and simply ask the boy directly about the weird rumors that preceded his visit to their town, to which the boy replied, "We've all heard the same weird stories as you have, but I can tell you for sure that my cousin knows a kid, not some rando, that went missing around Halloween, and he was pretty scared about it. He's usually not a flake like that. He hasn't been the same since."

They continued their discussion in earnest, even talking about Kwamee's favorite subjects like science and math, much to Ralph's enjoyment since he had a fondness for the same.

Out of the blue, Kwamee asked Ralph if he knew what hippopotomonstrosesquippedaliophobia was. Ralph excitedly answered, "Of course! It's the fear of long words and, ironically, one of the longest words there is! Not to be confused with hexakosioihexekontahexaphobia."

"Which is the fear of the number 666. The number of the beast, the Antichrist. Which also might be why people around here are freaking out," the twelve year old responded.

"Or maybe they just have coulrophobia, fear of clowns because of a bad childhood parade they experienced," said Ralph.

"Maybe, or casadastraphobia, the fear of falling upwards into the sky because of a poorly maintained public playground! Amazeballs!"

They both laughed aloud. Kwamee reminded Ralph of a younger version of himself, with an excessive number of firing neurons in his brain. He had a similar passion and quizzical mind and thirst for knowledge that couldn't be quenched.

"I can be pretty sleuthy, professor. I'll sniff around and keep my eyes and ears open for you," said Kwamee.

Ralph replied, "Please do not, I repeat, do *not* get into trouble, and by all means avoid any inkling of danger. Promise?"

"I'll promise if you'll promise to keep me posted and in the loop and get back to me. No FOMO. Anyway, I wouldn't worry. My mom said that I'm lucky because I'm a Sagittarius and was born on a Saturday," said the young boy.

Ralph didn't like to lend credence to any pseudosciences like astrology, but it seemed innocent enough, so he said, "I'm a Cancer myself. Hopefully not a diagnostic predestination. I was born on a holiday, though: the Fourth of July. Every year, I get fireworks on my birthday."

"For reals? That's lit," replied Kwamee. They both crossed their hearts and hoped to die, then spit in their palms and shook on their agreement.

After Ralph left his new young friend, he thought about what he had said. About the Antichrist. He looked up and noticed that he had wandered into the middle of an unpaved intersection. A crossroads. Perhaps instead of an irrational fear, maybe the townspeople were exhibiting a normal avoidance of the devil who had actually arrived in person to pay their little hamlet a visit.

He shuddered and vaguely remembered a Bible verse: "When I was a child, I talked like a child, I thought like a child, I reasoned like a child. When I became a man, I put the ways of childhood behind me." He thought, *They had it ass-backwards.*

# CHAPTER 38

Annie Hawthorne sat in her pet cage in the wicked witch's dank cellar, reminiscing about recent events. She missed her family. Mommy and Daddy and Emma and little Max. They had just a month ago visited Grandma Annie, whom she was named after. Her real name was Anastasia, but she just skipped formalities and went by Annie. Grandma would joke that she was the original little orphan, or sometimes Annie Oakley, the sure-shot firearms expert. Sometimes she'd say that they were named after the biblical Hannah, which meant "grace," or "favor," or "prayer" in Hebrew. Boy, she could sure use one of those now.

They both had the lucky number of seven, which was exactly how many hours she had been stuck in this cramped little cage drinking water from a pet feeder. It was time to get out.

She recalled being with her family at home a short month prior, hiding on the staircase like a little spy listening to her parents converse, uncovering crucial details. *I wish I could hear them arguing now*, Annie thought. They'd been unpacking from their visit with her grandmother.

"I don't think our children should celebrate Halloween anymore is all. It gives Emma nightmares. And it's based on some old pagan ritual anyway that we shouldn't promote," said Beth, Annie's mother.

"Are you serious? Soaping windows, toilet-papering stuff, and the occasional egg if they really deserve it. It's just kids having fun. Us too, you know? C'mere you, come to Daddy," said Mark, Annie's father.

*Gross*, thought Annie.

"Gross," said Beth.

"Did I ever tell you about that time that we went to soap my fourth-grade teacher's house on Halloween?" asked Mark.

"Actually yes, you did," said Beth.

"So, we sneak over there after dark, but not too late. I'm at her house by one of those square glass basement windows, and I'm rubbing the soap—my friend's mom made homemade soap, if you can believe it. And not some mamby-pamby, Amish-scented stuff, but, like, gritty pumice farm soap that would make your hands bleed just by using it."

"I wish I had some now," said Beth.

"Anyway, I'm rubbing the shit out of the window, soaping it so you couldn't see through it if you wanted to, and the window fell in and shattered on her basement floor! There she sat on her basement toilet that the window led to, I guess. She was taking a crap and screamed and I screamed and ran. If she saw me, she never said so or was too embarrassed. I can only assume that she finished her business. If I would've thought of it, I would've thrown her a roll of TP," said Mark.

"You guess?"

"C'mon. Annie loves Halloween. And so does Max. And so do you. Me too. We'll figure out something else to do with Emma. Fair's fair. Anyway, she's got that Christmas play in a month or so that she's all excited about. I'll unpack and you try to remember where the Halloween stuff is," said Mark.

"I know where the Halloween stuff is," she said as she sat down in his lap. "I wish I had some of that farmer soap now. I'd wash your mouth out with it, you dirty boy."

"Gross," said Mark.

Annie wished that she could eavesdrop now from the security of her home instead of being locked in a tiny cage in a dirty corner of that godforsaken basement. She looked at her grandmother's faerie broach, which had been handed down to her during the trip. *Thanks, Grandma. Little did you know you were gonna help me escape this wretched place.*

# CHAPTER 39

Annie Hawthorne had always been a precocious child. She liked climbing and crawling and was especially fond of escaping her brother Max's traps that he would set for her. For her last birthday, her twelfth, she had asked her parents to take her to an escape room adventure, which they obliged. It was over before her parents even found the first clue. She loved puzzles and problem-solving and had even read several biographies about her one true hero and role model, the master escape artist and magician Harry Houdini.

On Halloween 1926, at the age of fifty-two, Houdini died from sepsis due to a ruptured appendix. His last words were "I'm tired of fighting." Annie was exhausted, but still had some fight left. She was getting out of the witch's basement one way or another.

When she and her classmates from the school bus were herded down into the witch's dank cellar and deposited in their pet cages, she had seen her chance. Amongst all the hurry and fury and commotion, the cruel slubberdegullions failed to latch her cage lock all the way. Haste makes waste. She removed her grandmother's faerie broach that her mother had pinned on her that very morning, insisting that she not lose it such as it was a lucky keepsake.

Using the long broach pin, she finagled and picked the lock quite adeptly. She thought Houdini would be proud. Quietly yet swiftly, she crawled her way back up the old coal chute. As she climbed, she became covered in soot, giving her an ashen nighttime camouflage when she emerged outside undetected. Her war paint gave her a little extra confidence as she escaped through the woods behind the witch's house toward the busier neighborhoods. She had decided not to travel directly down the street for fear of being discovered by these demented maniacs.

Just as she was about to enter the open clearing at the end of a long block, she heard a whimsical, raspy voice: "Ladybug, ladybug, fly away home. Your house is on fire, your children will burn. Except for the little one whose name is Ann who hid away in a frying pan."

The old witch had never looked so terrifying as she did just then, standing there in the shadows. Her greasy, unkempt hair straggled down, covering half her face. Her bent, hairy wart on the top of her crooked nose was seen easily in silhouette. "And there's no such thing as faeries!" she said as she reached out with her arthritic fingers, poking the meat and removing the broach.

Within seconds, she had flung the ropey sack over Annie's head and torso and headed back to her house of horrors. Annie cried upside-down in the scratchy sack and wondered what Houdini would do. She came to one conclusion. He would have cried too.

# CHAPTER 40

Thanksgiving Day. A holiday celebrated in the fall around the country. A day of celebration and camaraderie between pilgrim settlers and Indian tribe natives. A day to give thanks for the blessings of the harvest from the previous year—a harvest festival, even though harvest in New England occurs well before late November. In Puritan history, numerous unexpected disasters or biblical threats such as plagues, droughts, and floods led eventually to days of fasting and days of thanksgiving.

Thanksgiving Day. Not usually a day to mourn the loss of your most precious loved ones, your offspring. Instead, a time of gratitude and reflection and remembrance of people past and present. Not yet the future because you can't be grateful for something that hasn't occurred yet. You can only hope. Hope that they find your kids safely before it's too late. Every week someone went missing. Sparse witnesses with nonsensical stories about mummies and monsters. Many probably just runaways or divorced parents settling their custody differences themselves.

It's the kind of thing adults tell their children so as not to scare them. When children ask if the boogeyman is real, you just lie. But children know better. Children still believe in things that adults don't. Out-of-network dental plan tooth faeries and egg-dispatching bunnies. Special toy-makers from the North Pole who leave gold in a fireside sock.

Thanksgiving. Harvest foliage decorated the streets and beckoned in the coming winter. A hand-drawn turkey, magnetically attracted to the fridge, guarded the treasures inside. The pilgrimage to satiety with cranberry cylinders was firing on all pistons. Anticipation of full bellies complemented by vociferous carnal knowledge of a seasonal bird and a pumpkin harvest put to the test. A husky corn cob centerpiece upstaged by the main event. Contentious cuisine and pretentious palates. All of the muse and notes hidden, hard and soft, from temperamental taste to opining appetites. Just say please to stinky cheese.

Napping and crapping the twilight away while loosened belts and burps announce a bountiful harvest. Breaking bread and bone. Green beans and brussels sprouts. Pumpkin pie and lattes greeted seasonally with spice and fervor. Baked and half-baked ideas not quite filling the pie or pilgrim's promise of progress. Giving thanks for the framework of freedom and the inevitable inequity. To the victor go the spoils. And leftovers. A sweet potato casserole of the dice. And everything nice. Except for the missing loved ones. A sliver of dessert cutting through appetite and intestinal fortitude. Basted and wasted, asleep on the couch in a serotonin coma. Hearth in hand, just thankful to be together.

Bridgett Bishop looked forward to Thanksgiving as much as the next person. She liked to cook, so she always made too much, with leftovers going to the mission or other homeless shelters. Just doing her part. In anticipation of the feast, she wore her yoga pants and an oversized sweatshirt. A wolf in wolf's clothing.

This year she was going all-out, preparing a green bean casserole, two pies, and, for appetizers, her famous Bridgett's balut deviled eggs, which weren't really eggs in the typical sense but rather the boiled fertilized fetus of a bird, in this case a pigeon. She had taro chips and tarot cards, and for the main course, she would prepare a turducken consisting of turkey, duck, and children. It was a cornucopia of villainous delight. Low and slow. She hadn't realized how much work actually went into making a turducken, let alone the spatchcocking. The wishbone was already broken and devoid of wishes. She was hoping for a lucky break and cussed the skeletal good luck charm, though it wasn't lucky at all for the provider of said bone.

She was using fresh, all-natural ingredients. From farm to playground to table.

The holidays really were for the children.

# CHAPTER 41

Count Dracula waited for the sun to subside and disappear below the horizon line. He could tell by the shadows that it was sinking like a rock in a lake, or a lagoon. *Loose lips sink ships*, he thought shortly after as he made his way to see the good Dr. Jekyll in his compounding pharmacy and emporium. Thankfully it was growing darker earlier as fall searched for its winter companion. He still wasn't quite sure what to make of Dr. Jekyll's previous manic outburst outside Castle Frankenstein. Maybe he was off his lithium. Perhaps he was just an overindulgent true crime show aficionado eager to play armchair detective.

Not wanting to wait to be invited into the pharmacy, Dracula surveyed the outside premises and set himself up for a good, old-fashioned stakeout, a term that he had hoped never to use.

Dr. Jekyll exited his store and fumbled with his oversized key ring until he had found the appropriate skeleton key, the one that comprised his entire security system. The Count approached Henry Jekyll cautiously, taking care not to startle him, then addressed him from a distance.

"Pardon me, dear doctor, but I was wondering if you could perhaps spare just a moment of your time. I would greatly appreciate it."

Henry Jekyll recognized the Count instantly and looked both ways carefully to be sure that they were alone. "Of course, but we must hurry. One never knows when he is afoot."

Dracula smiled and thought that he might include *paranoid delusions* in the good doctor's disposition.

"Hyde is suspicious," Henry Jekyll continued, "and he's not to be trusted. He's been following me, and I'm afraid of the despicable acts he's capable of if he knows I'm helping you. I could swear I saw him in the shadows of the alleyway around the corner from the shop. I could smell him even more so. The stench of him wafting across my nose was too close for comfort. I just kept moving with my head down and tried to keep my distance. Avoidance should be enough, right?"

The Count replied, "Please, dear doctor, let us have a seat and perhaps you can tell me what it is that you know."

The two of them walked to a nearby park that seemed comfortably anonymous and not well travelled. They shared a common park bench that held a plaque dedicated to some local inhabitant leaving a legacy of wrought iron in the rain. Dracula asked Henry directly, "I just wanted to know how it is that you came about your unusual accusations and warnings of dire events."

"Just between you and I, understand?" Jekyll said. "I overheard Mr. Hyde ranting under his breath all too audibly. Something about a local witch named Bridgett Bishop, and that they both had something to do with the missing children. I'm sure of it!"

"But why all of a sudden?" asked the Count.

"You might as well ask why is a snake a snake. I fear that their pent-up rage and hostility has been simmering for some time, and that their hatred and thirst for revenge finally reached the boiling point. All around the community, distrust and divisiveness have grown, allowing for prejudice and alienation to spread like a pandemic. The proverbial torch has been lit."

"I see," said Dracula. "Have you any evidence to support your claims?"

"Go to this address. I had already written it down in hopes of seeing you again," replied Jekyll, and with that he handed a folded piece of prescription pad paper over to the Count, who opened it.

It was the address Frankenstein was likely entering at this very moment.

# CHAPTER 42

Evil took the form of an old woman. Frail and lonely with a careful gait and tortoise pace. Her puppy dog eyes bore a forgetful gaze and pitiful demeanor. The old woman could be seen easily as a potential victim of the troubles and woes of modern society. Kids today. Perhaps providence. Not Rhode Island—rather, serendipity. Or just dumb luck. The masks of sorrow and fear cloaked her true toxic nature.

"Goosey, goosey, gander, whither dost thou wander? Upstairs and downstairs and in my lady's chamber. There I met an old man who wouldn't say his prayers; I took him by the left leg, and threw him down the stairs," the old witch sang as she stirred the pot. Then came another knock at the witch's door. *My, my,* she thought, *I am getting popular. Maybe a little too much so.* She opened the door casually, only to be greeted by a seven-foot five-inch giant covered in scars from head to toe as far as she could see.

"I'm so sorry to bother you, ma'am. My name is Captain Saul Frankenstein, and I was wondering if I might have a word?" he said, flashing his badge.

"Come in, come in deary, and please close the door—this weather is growing more unforgiving. Why, it's getting colder than a witch's . . . well, you know. Come by the fire while I fetch some milk and cookies," said Bridgett. She wore her Lululemon yoga pants and oversized UVM hoodie and slippers. She had noticed that her clothes had been fitting a little tighter recently. *Oh well, it's the holidays*, she thought.

The old witch did her best to insulate her feelings and true intentions. She returned with a tray of sugary circles and gingerbread men and women and two glasses of milk, which she set next to Frankenstein.

Saul had made a habit of never eating homemade food from a stranger. Partly because it probably wasn't kosher, but also, he remembered once when a patient he had saved brought in a holiday fruitcake to the EMS department just to say thanks. After everyone had been chatting and eating for a while, she revealed offhandedly that she had found the pastry in the dumpster behind a bakery. "I just don't know why they throw out good food all the time. It seemed a shame to let it go to waste," she said.

All of the EMS personnel stopped mid-chew and looked at each other with mouths agape. Saul could see that her intentions were sincere, but then noticed her fingernails, which looked like she had just cleaned a toilet.

Now, to Bridgett, Saul responded politely, "No, thank you, ma'am, I just ate."

Bridgett shrugged it off and asked, "How may I help you, Captain?"

Saul had been surveying the room discreetly for anything out of the ordinary and noticed that nothing seemed grossly amiss. Her humble furniture and homey decorations appeared right in line with what one might expect from an elderly woman in the twilight of her years. He was almost embarrassed to ask, but did anyway: "I was wondering if you or anyone you know had heard or seen anything out of the ordinary over the past few weeks? Maybe some children wandering around or playing where they hadn't before? Anything unusual at all?"

Bridgett coyly responded like a timid, shrinking violet. "Why no, honey, I haven't. Some lovely police officers were here not long ago asking the same thing; I wish they had stayed for supper. I try not to dwell on such dreadful things—I need my beauty sleep, you know. Are you sure I can't interest you in some hot cocoa, perhaps?"

Saul mentally crossed her off his list and was about ready to leave when, suddenly, a familiar voice whispered in his ear, "The children are in the basement."

It was Ralph. The invisible man no less.

# CHAPTER 43

Frankenstein immediately got up and headed toward the cellar door. The old witch's shy tone changed, and her voice cracked as she said, "I beg your pardon! You've no right!" Saul ignored her and ran around the halfpace, past the soundproof basement door, and down the dirty stairs into the dank, dark hole that was her cellar while Bridgett screamed, "I'm calling the cops! You don't have a warrant!"

And there they were. Lined up in cages, like filthy animals waiting to be euthanized at the pound.

He started tearing open the cage doors, freeing the kids who ran like mice on a sinking ship up the stairs and out the front door and down the street to freedom. Annie Hawthorne grabbed triple P's hand, and they ran with the rest of them, trying not to trample one another if possible. Annie started to tumble but Kevin the boy scout grabbed her just in time to help keep her upright as they all ran for their lives. Down the street and far away. And then some more.

The jig was up and the old witch was furious. By now she was standing over her cauldron, vexing and hexing familiars not so recognizable to the non-purveyor of sorcery. "You monster! How dare you interfere with my plans, you quilted freakshow! May the upside-down hanged man leave you askew. I'll yet make you part of my Christmas stew!" She chanted and conjured every shaman and neo-pagan she could reach to harness their powers.

Dr. Ellison attempted to grab the witch and disrupt her bewitchments. Bridgett grabbed a sack bag of thin lambskin filled with an unknown liquid from one of her shelves and smashed it over the head of her unseen assailant. Ralph reacted in horror as he felt the accelerant burn his eyes and mouth. The witch tossed a small wooden stick with ember and the invisible man was alight. He was no longer invisible since he was completely aflame, screaming in unfathomable pain.

As the witch's enchantments took hold, the ground beneath them began to tremble as if quake and aftershock were nanoseconds apart. A large sinkhole was opening beneath them, swallowing everything around it whole. Frankenstein looked to make sure that all the children were gone and safely away, then grabbed Ralph, fire and all, and ran up the back cellar stairs and kicked out the door.

Once outside, he rolled the fire off his friend, whose body smoked and smelt like burnt hair and toast. The witch had grabbed her broom and flew circuitously around and around after them like a devilish whirling dervish, assisting the vortex in collapsing and dragging the house and all of its contents into hell's sinkhole. She then flew off with her broom into the distance, screaming, "There's no place like hoooommee!"

Frankenstein held Ralph in his arms like the Virgin cradling the baby in an obtuse Nativity scene. No longer room at the inn, or an inn at all for that matter. Just an out. Barely escaping with their lives.

# CHAPTER 44

Luckily, Captain Frankenstein had driven his work truck to the witch's house. He quickly triaged and loaded his patient and semi-visible friend, then hit the emergency sirens and lights and sped onward toward the hospital. Saul raced through the streets, radioing ahead their upcoming arrival to the ER. The twinkling red and blue lights did little to enhance the mood or the holiday spirit.

As they cruised down side streets lined with tall pines, they passed numerous police and rescue vehicles heading in the opposite direction toward the address where the witch's house once stood. Where there was once the fresh clean smell of piney air, there now drifted strangling smoke exuding from the witch's open hellhole. 'Tis the season.

While Frankenstein drove through intersections with sirens blaring, he tried to notify Dracula and Aoife using voice to text on his smart watch. He yelled into his wrist trying to speak above the sirens and horns, but the dictation came back as autocorrected nonsense. "Ridiculous auto cat rectal."

The invisible man was partially visible with second- and third-degree burns over much of his body and remnants of the lambskin bag melted onto his skin in patches. He was in exquisite pain which was good in the sense that his injuries hadn't destroyed all of his nerve endings that conducted the uncomfortable signals to the necessary synapses. Pain was predictable and indispensable, if nothing else.

Ralph lay there bound to the stretcher suffering in silence, listening to the decibels of sirens droning on. He recalled in his head the events which led to his present state. He had deviated from his usual strict protocol—observance—and made the conscious decision to attempt the physical trial sooner than planned. Patience, he'd learned, was a virtue.

He remembered tapping his antecubital fossa while chewing on the rubber tourniquet, stretching the limits of science. The injection into his left nondominant arm hit the vein without blowing it and infiltrating his trusting flesh. Off came the tubing while the cotton ball and band-aid played tamponade. Ralph had made a fist several times and decided to remain sitting just in case.jic. He had felt fine. Actually, unchanged. He'd wondered about the vial's compound date.

"The onset of effects should begin fairly rapidly unless I infiltrated..." But as he went to check the venipuncture site, removing the bandage, he noticed that there wasn't anything under it.

"That's strange," he said now. "What happened to my arm and, now, me. Trippy. Vitals seemed okay. O2 was 98 percent. Vision's still weird. Or my brain trying to process the different pathways. It's odd. I'm not blind. I can clearly see. Just not me. Or what and where I perceive me to be. It's starting to make my head hurt. Kinda like wearing VR too long. Spreading quickly—my skin feels hot. Metallic taste in my mouth. No discernible skin. Don't freak. Calming down. Thermogenic effect fading to tingle. Ha. Hahahateeheehee. Crazy cool. Until the witch and the fire. HAAAHHHHHH! This pain is now!"

Suddenly it was unbearable beyond belief. The simultaneous stimulation of large areas of pain receptors firing and filling synapses, pushing Dr. Ellison toward passing out. Too much of a bad thing. Misplaced misfortune. The semi-invisible man looked up groggily from the swaying stretcher as the emergency vehicle drifted around, narrowly avoiding the oncoming horns of traffic.

They were greeted at the ER doors of St Mary's, at which point stretcher and patient were rushed in. The staff quickly placed an IV with Ringer's lactate into one of Dr. Ellison's arms using Doppler-guided fluoroscopy and administered oxygen. Monitors and blood pressure cuff were put in place to evaluate his vitals continuously. His BP was low and heart rate sinus rhythm but tachycardic and he was going into shock.

By now Dracula and Aoife had made it to the hospital and Captain Frankenstein invited them in. He gave them an update and they went about getting settled in the waiting room to do just that. Aoife filled them in on her own adventure at the lagoon, and Dracula likewise gave a briefing on his meeting with Dr. Jekyll. After a bit of time had passed, they were greeted by the ER doctor.

"You weren't kidding about his unusual visibility. He's been unconscious, so I can only assume that he has no control over that aspect of his physical being. However, he is still susceptible to most imaging studies and bloodwork, and I believe that, for the moment, he is stable." A sigh of relief rotated around the circle of friends.

The emergency room doctor continued. "When a bed becomes available, we'll transfer him to the burn ward for further evaluation and follow-up care. You should be able to visit him then if you're wearing the appropriate PPE. One of his greatest risks will be sepsis, since skin is usually one of our first lines of defense against infections. We're already treating him with some broad spectrum IV antibiotics empirically."

The monster friends expressed their sincere thanks and gratitude and the physician disappeared back into the controlled chaos that was the ER.

Several hours had gone by when they were finally notified that Dr. Ellison had been transferred to room 421 in the burn unit, and they promptly went up to visit. There he lay, partially visible like an unfinished portrait, his scratchy voice barely audible between the hissing of pumps and mechanisms. He looked at them with his one open eye and whispered, "I guess I should have taken better care of the flesh."

"You've done admirably. A better friend one could not want," said the Count.

"How can we help, Ralph?" asked Aoife.

"Why, it's as plain as the nose on your face." Ralph snickered and grimaced since he had no visible nose. "Also add pyrophobia to my list of differential diagnoses. My visual deficit supersedes your present visual abilities, or more accurately, your interpretation of them," he continued. "I can't help but feel that I'm not here...maybe I never was?" He spoke through a fog of pain meds.

The Count reached out and gently held one invisible hand while placing his other gloved hand over the space where his friend's heartbeat was most pronounced. It was rapid, but had a strong, regular heart rate and rhythm. "You must know by now, my good friend, that you are never alone. You are always in our hearts and minds as we are in yours," said Dracula.

Aoife continued, with uncertain tears in her eyes, "And that's not some kind of weird vampire mind trick, to be sure. You know it to be true. Please rest, hydrate, repair, and do whatever it takes to come back to us. We know how strong you are."

Ralph managed a partial, visibly crooked smile, though it was easy to see the tears making their way from invisible cheek to pillow, leaving a wet indentation on his pillowcase.

"You risked your life to save me and the children," Ralph said to Frankenstein. "I know that you're used to it, part of the job and all that, but I'm not. I can never repay your selfless acts of heroism. I love you, Saul. And the rest of you, too. I'm so proud right now to have friends like you." The invisible man cringed in pain quietly, as though no one could see.

Aoife gently kissed his invisible left cheek, barely outlined by the sprinkling of her tears, and said, "*Gra, dilseacht, cairdeas.*" *Love, loyalty, friendship.* She removed the Irish claddagh friendship ring from her finger and placed it on his right-hand pinky. Heart, crown, and hands.

The three of them left the room and made their way down the hall to the elevator doors. Just as the door dinged open, the overhead speaker announced, "Code blue, burn unit room 421. Code blue, burn unit room 421." They rushed back down the hall and were stopped outside Ralph's door while scrubs scrambled frantically. They could see through his partially obstructed window that their friend's heart monitor showed only a flat line. They listened and heard the familiar, unwavering monotone that sang infinitely and inexcusably of death.

The surreality was hard to fathom. The invisible man had drawn his last visible breath and exhaled blindly into the next. The Count and Contessa Aoife and Captain Frankenstein held each other more closely than they ever had before, for seemingly forever.

No one saw it coming. In part because they didn't want to believe. Not seeing is not believing. They say that people see what they want to see. But sometimes they just don't have a choice. Death sets its own pace.

The temperature and mood around them were bone-chilling. Aoife looked to see if she could see her own breath, but she could not. After a while, they made their way slowly toward the exit. They bridged the gap in their vacant hearts with a profound solace and quiet as they ventured outside into the cold and unforgiving night air.

A blustering gust of wind scythed at their necks and nerves. Aoife snarled and finally let out a blood-curdling primal scream that drowned out the wind. The Count covered her in his cape in shame that he was cold-blooded and could not comfort his love with body heat.

Tomorrow was going to be different. Somehow. Someway. They

were going to find the missing witch and monster fiends and stop them from harming anyone else.

The night sky howled on with a pessimistic full moon halfway to the horizon.

# CHAPTER 45

The ill-fated Green Mountain latched onto the succubus's nipple, nursing death with time. Huge pines whispered amongst themselves, leaving the faintest psithurism for eavesdroppers to decipher.

Even with the old witch's disappearance, the impending threat still loomed in this small town, as Bridgett Bishop remained at large. The loss of her house and the kidnapped cache of children did not deter the witch from her plans. She used some of her favorite necromancements to call upon the goddess of the dead, Nephthys. The Egyptian mummy rose to the occasion, as she did in her life before and after. Hyde and the black lagoon creature had already left and were on their way to get a good seat.

Today was the annual holiday parade taking place down along the Rockwellesque Main Street of Killington. Local food trucks and restaurants had their eateries on display. Sugar on snow, fried pickles, fresh-baked doughnuts, and honey that was the bee's knees. Vendors solicited all kinds of frightful sugary delights. One truck even sold the inedible confection candy corn. They looked like rotted meth teeth that fell out from abuse. CBD gummies for the gums, and THC edible undies for the hell of it. Gummies for their gams—the delicious atrocity of a high-fructose corn syrup diet.

Though small by comparison to larger municipalities, the parade was still a chance for parents and children of the community to partake in a traditional holiday event together. There were the local police and ambulance vehicles with sirens blaring, car dealerships showing off their latest overpriced cars and daughters, the high school marching band, and plenty of tossed candy pieces that fell to the ground to intermingle with the FFA horses and manure that littered the streets.

There were also a small handful of papier-mâché floats from church groups and other nondenominational organizations. There even was a single huge inflatable balloon of the new Rutland City High School mascot, the raptor (the team having recently changed from Raiders because state legislature required all schools to stop using potentially racist imagery). The small band of walking volunteers towed it by the numerous strings attached to key points of its anatomy as it floated along like a drunken puppet.

Golden streaks of sunshine bled through the cracks in the trees, greeting the dormant believers with the possibilities that a new day might bring. A gentle breeze waved away the gloom while welcoming the hushed foreboding of the cycle of life. The grayness strolled in across the tree-covered hills—barren trees and wombs, waiting to be fertile with spring again. But first, there was the winter wonderland and chill to contend with, which ran up and down their spines. The main downtown thoroughfare was decorated with oversized Christmas ornaments, accenting the streetlights which guided the path of the annual holiday parade to its final destination at city hall.

The witch Bridgett had always enjoyed the holiday parade. However, this year, she would become more of an active participant. The old witch had her own plans for celebrating the family-friendly festivities. Time for a new tradition.

# CHAPTER 46

*Baa, baa, black sheep,*
*Have you any wool?*
*Yes sir, yes sir,*
*Three bags full!*
*One for the master,*
*One for the dame,*
*And none for the little boy*
*Who cries down the lane."*

The old witch Bridgett Bishop recited the nursery rhyme to herself as she put the finishing touches on her latest spell. The annual holiday parade was a community event, and she just wanted to do her part. To date, Bridgett was content with the success of her mission of revenge. The abominations that she had resurrected were performing up to par so far. Sure, there had been some setbacks, but she was just getting started. Bridgett was proud of herself, so much so that she danced an ungainly jig, clapping and stomping out heartbeats in her mind.

Parades have been part of human history for a long time. Cave paintings dating back thousands of years depict prehistoric men triumphantly parading their fresh kills in front of their cave-dwelling onlookers. Since 3,000 B.C., religious and military parades have celebrated soldiers going into battle, showing off to their people captured prisoners and conquered booty and treasure.

The annual Killington parade always rang in the official opening to the holiday season. It offered local organizations a chance for recognition and commerce while giving the community a chance for some good old-fashioned fun. There were marching bands with instruments lined and lit with battery-powered blinkers of all colors. There were floats, clowns, and antique cars from locals showing off their passions and hobbies. Hot buttered rum warmed bellies and a nip of schnapps took the bite out of the crisp, clean air. Candy was thrown and picked up out of the gutter for consumption. Fire truck sirens and openly shitting horses followed behind the floats and marching groups, with the parading pooper-scoopers batting clean-up.

The homecoming queen and her court of consorts drove by in convertibles doing the royal wave, satisfying fans and carpal tunnel with the flick of the wrist. Santa always brought up the rear in the last float, waving his good cheer jubilantly to the less-than-packed audience of childhood attendees. And of course, the Chamber of Commerce was represented accordingly.

Mayor Dorschel sat with his well-dressed peers at the table of honor, preparing for the feast. They were dripping with Valentino and Prada and watching the parade from the balcony suite of the finest hotel overlooking the Main Street route. Best seats in the house. Nothing too good for their bougie expensive tastes. When it came to gluttony, the more the merrier. Lying on the street curb directly below was a homeless man, holding a sign that said, "Anything will help," burning an image in any bystander's mind that couldn't be cropped.

The town council's chief financial officer Barry Benington was particularly obsessed with germs and excrement, so he appreciated the extra niceties and modern conveniences that were included inside the oversized honeymoon suite. He removed his Patek Philippe wristwatch and placed it on the sink counter. It was given to him as a gift by the city for years of service and was worth more than what most of his employees made in a year.

After washing his hands in preparation to eat, he splashed cold water onto his face from the modern, touchless bathroom sink. Barry looked himself over in the mirror and saw that his face was as flush and pink as a baboon's ass. *Need to slow down on the browns, it's not even noon*, he thought. Even though he was there on business, he acknowledged the lavish and lush finishes, which set the tone for a pair of newlyweds to consummate their first night of matrimony. A blue light and luminol would have shown exactly just how much consummation had occurred there over time.

Certainly the proprietors of this fine hotel establishment had spared no expense. Even the bathrooms had the latest and greatest Toto comfort height, self-flushing, hands-free bidet and toilet with Bluetooth and heated seats. The CFO dried his face in the mirror while he thought of the silly stories and childish tales that haunted their local municipality.

"Bridgett Bishop. Bridgett Bishop. Bridgett Bishop." He laughed to himself without a care in the world. Don't say her name three times into a mirror or she will appear.

And she did. She was floating behind the sterile, white, semitransparent cloth shower curtain. She'd been there the whole time, stalking this group of prominent political leaders and snollygoster throttlebottom guests but couldn't resist a dramatic entrance. Her willowy wisp of mothballed nylons and transparent threadbare gown left her drooping, scratchy, witchy teats on full display.

As he opened his mouth to scream, she flew up to him and shoved a rather large and angry brown recluse spider into his pie hole and held his jaws shut. He struggled against disbelief while the flesh-eating toxins went to work. By the time she had allowed him to open his mouth again and say "ahhh," the front half and side of his tongue had dissolved into a yellowish green, fetid mush. "Itsy bitsy spider went up the waterspout," she said as she closed in for a kiss. No tongue, though. The string of malodorous mucous and rotted flesh formed a slender bridge between their lips as she held her reticent and reluctant lover in a close embrace.

The CFO shit himself, and with the deluge of liquid feces streaming down the leg of his Giorgio Armani suit slacks, he ran out onto the balcony just as the mayor was about to carve their cooked goose. His unintelligible, pauciloquent speech came across as codswallop and gurgled, mush-melon nonsense. He tried in vain to make his no-longer-present tongue utter discernible words and syllables. His body language, however, warned of some unspeakable terror.

The mayor himself stood to do the honor of dissecting the sacred bird. He sharpened the carving knife against the honing steel several times for good luck and made the initial cut.

The goose exploded from the inside, erupting with hundreds of angry bot flies, which attacked the festive diners. The gaiety turned gruesome as arms waved and thrashed in horror. He saw the swarm of bot flies engulf his face.

The creepy crawlers burrowed into his lower lip. They dug and bit and tunneled and tore the superficial flesh from the underlying dermis. They left bloody, fluid-filled sores all over his cheeks and swollen lips. The itching was overwhelming. The formication screwed with his mind. It made him itch so bad that he grabbed the sharp blade and filleted his lower lip off, down to the bone. With his bloody lower jaw exposed, he looked like a deformed ventriloquist dummy in some vaudevillian act from hell. He screamed, but you never saw his lips move. His blood poured onto his plate mixing cranberries with red blood cells and spilled merlot. *Cin cin.*

The CFO was on his knees now, puking up bits of tongue and his breakfast bagel, along with blood since by now the flesh-eating toxin was working its way down his esophagus. Hardly an opportunity for a silver-tongued politician to be loquacious when he was missing a lip. Or a tongue.

Down the road a bit, a festive snowflake-patterned tablecloth lined with fresh evergreen and holly covered the desk where the local television announcers had set up to film their broadcast. They were to introduce the participants and organizations as they rolled by the live TV camera, providing uplifting commentary and reviewing parade contestants. Framing them in the lens, they sat just outside the large toy store decorated with Christmas dressings, leaving an appropriate backdrop imprinted in viewers' minds.

After a brief hair and makeup touch-up, the cameraman performed a light meter check and fingered the countdown—*three, two*—and pointed. The camera was red-lit and focused on the perfectly symmetrical faces and lips of the anchorman and anchorwoman. They both were easy on the eyes as well as the camera lens, which was focused on them when, suddenly, there was a distracting movement in the large toy store window behind them. It appeared that someone was walking around with a flashlight—perhaps looting the place?

The creature was green-lit from the blinking holiday lights when it smashed into frame, the camera filming all the while. It placed its huge palm on top of the blond anchorwoman's forehead with claws splayed down into the skin and eyebrows and tore off her face like skin off a grape, leaving an accurate anatomical head with lidless eyes screaming just like the mouth.

It all happened so fast. The cameraperson couldn't hear the producer yelling, "Cut, cut! Go to commercial!," instead frozen in disbelief. The attractive blond anchorwoman was no longer symmetrical, and her perfectly proportioned facial features were in the creature's mouth, disappearing before her very eyes. The TV viewers were treated abruptly to a commercial of a monkey peeling a banana and tossing the skin onto the ground, left wishing that they could edit their memories of that which can't be unseen.

The parade was already in full swing when Mr. Hyde appeared from a nearby alleyway. He was brandishing one of the rare and quickly sold out Elon Musk's Boring Company Not a Flamethrower flamethrower. Limited to twenty thousand pieces with a range of twenty-five feet, they were Twitteriffic. Musk himself was quoted as saying, "The rumor that I'm secretly creating a zombie apocalypse to generate a demand for flamethrowers is completely false." His new Twittereens might now have been rethinking that.

Hyde let loose with the Not a Flamethrower, which hurled a flaming tongue over twenty feet into the air, licking the papier-mâché float crossing his path. The float, ironically, depicted a group of scouts roasting marshmallows on a campfire, representing diversity and unification. It lit up like a child's eyes on Christmas Day, spreading fiery pieces of paper vomitus to everything and everyone around.

The scattered fireflies of burnt papier-mâché reached the huge raptor balloon filled with helium, releasing a voluminous explosion that shattered nearby shop windows. The nearby human bags of blood were crushed easily into collateral damage. Vertebrae and veritable flies in the ointment. Panic and mayhem followed, which only further filled Hyde's belly with laughter and joy. A procession of predators parading around.

As the other end of the parade snaked and sidewinded through town, the mummy Nephthys popped out of the window of Red Riding Hood's grandmother's house floating down the street. The costumed child actors on the float ignored their marks and took their cue to dive off and run for their lives in any and every direction.

Nephthys was the last of the three reincarnated mummies, and her weapon of choice was the ball and chain flail, or the holy water sprinkler. It consisted of a bronze ball covered in sharp, deadly spikes, attached to a chain and then to a metal handle that resembled a police baton. It was meant to be swung in a circular motion over-head, building up centripetal force that was then transferred to the object of impact, delivering incredible energy sufficient to collapse a shield or cranium.

The first law officer on scene drew his weapon and pointed it at the mummy, commanding it to stand down. The mummy responded by swinging the flail down onto the officer's head, where the spiked ball stuck firmly. The mummy let go after impact, allowing the chain and handle to swing back and forth like a bloody brain bits-covered pendulum. It ticked on until the cop corpse fell to the ground.

The next officer was Holt, who discharged her SIG Sauer forty-caliber service semiautomatic and spewed round after round into the mummy until the fifteen-shot magazine was empty and the slide clacked open. The ammo squibs exploded dust and moldy flesh at their points of impact, which was of little consequence to the mummy. She proceeded to approach the young officer, whose face was one of shock and confusion, and then carefully twisted her head around the base of her skull and neck.

Around and around and around Nephthys twisted and turned the officer's skull like winding up a toy. One half-expected the head to spin back full circle upon release like a top, but instead Holt's rag doll body just went limp while her bobbled head stared off in the opposite direction.

Initially shocked and repulsed, the third law-enforcement officer got behind the mummy and put it in a vice-like headlock and choke-hold. It was Officer Dailey, and he felt confident in his countermeasure, since it had yet to fail him. Unbeknownst to him, an Egyptian cobra was living within the husk of the mummy, and now it slithered out and around the neck of the officer. The venomous asp stared him directly in the eyes from mere inches away and flicked its forked tongue across his cornea.

He screamed in terror and instantly released his chokehold on the mummy as the cobra's coil tightened further around the boy in blue's neck, further blocking off his airflow and stifling his cries for help. The mummy turned around to face her attacker and smiled and opened wide. Her decayed, yellowed teeth were somewhat intact when she bit off the policeman's nose and chewed. Blood flew everywhere from the empty hole in the face that connected the cop's oral cavity to its sinuses. A few remnants of the mummy's teeth and oral decay remained sticking out of the hole. It resembled a leprotic manifestation of the sort that disfigured its victims, leaving them without a sense of smell or a discernible face.

The mummy then grabbed the head and tail of the encircling asp and pulled tight, strangling Officer Dailey with the snake itself. The *Naja haje*, or Egyptian cobra, was the symbol of royalty and had been used in executions for centuries. Today was no different. The necklace that Nephthys wore depicted a serpent goddess whose diamond eyes glowed and shimmered. This meant little to the panicking crowd who were stampeding and crushing each other in an attempt to flee. Every person for themselves. The trampled and injured were stepped on over and over in the fearful flight to safety. Babies cried and old men died from heart health or just outright terror.

The witch had fled on her broomstick while the other three monstrous villains climbed casually into the utility van and made their exit out of town. An unholy trinity of terror. A harpies' delight. The enthusiastic and misanthropic energy in Hyde was palpable. Knowing very well that the black lagoon creature didn't understand him, and he wasn't sure about the mummy, Hyde looked at them anyway and said, "Don't you just love a parade?" He didn't wait for an answer and just laughed out loud as the oversized vehicle sped away and along to their predestined destination. The holidays were just getting started.

# CHAPTER 47

The clouds brushed across the moon like velvet, leaving a shiny ball of geomagnetic proportions. Halfway to there, no turning back. A full moon at high noon. Aoife loved it. Dracula not so much, as he hid beneath the promise of salvation that the oversized umbrella had granted him, along with gloves and clothing that covered his photosensitive skin. It was the equivalent of SPF 1000.

The couple had traveled downtown to the site of the parade debacle to get a glimpse firsthand of the destruction caused by their monstrous nemeses. They walked past the bells of St. Mary's Church. The chimes rang every hour on the hour, indicating the time of day. It lent an innocent charm to the family-oriented community and was a pleasant, welcoming part of the local landscape. As the digital bells faded, they were replaced by the distant memory of echoes from a faraway train traversing the mountainside. The bells rang twelve times. The bewitching hour, a.m.

Suddenly, Aoife noticed an unusual shadow cast from overhead moving rapidly across the sky. It was the old bitty witchy herself, flying on her broom, straddling it in a scopolamine-induced high. She wore a plaid schoolgirl skirt commando-style, which horrified Aoife even more as she gasped in disbelief.

Many who were deemed to be witches in the past were merely

women enjoying the hallucinogenic pleasure of a scopolamine trip by absorbing the drug through their vaginal mucosa. The witches' salve or flying ointment was applied to a broomstick handle to produce the sensation of flying or altered states of consciousness. Black henbane, the witches' plant from which it comes, could send one on a flight to the sabbat or the devil's dream of deadly nightshade.

The old witch wasn't trying to impress anyone special. She'd just woken up feeling sexy and confident after her success at the parade, so she'd gotten dressed sans panties in her skeezy schoolgirl outfit. Plus, it had been a while since she partook of the devil's ointment.

Her dirty matted gray hair was tied into pigtails, which waved trailing in the wind, and an overdose of pancaked blush blew off her less than rosy cheeks, leaving a small cloud of dust behind as she rode her broom across the sky.

Her ensemble was completed with a button-down cotton shirt underneath a filthy mothballed cardigan which no longer fit, probably since it was never hers anyway. Likewise, her leggings fell down and rolled about her cankles, exposing every wart and liver spot bespeckling her wrinkled, hairy skin. The old school-gal had haphazardly applied an exaggerated portion of bright, ruby-red lipstick to match her knockoff ruby red slippers, which gave her more of a scary clown vibe as opposed to sexy.

The witch Bridgett flew her broomstick circuitously around the pinnacle of St. Mary's Church, coming to rest in the open bell tower and disappearing inside. Aoife raced up the church steps while Dracula followed behind, shielding his eyes from the cross sitting atop the tallest building in town.

The werewolf threw open the large church doors to reveal the witch at the altar in front of the pews, confronting the holy bishop himself. The witch held her broom raised to strike down the church patriarch, and as his eyes met Aoife's, his expression was one of fear and terror.

The she-wolf sprang into action and pounced in on all fours and ran toward the raised altar adorned in gold ideology.

The Count stood at the open doors, uninvited for sure, and hissed and bore his fangs, quickly shielding his face with his cape when he saw the huge crucifix hanging soulfully on the back wall. He promptly retreated, circling around the outside of the church to cover a rear escape while his wife went on the attack.

It appeared that the witch was targeting anyone, anywhere at this point, even a holy man of the cloth. The bishop looked shocked and confused and fled for dear life into the back vestibule as Aoife charged down the main center aisle.

The old witch hissed, "Here, kitty, kitty," as she twirled her hands above her head, sprinkling a most foul-odored powder above the nearest holy water receptacle. The water turned into a milky liquid that smoked and sizzled and burst into flame, turning the air putrid.

She clapped both hands together and the four holy water receptacles in each of the large room's four corners filled with the flaming milk and flew across the room, splattering fiery, off-white milky substance everywhere.

Aoife bobbed and weaved to avoid the now acidic, unholy liquid spattering and plashing around her. Splashes of the substance singed the werewolf's fur and her painful howls echoed throughout the large-domed chamber. She yelped, crashing into the first five pews, knocking them over like dominoes.

The witch mounted her broom and flew along the curved ceiling, decorated in exquisite wallpaper detailed to mimic the Sistine Chapel. Aoife lunged upward as Bridgett flew overhead, latching onto the brushing bristles of her broom. The wide-eyed, befuddled witch flew on over the pews with her werewolf cargo in tow toward the open front doors, screaming, "Bad kitty!"

There was a large, circular stained glass window just above the front doors of the church, and the wicked witch flew full speed straight through it. Shards of colored glass shot off in all directions while Aoife tumbled down onto the church steps outside, rolling over and over in glass and defeat. The witch cackled and laughed and flipped off the werewolf with her crooked middle finger.

"By the witch of Endor and all of her ilk, transform the rain into a storm of milk. Nursing demons and fiends from your unholy teat, summon the thunder for vengenace complete."

The clouds above opened up and produced a thunderous boom, followed by a torrential rainstorm mixed with hail. Except it wasn't clear rainwater at all, but rather a dull, white downpour of milk. Sour as the witch's temperament and smelling most foul, covering everything in a square block with acrid sentiment and scent, denting every surface with pelted little smelly, milky orbs, the golf ball-sized frozen milk spheres pitted and patted the surrounding parked cars, smashing windshields and setting off car alarms as Aoife dove for cover back inside.

As the Count reached the rear of the church, the back doors flew open and the bishop himself fell into his arms. Shocked and surprised at the sight of Dracula, he fell to his knees, dumbfounded. Dracula picked him up and said, "My word, are you all right?"

The bishop stuttered and said, "Thank God you arrived when you did. No telling what that mad witch is capable of. This is complete madness."

"You're okay. Let's get you out of here," Dracula said. "My wife will handle her, I'm sure."

By now the sour milk rain and hail had spread to reach them both as Dracula whisked the shocked bishop away from the blasphemous scene into the nearby tree line, seeking cover.

A few minutes later, Aoife abruptly exited the rear of the church and made haste to the thick pines out behind St. Mary's, joining her husband and the holy man. Dracula asked with concern, "Are you injured, my love?"

"Just my pride. She certainly has some tricks up her sleeve," Aoife replied.

"Thank you both. I can never repay you for what you did today. It smells so terrible. I guess I need to get a cleaning crew in before morning mass," said the bishop.

"Glad we could help. Perhaps you should lay low for a while. At least until the mad Druid is stopped," said Aoife.

"That sounds great," the bishop replied, "but I haven't missed mass or keeping up with my responsibilities in years and I won't be frightened away now. Or anytime soon."

Dracula replied, "We can respect that. What did she want? Did she say anything?"

"I have no idea. I was rehearsing my sermon for tomorrow's mass and she flew in on her broomstick from upstairs and nearly frightened me to death. I heard her mutter something about giving the town last rites. She's as crazy as a bat. Oh, sorry."

"Not at all. We're just glad that you're okay," said the Count. "We'll leave you to your service, then."

By now, the stinky storm was subsiding and the old witch was long gone, leaving more chaos and destruction in her wake. The two monster mates slipped back again into the upcoming twilight. The calm that never preceded the storm. Aoife was about to say *what in the world is tomorrow gonna bring* when, suddenly, a black cat ran directly across their path. The two looked at each other, then walked on in silence.

# CHAPTER 48

After the shit show of a parade and the church calamity, the town was pretty much shut down and curfew was put into place. Roadblocks and checkpoints set up perimeters and countermeasures while the National Guard was notified of the situation. Bridgett and her troupe of transgressors had made a hasty escape to their new home away from home. A ghost town in the middle of nowhere. Glastenbury. Don't blink. Still perfect cover for those things that thrived in the dark.

As if on cue, the weather had turned and snow had beseeched to the land yet again the promise of death and decay. The old ghost town was deserted, with limited access during hostile weather. The rustic area had long been entrenched in folklore and shrouded in mountains of mystery.

But before settling there, the old witch had a previously scheduled engagement to attend to. She bundled up in her snow parka and boots and flew on her broom to see an old friend.

The witch rode her broom across a starless sky amidst the flakes and wind to the opera house in Rutland, which was where her friend resided. She had always considered herself a patron of the arts, the dark arts at least. She knew Erik from the old days when she used to frequent the stage productions of which he was intimately involved.

Bridgett had no need to "convince" him with her spells, potions, and portents. Rather, she knew full well of his animosity toward the locals after the way he'd been hurt by them. It was simply a shameful and disrespectful way to treat his creative genius. He wouldn't lose sleep over a handful of townies taking dirt naps. She hoped to establish some form of an alliance as they had occasionally done in the past, with the common goal of retribution and revenge. An axis of evil tilting the good earth and changing its polarity.

She also knew that she could avoid nosy neighbors and busybodies by meandering the infinitely complex tunnel system beneath the walls of the Center for Performing Arts.

The Phantom greeted Bridgett at one of the stage rear exit doors after hours. "My, my, if it isn't my old chum, Miss Bishop. Pray tell, what brings you here at this unholy hour?" said Erik.

The witch looked around and answered, "Stop dillydallying, you fool. You know exactly why I'm here, unless you've been living under a rock … Well, even so, you know what I mean. It's cold out, let me in before I become a fartsicle, you old crap sack."

"You always were a smooth talker. Come in, please, this way," he said as he illuminated the way with an electric torch. They walked and talked and got reacquainted. "Do you remember when we first met, Bridgett?" asked Erik.

"Of course I do. It was at a performance of *Macbeth*, my favorite play of course because of the three sisters. They remind me so much of my own. Bubble, bubble, toil and trouble and all that. Witches indeed," replied Bridgett to the Phantom, who smiled a twisted smile under his mask. "Let's just say that we had a lot in common back then. You truly were a virtuoso in a classical sense."

The Phantom crossed his cape and took a bow. They walked on through the catacomb-like tunnels in silence while the torch cast shadow and doubt upon the old, cobbled rock walls, distorting image and justice alike.

The two miscreants wandered and wove carefully through the underground labyrinth until they arrived at Erik's private chambers, which was essentially a cavern connected to an underground spring. No one really knew where he lived—just that his service and meticulous care for the theater was outmatched by none.

The floor wept with dampness while the cavern's rock wall was highlighted with exquisite procured art from a variety of periods. From Manet to Monet, from Dahl to Dali, the eclectic art was mirrored by their instrumental counterparts strewn about since Erik was fluent in most musical instruments. Though he played the piano and harpsichord effortlessly, he preferred the violin, and his confiscated Stradivarius was his prize possession.

"You have to admit, since our chance meeting, we've been of assistance to each other a number of times. Our goals have been mutually beneficial and agreeable," Bridgett said, and he agreed. "Do you remember that once I took care of that very small problem for you? She only weighed about 120 pounds. I'm here to collect on my debt."

"Christine," whispered the Phantom.

# CHAPTER 49

The Paramount Theatre or the Playhouse in Rutland, Vermont was built in 1913 by George Chaffee. Resembling a Victorian-era opera house with lavish decorations, it allowed for over one thousand patrons to hearken back to the day when dramas and plays relating to social problems were presented openly. A period when literature and theater flourished, and where the middle class started to challenge the hierarchal order of the country. The Victorian Era spanned Queen Victoria's rule in England from 1837 to 1901 and expanded the horizons of education and literacy, as well as a desire of the people to question religion and politics.

Captain Frankenstein had responded to calls to the theater before in the line of duty and was familiar with the area. This morning he had received a cryptic text message from an old acquaintance by the name of Erik Raeder to come there at once. It was a matter of an urgent nature. He remembered Erik from one of his past nine-one-one responses, as he was a primary witness to an unfortunate accident.

A few years ago, a young woman had fallen from a great height and was DOA, despite Saul's attempts at advanced cardiac life support measures. Erik was uncontrollably distraught and devastated by the terrible tragedy, as one would expect from a close friend of the deceased. Saul had the opportunity to interview him at length and was impressed by his intellectual candor and numerous talents, not the least of which were his accomplishments in musical theater, art, and choreography. He was a master of numerous instruments in a classical sense and had a penchant for mentoring protégés, of which the deceased apparently had been one.

Erik Raeder Jr. spoke with a slight European accent, although one couldn't tell by his musical prowess in performing with a variety of dialects. Apparently disfigured at birth, Erik wore a full facial prosthetic mask, not unlike that which severe trauma victims had at their disposal. In part for protection against microbes and supersensitive nerve endings, and in part to conceal his disfigurement. Saul couldn't help but relate to some of the emotional courage needed to offset the off-putting public eye. Not unlike Saul himself, Erik was familiar with the fact that he was a foreigner in his own town.

Frankenstein got into his work EMS vehicle and buckled in for safety. Little did he know how unsafe the future was, and what little protection the belt and airbags actually would provide.

# CHAPTER 50

Shadowing the gaunt daylight in an attempt to subvert the dawn, the winter solstice was succored by the dying fall. They met backstage in the theater as twilight became night. The first performance of the annual Christmas production of *The Nutcracker* was about to get underway and Erik was putting some finishing touches on one of the stage sets. Apparently he was also a skilled craftsman at stage production. Erik greeted Saul with a firm handshake and partially hidden smile behind the facial prosthetic mask he bore as a burden.

"Captain, thank you so much for coming. I'm afraid that we meet again under less than social circumstances," he said.

"Mr. Raeder, it's my pleasure. What seems to be the problem?" said Saul. The offstage banter among the cast and musical director was shielded from Saul and Erik by the large velvet curtains that delineated the back from the front of the stage.

"I hope that you'll pardon my being blunt and forward," Erik replied, "but I believe in getting to the point. Time is the one valued asset that no one can have enough of."

"Truer words were never spoken. So what's up?" Saul asked.

Erik spoke directly. "As you well know, certain events of social defiance and civil disobedience have been occurring in the vicinity."

"I'm not sure that I'd phrase it that way, but what do you know?" asked Saul.

"Throughout history," Erik said, "people have had to rise up against oppressive governments and social norms, reestablishing themselves as a force to be reckoned with. Being a government official, you of all people should know the corruption that runs rampant. Elections can be stolen, lies become truths, words minced like minds, weakening disposition and temperament. The time for poise and restraint has passed. The hour is nigh for those of us with the right determination and strength of character to take the reins. The meek shall not inherit the earth. What say you, Captain? Will you enlist in our crusade against those who disservice us?"

With a frown, Saul said, "Erik, you know I can't do that."

"Why, Captain? Why not stand up to help and assist in controlling those who are weaker and meeker? It's what they expect and count on."

Captain Frankenstein recalled performing a basic background search on Erik Raeder Jr. when he was witness to that accidental death. It had revealed that Erik's birth father was a card-carrying SS officer of Hitler's Nazi Germany. The elder Raeder held dearly a love of fascism and disdain for democracy and the parliamentary system of governance. When he said "heil," what he really meant was "kneel."

His name was Erich Raeder, and he named his son, albeit estranged, after him as well. Erik Raeder Jr. had kept his father's name out of pride for his white supremacist heritage and rigid, back-breaking discipline. Like father, like son. Erich Raeder Sr. was tried by the Hague for Nazi war crimes. The International Court of Justice and International Criminal Court resided in the Hague, and they were the principal judicial courts for the United Nations to prosecute those accused of crimes against humanity. The fact that Erik's father was convicted there was no small feat.

These facts gave Saul pause, and he couldn't imagine the challenging effects it could have had on the development of a young, impressionable mind. He had only wanted to help Erik as he would any of his other trauma victims. *To love thy enemies as well as one's friends is the truest test of one's character*, he had reminded himself.

Making certain eye contact and speaking in a soft, nonthreatening voice, Saul said calmly, "Erik, I know that you had a rough childhood. I can't imagine having to grow up with a father like that."

"My father was a great man!" Erik said with pressured speech. "Make no mistake. He was demonized and persecuted, just like your father was. My father taught me to be a man. When I was but a boy, our beloved family pet was a German shepherd named Blondi, whom we had since birth. I imprinted myself to her, and she to my heart. She grew to become my best friend. We went everywhere together, and due to my parents' important pressing engagements and frequent absence, she was often my sole company and companion. She grew rather large and would do anything to protect me from danger. She was a comfort to my soul. As she got on in years, my father decided that she was becoming too old to be useful, so he took her outside and shot her in the head with a German nine-millimeter Luger. I was beset with grief, not sure what to do without the best friend I'd ever known. I sat there crying to myself. My father viewed this as a sign of weakness, you see."

"Above my sobs, I heard scratching at the front door. To my surprise and amazement, there was Blondi, with her right eye hanging down onto her cheek still tethered to her orbit amidst the matted blood. Her tongue was dangling sideways, but she was smiling and wagging her tail because she was happy to see me. This disturbing reunion had me taken aback until my father handed me the Luger and told me to finish her off. So instead of inviting my friend inside to care for her wounds, I shot her twice in the head as she stood there on our front porch. I always loved that dog, but I had the courage and fortitude to be a man and do what had to be done."

Saul looked down in sorrowful silence, not sure what to say. Erik saw this and said, "Don't worry, old sod, there comes a time to put away childish things. My father taught me that."

Saul forced a tearful smile and sent it Erik's way. Every dog has its day.

Erik looked Saul straight in the eye. "Captain Frankenstein, you know very well firsthand what it's like to be made the butt of every perverse joke by these people whom you call neighbor. They mock you and fear you at the same time. You are simply a monster to them and always will be. Come with us, brother, and we will rise above these insects who have no true appreciation for what we are."

Saul replied, sincerely, "Don't you understand? There are numerous plastic surgeries that can help address your scars and deformities."

"Not the ones on the inside, I'm afraid. Those will never heal, nor would I want them to. It was hatred and grief that molded my darkened soul to the creature you see before you. You see I can no longer feel anything. No forgotten dreams nor unfulfilled ambition. Neither highs nor lows. Just in-between. You choose heaven or hell. My purgatory is of my own design. It's too late for me, and alas, now it's too late for you."

The orchestra went about preparations as usual, subtle harmonies adrift in the incidental milieu to a tempo lost long ago. The music of the night. Hold me closely. All I ask of you. Erik's thoughts were adrift. "My lovely ballerina Christine has died, just like my soul. At her last, she couldn't even bear to look at me. My disfigured countenance, a wretch of a man, was too much for her innocence to bear. So yes, I threw her from the precipice into the abyss. The witch tricked her to the most pristine and beautiful spot atop the mountain overlooking all that could have been but would not be ours. Now, I perform to an audience of one, desperately hoping for ghostly applause from the canyon below. I sometimes think in my mind's eye that I hear the resonance of her voice. Alas, they are just echoes of a life never lived, just teased. I was her creator and harshest critic and her most zealous fan. I longed for her sweetly from afar and admired her closely in my heart. I should have been her Adam, but instead I was the fallen angel."

"Of what strange nature is knowledge? It clings to a mind when it has once seized on it like lichen on a rock. I was benevolent and good; misery made me a fiend. The fallen angel became the malignant devil. Yet even that enemy of god and man had friends in his desolation; I am alone. Only someone as ugly as I am could love me. We are fashioned creatures, you and I, but half made-up. It is true, we shall be monsters, cut off from all the world, but on that account we shall be more attached to one another. How sweet is the affection of others to such a wretch as I am. I believed myself totally unfit for the company of strangers. How mutable are our feelings, and how strange is that clinging love we have of life even in the excess of misery. I truly am a phantom. A nonexistent specter who's merely an apparition and shadow to a demon."

"Erik, it doesn't have to be this way. Please let me help you," Saul pleaded.

Erik's disturbed voice and face were camouflaged by his full mask, distorting the sound of his retort. "My own existence should never have been. My mother bore a son whom she didn't want. Since abortions were illegal, she tried to do it herself. She drank poison while I hid in her womb, not wanting to be born at all, not any more than she did. My mother's efforts didn't kill me, but rather left me as the hideously deformed freak thing that you see before you. More monster than man. My early life, like yours, was fraught with difficulty and pain. I was born in a small town, just outside of Rouen, France. After my father was imprisoned, I was abandoned and unwanted by my mother, so I ran away and joined a gypsy caravan and became part of their traveling freak show to earn my keep. *'Le mort vivant,'* 'the living dead' was how I was advertised. 'He walks, he talks, he wants to be your friend' for a pittance."

"My mother was a meth head junkie who couldn't stop, so I took from my father's strength to do what needed to be done. Yes, he was an SS officer who went to prison for hate crimes, but is it a crime to hate those that are inferior to oneself? Especially if they mock you? I should think not. Through my formative years and travels, I learned the arts of illusion, architecture, and ventriloquism. As I grew older, I became an obsessive aesthete and mastered the finer arts of music and opera. Later, with the aid of my engineering and craftsman skills, I even helped restore the Opera House that we are standing in, as well as others."

Erik Raeder Jr. wanted and demanded Frankenstein's unflinching loyalty and devotion, not unlike his father's dedication to the brainwashed causes of the Third Reich and the Nazi movement. Blind obedience and servitude while goose-stepping on thin ice. Saul responded to this absurd request. "You know that I'm the captain overseeing emergency medical services for the county and state. I took an oath to protect and save people, not the opposite. I take that obligation very seriously and would never betray the public trust or my word."

"Either you're with me or against me. Friend or foe. Not in-between. Choose carefully," said Erik as he held out his gloved hand. While reaching out, he brushed open the front of his cape, exposing his lapel pin. It was a swastika.

"What's that on your shirt?"

"This? It's an old family heirloom from my father. It's from the war. Why do you ask?"

"You know, Erik, that my father and I are Jewish?" Saul said. "That symbol represents the true horrors of the Holocaust, one of the best examples of the worst of mankind. I cannot be any party to that evil madness."

"If that's the decision that you choose to live by, then you'll die by it as well," said Erik as the look on his face changed from admiration to admonishment and disgust. "The eternal Jew. *Der untermensch.* The Jew has always understood how to hide behind varied masks. Now it is I who wear the mask of Aryan supremacy. The Jew corrupts pure-raced peoples with his bad blood."

"I'm O-negative myself. The universal donor. My blood is compatible with everyone, just like my viewpoints," said Saul. Saul was trying to deescalate the situation and talk down the now hyper-manic Erik, just as he was trained to do.

"You're a fool, son of the Jew Frankenstein. You will die the fool. Judah and its world must die! As you must, *heir Judah*," Erik crowed.

Background music resumed playing as the orchestra warmed up for the evening's opera. The musical notes and symphony blessed the backdrop with the growing crescendo of their cracked voices. A cello and violin made love in the back of the pit, reposed and postured toward a life as far distant as a cry for help. The glockenspiel and wind ensemble breathed a precious sigh of relief as the notes fell out around them. Tones tweaked amongst the tuning instruments like a group of children talking together before school. This was followed by the maestro's familiar call to attention by rapping his vintage rosewood conductor's baton upon the podium, not unlike a grade school teacher letting her students know that class was about to start.

The amphitheater seats were full and the chimes dinged to notify all of the patrons to take their seats. Frankenstein recognized the situation as untenable. He looked at Erik and backed away, fearing for the safety of this public populace, and removed himself before the actual curtain call revealed the two man-monsters hidden just behind out of view. *Exodus, stage left*, thought Frankenstein.

Erik scowled and scurried off backstage into the shadows of the playhouse, well aware that befriending a Judah vas verboten. *Jawohl. Sieg heil.*

The old witch watched from the catwalk and had overheard everything. Not wanting to pull focus, Bridgett had fought back the urge to kill Frankenstein that remained from their last encounter. She had let Erik attempt to persuade the monster to assist in their crusade, knowing that it would be a bust. She instead focused on the prize at hand: the cancellation of Christmas and any semblance of holiday spirit.

The heavy velvet curtain rose up squeakily from behind the proscenium arch, allowing audience and stage to become one. The crowd applauded as Saul looked back from the theater wings, only to see no trace of the Phantom. For that's truly what he was. A phantom of the opera.

# CHAPTER 51

Gusty belches of northeastern wind swept across the hills, which looked upon the mountains for relief. A token sigh of similitude for the flatlands to share in the same winter's night. The equinox event rip-tiding the calendar pages, counting down and ahead to a new day and familiar beginnings.

The glittering hint of frozen rain took hold and entombed all that it surveyed. Sheets of sleet rained down like shrapnel covering flora and fauna, yielding an idyllic snapshot preserving time in ice. It somehow made everything seem new again. The crunch with each step harkened the difficulty in traversing the slippery slope of Frankenstein's long driveway, which he shared with the other forest creatures. It was simply breathtakingly beautiful. A preserved pastoral postcard that homogenized both home and stead. The heavy added weight of the ice-covered tree branches spoke loudly with cracks and groans and the occasional boom as timber broke and fell like decrepit old bones.

Aoife slipped and fell, letting out a curse and a growl as she made her way timidly to the familiar doorstep. The frozen stalactites that lined Frankenstein's gutters resembled a glistening iron maiden with open and welcoming arms. With the resounding boom of the antique cast iron front door knocker, a handful of icicles became dislodged and fell down upon the Count. One even pierced the skin above his cold heart.

Aoife kissed his superficial wound and said, sardonically, "At least it wasn't made of wood."

Dracula looked at her with a raised single brow. "You're hilarious."

"I know."

Frankenstein opened the heavy doors invitingly. "Hey guys, come inside, please. We've much to talk about. Be careful—it's slick out. I almost fell on my ass earlier."

"Cringe," Aoife said, smiling at the Count.

"Hanukkah sameach!" said Dracula.

"Oh, thanks. Chag sameach! Happy Hanukkah to you two as well," said Saul. "I only wish Ralph were here to celebrate with us."

"Us too," they somberly replied.

"I was just about to light the menorah. It's a family heirloom. Please, come in. I've made some latkes and pastry." Just inside the front entryway in a glass display case was the mezuzah, a small parchment scroll with the text from Deuteronomy 6:4-9 and 11:13-23 written on it. Frankenstein wore the traditional yarmulke, while Dracula wore a kippah and Aoife covered her head in a tichel out of respect for their very dear friend. After their house fire, they'd been left with the clothes on their backs and a handful of storage lockers scattered across memories of times and places before. A change of clothes and currency and they were as good as yesterday's news.

They all made themselves at home while Saul lit the appropriate candle, saying all three prayers to himself including the *shehecheyanu*, as it was the first night. The next seven nights would require just the first two blessings. "Baruch atah Adonai, Eloheinu melech ha'olam, asher kid'shanu b'mitzvotav, v'tzivanu l'hadlik ner shel Hanukkah."

He went on to recite the *hanerot halalu* aloud. Then Saul placed the lit menorah back in the front window to display his faith. He couldn't imagine anyone being angrier than they already were since he was the son of Frankenstein. They weren't successful before in lynching him and his father and burning down their castle, so he'd be damned if he'd allow them to control him now.

They all went to wash their hands and Saul said the blessings before they partook in the food that he had prepared.

The smell of pancaked potato carbohydrates warmed the air and senses. The crisp outer texture hid the succulent, savory innards while the kosher salted butter melted in their mouths. Frankenstein, Aoife, and Dracula smiled at each other, enjoying the feast and the comfortable silence between them.

Frankenstein reminisced. "I think of us as family today, but I remember many years ago when I still had living relatives that would get together to celebrate the holidays. One time, my Auntie Eva and Uncle Hyman came to visit for Hanukkah. I had accidentally left out some gold pieces of eight I discovered on a dive trip off the coast of Caesarea. My uncle Hyman ate one, thinking it was gelt! Granted, he was getting older, and his vision maybe wasn't so hot."

They all chuckled, and Aoife said, "What about his taste buds? And teeth? And the wrapper?"

"We laughed and laughed," Saul said. "He was a kind and gentle man. Always nice to me, even though genetically they weren't *meyn feter aun meyn mume*. Eventually congestive heart failure got the best of Uncle Hyman and he drowned within himself."

The room got quiet until Aoife broke the awkward pause. "These are the best potato pancakes that I've ever had, seriously."

Saul smiled. "Well, thank you. My father taught me how. This was always a special time for us together."

"I'm sure you miss him dearly," said Aoife.

"I guess we all have special loved ones who are missed."

All three shook their heads, thinking of Ralph.

The Count said, in Hebrew, "Over the centuries, I've respected and praised any and all religions that practice love, kindness, and kinship.

I've spoken many dialects from many different cultures. It matters not when or what part of the globe your tribe descended from. Using religious preference as an excuse to justify evil deeds is the opposite of any true spiritual belief that I've encountered. Most people everywhere just want the same thing. Civility, love, peace, and the ability to raise their families without fear of repercussions or recriminations. Call me whatever you will."

Aoife kissed him gently on the cheek and fed his eyes with her smile. Saul warmly replied, "It's a mitzvah."

"Gentlemen and women, to the task at hand," said Dracula. "From this day forward, we vow to end this nightmare not of our doing for the sake of that which we hold dear. Our character and principles are at risk should we fail in this undertaking."

"As well as the lives of countless families and children," Aoife added.

Just then there was an alert from Saul's doorbell to his watch. He looked, but no one was on screen. But the camera showed that there had been. He reviewed the footage to see Dr. Jekyll himself leaving a package on the doorstep and then promptly flitting away. Frankenstein opened the door to only empty shoe prints in the snow. Strange. He picked up the package, which was gift-wrapped with a big red bow on top holding a card in place. It read, "Merry Christmas and Happy Hanukkah to you all."

He closed the door and returned to his friends by the fire, carrying the present. He shrugged and thought that it was meant to be opened now, so the three of them made haste like children on Christmas morning. Openly detached from clocks and timetables, they hoped for the one wish that would never come true without their help.

God bless us all. Everyone. And monsters too.

# CHAPTER 52

## DECEMBER 17, 2018

They were poor, but so was everybody in the old neighborhood in the old days. The Ukraine was supposedly the breadbasket, but some had more bread than others. Maria Claudia Luminita was making a special Ukrainian birthday cake for her daughter Ivanna's sixteenth birthday. Humble surroundings, but they had each other: Maria, Ivanna, and Dorian.

"Dorian G. Luminita! I told you to keep your hands out of the cake. It's your sister's birthday. I wanted this to be special for her. Where is she anyway?" said Maria.

"She's down the street, kissing all the boys," said Dorian, Ivanna's precocious eight year brother.

"Oh, stop that. You tell her to get home, we're having dinner soon."

"Yes, ma'am," said Dorian.

"I need some candles for the cake. I'm going to Crina's. I'll be right back," said Maria to Dorian's salute.

The Rusu's lived three houses down on the left and included a sweet little old woman named Crina, who was married to her husband of seventy-two years, Bobik. They gave the old neighborhood a sense of charm and a hint of the generations of Ukrainians who had come before.

Bobik was severely hearing impaired but refused to admit it. He was a proud Ukrainian, like his father before, and so on. He could get by with basic lip-reading in familiar situations.

"Good morning, Bobik. How are you?" said Maria.

"A fine day it is. You look well, Maria," said Bobik.

"You too. How is your hearing doing?"

"You better believe it," Bobik replied.

"Maria, would you come here please?" said Crina.

"Good morning, Crina. I was wondering if I could borrow some candles for Ivanna's birthday cake. How are you today?" Maria asked.

"Fine, fine, except we have a bit of a problem."

"What's that?"

"Do you know our granddaughter Ion?" Crina asked.

"Yes, of course. What a sweet dear. Is she okay?" asked Maria.

"Yes, yes. She's fine. She was here visiting this weekend and, oh, did we have a good time. She got to play games with Grandpa, learn how to make goulash—oh, she is so bright. We even made a cake together. The devil's cake," said Crina.

"Devil's food cake?" asked Maria.

"It was so good. I saved you a piece, but mister you-know-who got to it in the night."

"Thank you just the same, said Maria. "So, what's the problem?"

"Do you know her pet? That chicken that follows her around?" asked Crina.

"Yes, how adorable. She loves that thing. She named it Susie. It rides on the handlebars of her tricycle. It's the cutest thing," said Maria.

"Grandpa ate Susie last night."

"What? No!" Maria exclaimed.

"And he gave some to Ion and she ate her too. She didn't know. I told her Susie ran away, so if she says anything, just say she ran that way," said Crina, pointing down the street.

Maria wasn't sure what to say other than, "Okay."

Crina started ranting in gibberish that Maria Claudia couldn't quite understand. Finally, she said, "Come, sit. Have some tea with me."

"Why, thank you," said Maria, taking a seat.

"I want to tell you something you already know in your heart," said Crina.

Maria wasn't quite sure what to make of this but said, "And what's that?"

"That you're descended from gypsies!" Crina exclaimed.

"Descended from? We're two months away from living in a caravan now!" said Maria as they both laughed.

"I'll try to teach you how to pick a pocket," said Crina. They both continued their jovial laughter.

"Oh my. Poor Susie," said Maria.

"Eh, she didn't taste that good anyway. No matter. But there will come a day when you realize who you are as a person. You, Maria, are your mother's daughter. God bless Papa," said Crina as she made the sign of the cross. "I have something to give you."

"Oh, what's that?"

"My library books. My sight is failing, so I want you to have them. Maybe when I'm blind, you can read to me," said Crina.

"Don't say that!" said Maria.

"No, it's okay. But these books are special. Read them carefully. They need a good home."

"I don't know what to say, but thank you," said Maria.

"Good. Now they belong to you," said Crina. Maria gave her a hug as they shared in the spirit of fellowship.

"Oh wait. One more thing. Here, take this," said Crina.

"Champagne? Oh no, I couldn't."

"It's your daughter's birthday. Anyway, it's the cheap stuff. What, you think mister big shot spender here is going to Paris anytime soon? Please, take the bottle, and have fun. And here's some candles for the cake. Kiss your babies from me."

"Thanks, Crina," said Maria as she gently kissed her forehead and held her fragile, aged hands. Her skin was so thin she was afraid that if she squeezed too hard, Crina would burst. The two women shared a smile that connected them as true as the earth is connected to the sky and the sea itself. They waved and said goodbye until tomorrow.

# CHAPTER 53

All three of them huddled in a circle around the present like giddy schoolchildren. "What if it's a bomb, or anthrax, or Covid?" asked Saul.

"I'm pretty sure that I could smell those," Aoife said.

To which the Count replied, with a smile, "You should work at the airport."

No one else smiled. They tore open the festive wrapping paper and opened the box. Inside was a beautiful ballerina poised to perform a pirouette.

Aoife wound the key on the bottom of the pedestal and shook the snow globe. The tiny dancer twirled gracefully en pointe while the snow cascaded gently around her, somehow keeping time to the tune that resonated from its base. The music box clicked away the traditional Russian and Ukrainian folk dance called the trepak, from the second act of Tchaikovsky's 1892 ballet *The Nutcracker*. Saul knew immediately what this meant. This was worse than he thought. He told Aoife and the Count about his earlier encounter with the mentally disturbed Erik Raeder Jr. Saul had made an official report and contacted the appropriate authorities, but nothing rose to the level of a search warrant.

There was a card inside with the gift which simply read: "Late show, tragedy tonight. B.B. has been recruiting to increase her rank and file. New headquarters is the abandoned ghost town of Glastenbury. Beware!"

The ominous card was signed with a "J" which, in cursive, almost looked like an "H." Dracula looked at Aoife. "Are you up for a road trip, my dear?"

She replied, "Try and stop me."

"Then I guess I'm going to the opera," Frankenstein said. "Too bad they don't make tuxes monster-size." They all put their hands together for one last prayer and wished each other the best of luck and safe travels. Saul couldn't help but think that they were going to need it.

# CHAPTER 54

## DECEMBER 17, 2018

That night, the Luminitas celebrated Ivanna's birthday party. They had a roast chicken without a name, potatoes, and, for dessert, a devil's cake. Ivanna closed her eyes and made a wish and blew as hard as she could to extinguish all the candles in one breath. Ivanna's birthday finale was the bottle of champagne from Crina. She slowly popped the cork, which ricocheted near Dorian's head.

"Hey! Watch it!" yelled Dorian.

"Sorry," said Ivanna.

Maria raised her glass and toasted her most precious daughter who was growing older faster than Maria herself. "May your belly always be full, and your champagne glass never empty. Happy birthday, my dear."

They clinked flutes, and the lights went out and the air raid sirens screamed full on.

The winding up of the emergency horn to its best decibel gave way to the whistling of the rocket as it descended toward them. The ground shook like thunder, and rubble dust shook loose from the ceiling above. Maria held her two most dearest heartbeats in her arms to shield them from death, which thankfully missed the beat. They stayed huddled to finish their prayer. Maria checked them both for injuries and the three exhaled sighs of relief.

"Thank heavens," said Maria.

"No way. Crazy. That was so scary!" exclaimed Dorian.

They went outside to take in the air and see how everyone else was. Three houses down on the left, where a home once stood, was now a smoldering impact crater in the earth. Just another hole in the ground. Or a shallow grave. Maria held her two even closer as she noticed that Ivanna, frozen with terror, was still tightly clutching the champagne, holding on for dear life.

# CHAPTER 55

It was dark when the young woman arrived at Henry and Edward's Apothecary and Compounding Pharmacy. She was running late as usual and sped through a couple stop signs to get there before closing. Looking after her younger brother Dorian always made for unexpected surprises to her time management. He was buckled in the passenger seat, but he might as well be tied to her hip as far as he was concerned.

"Wait here, please," said Ivy.

"Don't boss me, just because your my substitute teacher. I'm still thirteen, And hurry up, I gotta pee!" Dorian exclaimed.

"Well, whose fault is that? I'll be quick, I promise," said his sister.

The good doctor was just closing up and locking the door when she reached out to tap him gently on the shoulder.

"Excuse me, Dr. Jekyll, but please, can I still pick up my mom's prescription? I'm so sorry to bother you like this."

The looming figure turned to expose the shocking, distorted, and bizarre Mr. Hyde. He wore only a displeasing smile beneath his top hat and cape. Otherwise he was completely nude. Tipping his hat, he said, "Oh I'm afraid he's not here. Now how shall I accommodate you? Pray tell, what's your name, my dear?"

The young lady was shocked and taken aback, not understanding what the hell was going on, and said, "Ivy. Champagne Ivy. Least that's what my friends call me."

Hyde sneered. "Of course it is, my dear. Of course it is…"

# CHAPTER 56

Ghost town. Big schlemiel. Thirty miles outside of Rutland remain the remains of the town of Glastenbury. The old witch would blend in like a comfortable butt blemish in this barren of places. In the 1880's, Glastenbury was a thriving town nestled at the base of the Green Mountains. The lumber industry had led to commerce, sawmills, and about 250 residents. But a major flood destroyed most railway lines and bridges. The local Adnaik Indians avoided hunting the area because of a dark presence. They only used Bennington Mountain to bury their dead. One big Indian burial ground. Welcome home.

Numerous strange disappearances had occurred here over the years. Dating back to 1879, when a stagecoach driver was attacked, there had been countless reports of eight-foot-tall hairy monsters—some called them Bigfoot or Sasquatch. In 1945, at least four separate hikers of all ages and backgrounds went missing and were never found. People said not to wear red while hiking, like Paula Weldon, who disappeared too. Little red riding hood never made it out of the forest.

The Bennington monster lived in the Glastenbury Mountains. A haunted, terrifying place that would scare the shit out of you if you only knew the half of it. The stuff you don't tell your kids without spelling out certain parts. They wouldn't understand. Just like you. Jesus, Mary, and Joseph. The Patch Hollow Massacre, Chittenden,

Ricker Basin, and Castleton where the old First Church of Bennington used to be. The area eventually turned away more than it took in or rather swallowed up. The Glastenbury Ghoul. Sasquatch. Who the fuck knows what crazy-ass shit was happening deep in the heart of those Green Mountains? It wasn't gonna tell. Did you know? Could you know? Would you tell? No one really wanted to know anyway. Sleeping dogs.

The old witch stared into the cauldron. Her eyes, wandering through the void, were as dead as her soul if there ever was one in that decrepit, mangled simile shell of a person. It was the absence of any warmth or feeling that made her so disturbing. She could be cooking in a cauldron and converse as comfortably about changes in the weather as eye of newt. "Eeper Weeper, chimney sweeper, had a wife but couldn't keep her. Had another, didn't love her, up the chimney he did shove her," she muttered as the coal-black smoke rose forth from the long, barren chimney to fill the sky with disgust.

"With all this snow and cold, I feel like we're attending the Donner party. And they knew how to throw a party. They killed and ate two of the Washoe tribe members who came to rescue them. Now that's hospitality. As I recall, the last man to be rescued was sitting around the fire with a pot just like this eating his neighbor's femur while he had cattle outside. When asked why, he just said it was 'the sweet meat.' Let's just say he had good taste," she said with a smile.

Gulped, guzzled, slurped, and bibbled. They engorged themselves in gluttonous crapulence. It was a potluck so Mr. Hyde had made a pitstop at a daycare on the way out of town. The handful of hungry children were backed into a corner while the small circle of frenemous fucks ate everything but the grace. Handsomely disfigured, Hyde's beleaguered, grotesque features were consummated with inhuman temperament and voracious appetite. The boiling cauldron bubbled up tiny bones. All the while, the witch's disposition sous viding slowly.

"Salem witch trials indeed. I'll give 'em a holiday to remember, or try to forget," the witch mumbled to no one in particular.

Her black cat was showing signs of her age, with splotchy salt and peppering of her fur. She was moving more and more slowly, but knew enough to hide away quickly when Bridgett was like this, not knowing for sure how many of her nine lives had been lost.

The diabolical creatures sat down to celebrate their first meal together in their old, new abode. A monster holiday. Bridgett had even dressed for the occasion and dug out her old winklepickers from the back of the closet. She had previously been skeptical about wearing her pointed witchy shoes for fear that someone might drop a house on her, but she was feeling more comfortable in her own skin. Not that she was opposed to wearing someone else's, of course.

The old witch had a rapacious appetite and cleaned her plate, xertzing down the last bit of dregs and tittynopes. With a full belly and empty heart, she sat down by the roaring fire to thumb through her old cookbooks. "Snips and snails and puppy dog tails; sugar and spice and everything nice. That's what little children are made of. Scrumptious. And sometimes, a bit of grotty, gristly cartilage.

"A pinch here. A dash there. And a hell of a lot of screaming." Blood sausage and blood pudding were a regional holiday treat cooked up by some of the more geriatric ethnic populations to remind them of the smells and tastes of holidays past. A simpler time when eating offal wasn't so awful. Liver, tongue and tripe were merely that. Sustenance and surviving meant embracing the bad with the good. The yin and the yang. The baby and the bath water.

Speaking of which, it was time for dessert. When it comes to a meat soufflé, timing is everything.

# CHAPTER 57

Bridgett Bishop and her crew of psychopathic monsters were just getting settled in their new digs in the ghost town of Glastenbury. The old witch had learned a long time ago that one of the best ways to avoid detection from suspecting eyes was to keep moving to new locations without giving a forwarding address. She knew that it was time for a more private homestead, especially once the Phantom carried out his less than subtle plan. At least he would keep his promise and deliver the goods as agreed. Meals on wheels.

This deserted ghost town with its rundown buildings certainly didn't even have addresses, and given its history, sightseers would naturally avoid it for fear of becoming part of a ghost story themselves. It was perfect. She and her cohorts just relocated their base of operations into the middle of nowhere. When winter came, it was barely accessible at all.

The old, abandoned two-story house was in a tatterdemalion state, with missing shingles and shutters. The dwelling and its new tenants were all condemned. It had good bones though, like a child's skeleton who has yet to expereince osteoporosis. The main structure had an intact cement floor and solid support beams from which to attach iron chains and shackles for the unwilling students of their new nursery and daycare. It could use a new coat of paint and indoor plumbing, but she'd seen worse. Yes, this would do nicely.

The old witch considered the events and her progress so far. *Not too shabby*, she thought as she set the table. "So, a vampire, a werewolf, and Frankenstein's monster are going to try and put the kibosh on my holiday plans. How ignorant and blind they are. Three blind mice running around. Just like the rhyme. 'They ran after the farmer's wife. She cut off their tails with a carving knife. Did you ever see such a sight in your life as three blind mice?'"

She explained to her guests and cohorts Mr. Hyde, the creature from the black lagoon, and the mummy goddess Nephthys, "Did you all know that rhyme is based on a true story? Long ago, there was a Catholic queen called Bloody Mary, 'cause she had a nasty habit of mass-murdering Protestants. Once, she caught three of 'em plotting to assassinate her, except she didn't cut 'em at all. She burned 'em alive at the stake! Medium rare, I hope!" She laughed and hooted and hollered.

"Now let's go over our frightful plans my fiendish friends. The holidays are around the corner and we wanna make sure everything goes off without a hitch. Including spreading tidings to Dracula and his patchwork monsters. Bad tidings for sure," she said as her laughter resounded throughout the drafty room.

# CHAPTER 58

Christmas season. It was a time when people harkened to simpler days. So many of the homes had already resurrected their artificial Christmas trees decorated with tinsel and glitter and a big, bright, shiny star atop. Crafting candy canes and popcorn into never-edible ornaments. Nostalgic musical remixes and modern footnotes for carolers zooming in the yuletide spirit. To hear the angels sing.

Many in the town of Killington spent Christmastime longing for loved ones and yearning for truth. Traditionally, they loaded their family into the car to sightsee the displays of friendly Christmas lights while listening to holiday music. Instead, this year, they drove around searching and calling out names heard only by the silent houses and alleyways.

The snow dripped from the clouds as though the sky were melting. Splotching and splashing slushies onto Gucci boots and Jimmy Choo's. The mall and Santa's workshop within were usually packed with last-minute shoppers and a final opportunity to plead one's case for nice versus naughty on the jolly fat man's lap. Santa went home early this year. One person left a Christmas letter at his doorstep, which simply read, "HELP."

Endless wish lists justified by confabulated memories or outright lies. Temperatures rising in the thermometer of guilt or innocence. Dash away, dash away, dash away all. Ugly sweaters were outdone by the ugliness that pervaded the community. Wishing for a happy and healthy holiday season. No chance in hell.

The days grew a little shorter as their lives grew ever longer. Longer in tooth and nail, like the mortal illusion of forever. Calendar years blown away by the gentle breeze of time. Lurking was the timing itself, so derivative and unkind. It's beginning to look a lot like Christmas.

Captain Saul Frankenstein logged his target location into his GPS and was on his way. The orange rays from the outstretched sun reached between the fingers of the trees and harassed his eyes with a strobe effect. He drove his work vehicle past his distant neighbors and, frame by frame, he saw tree lines passing like filming a seizure. The relativity of his inertial frame of reference clicked by in rapid stop-motion photography.

Endless pines towering and standing at attention by a manicured six-foot critical distance. The gentle dusting of snow onto thick ice was enough to break a camel's back. Even with four-wheel drive, the tires and traction were splotchy. A grave invitation to a black ice affair. Frankenstein was chill. There's no dress code in heaven anyway. Rear wheels sliding by the frosty front yards, glancing at a neighbor trying to play fetch with a dog that just won't hunt. It's just cold. Cold as life or death. Or the grave itself. At least he was making good time.

# CHAPTER 59

The night janitor of the opera house received the EMS captain as agreed upon. No sirens, no screams, no *shmegegge*, no shit, for once. Silent sounds and lights were off as Frankenstein made his way along the subterranean passageways that echoed his whispering voice. The night caretaker warned, "He's here. The demon you seek. He can hide everywhere and does. Weird things happen when he's around. I can take you to him. The underground tunnels aren't even known or mapped because they're so old. I once got lost down there myself looking for a missing cat. When I found it, the black cat was completely gray! And ever since then, that noisy feline has never made a sound. It's as if it were scared near death. I think it lost all of its nine lives plus one."

The skeevy custodian looked older than he should as well. He smelled of heavy drinking and light lifting, and even though mixed with disinfectant, it pretty sure seemed like he had shart himself, or at least never wiped. Saul was worried this *meshuga* drunkard was full of it, but continued to follow him through the maze beneath the playhouse. He accepted his mission objectives, but wondered, *What the hell have I gotten myself into, and can I get out?*

The two of them walked along pressed against the wall. They walked and walked and counted their breaths while they walked along the methodically chaotic route following their own oversized silhouettes leading the way. Frankenstein's enormous shadow appeared to be stalking the smaller silhouette before him. Saul was starting to rethink this whole *farkakteh* idea when the aged young man escorting him darted down a dark corridor toward the reverberating symphonic sounds. The evening's performance had begun.

"*Yalla*," said Saul unenthusiastically as he raced to follow in silence. A night at the opera. He was hoping for Handel. No such luck.

# CHAPTER 60

The winter ranch had rentals for cross-country skiing, snow-shoeing, and even dogsledding, which was what the Count and Aoife were interested in. The treacherous trip to the ghost town in the middle of nowhere at the dawn of winter would require preparation and discipline. The snow cabin and yurt rentals usu-ally brought in good tourist dollars and were accompanied by a gift shop and small petting zoo of sorts with a herd of six muskoxen that looked like something from a faraway planet. The muskoxen had been brought in from Canada and Alaska and were well maintained on the hundred-acre property.

The Inupiaq-speaking Eskimos called them *itomingmak*, mean-ing "the animal with skin like a beard" in reference to their long hair that hung to the ground. The Inuktitut name *umingmak* means "the bearded one." They normally roamed the frozen tundra in search of roots, mosses, and lichens, and the male's thick coat and musky odor attracted females during the seasonal rut. The Inuktitut regularly hunted them for food and wool. These husky creatures were able to sur-vive the end of the Ice Age when most other large mammals died out.

Apparently, the sled dogs didn't agree with their presence and had to be separated from the muskoxen for fear that the dogs would kill them. "Yeah, they seem pretty feisty," Aoife said. "I'm sure we'll get along fine. *Allons-nous mushing, mon cher?*"

"But of course, my love," said the Count. He took the time to notice a rather unpleasant group of homegrown gentlemen next to a barn staring them down vehemently, like hyenas waiting for a bone. They even laughed like hyenas.

The Siberian huskies and Alaskan malamutes secured to the snow sleigh were quite uneasy and restless. The canines were none too happy to have a werewolf at the helm and excitedly barked and howled until Aoife let out an ear-piercing howl of her own. The leader, point, swing, wheel, and team dogs all whimpered and cowered back in place, awaiting the wolf's next command.

As the Count climbed onto the dog sleigh, he looked over his shoulder toward his wife, holding the reigns behind him, and said, "If you say, 'On Dancer, on Prancer, on Comet, on Vixen,' I'll bite you."

Aoife replied, "I'll give you Vixen."

"Tease."

And with that she yelled "Mush!" with a crack of the whip above the dogs' heads. They were off. She was truly grateful for their help and sacrifice and promised herself that she would protect these sled dogs with her very life. That's if they made it out alive themselves. The sled dogs raced all the faster, attempting to gain distance from their sharp-toothed benefactors.

The Count was caught in-between the dogs in front and his wife behind him as he huddled on the bed of the sled. His eyes were locked onto the path ahead and helped to mesmerize the dogs into submission. The vampire and werewolf charged forward with their mongrel companions, darting and dashing and prancing as if there were no tomorrow. And there just might not be, if they were too late.

# CHAPTER 61

Intimate yet charming and reminiscent of bygone days. The annual stage production of *The Nutcracker* had always played to a local sellout crowd. Family members awaited the stage introduction of their little ones, who played mice transformed into Chicago-born ragamuffins and hooligans who enlist in the Rat King's army. The Rat King, garbed in an oversized cloak, strolled into position and proclaimed, "That's just unfair. You always interfere with my plans. But just you wait. Sooner or later, I will destroy great Elohim and crush you all. Just you wait."

> *"Tick-tock, tick-tock—*
> *Now softly purrs the clock,*
> *Little Mouse-King's ears can hear,*
>    *Whir, whir, whir,*
> *Sing him the songs of yore*
> *For soon he'll be no more.*
>    *Strike, clock, strike!"*

• • •

Emma Hawthorne hated Halloween. It was just weird and creepy and scary and it didn't make any sense. She knew Annie and Max liked it, though, so she tried to bite her tongue to keep the peace.

"Free candy? Who cares? I can have all the candy I want but I don't want dental caries, please forgive me," she said to herself sarcastically. She just wanted to get past that waste of time and let's get on with Christmas.

Emma thought of Annie and the insanity of her kidnapping and rescue. But that was over. Her sister was back home and fine. Now it was her time to shine. She had worked so hard to try and regain some semblance of the holiday spirit that had been lost to so many; she refused to give up. Like a dying ember that needed a flame or breath of air.

The only thing she was truly looking forward to was performing in *The Nutcracker* onstage for the holidays. She had done it before, so she figured on giving the new kids some pointers on how best to emote the character of a rat soldier, servant to the Rat King. They would hide under the oversized conical robe of the Rat King, and when he opened his cloak, they would scatter and run across the stage. It was always a crowd favorite. Especially among the parents of the new child performers who would fantasize about beauty contests, cereal commercials, and product influencers.

Through all of the recent madness and mayhem, Emma knew that the people of Killington still wanted to believe. To hope and harbor faith in something more. She thought to herself, *WTH man. It's showtime.*

# CHAPTER 62

A mishmash of hometown rednecks and white trash formed an impromptu vigilante posse to eke out their own unlawful brand of frontier justice. It was the hyenas from the winter ranch rental place. They decided to become judge, jury, and executioner without a judge or jury. No prospect for pardon. Some of them had attended the town meeting, while others were just looking for an excuse to feed their bigoted hate of all monsters. They believed in some crazy half-assed conspiracy theories that the Count and Contessa were responsible for the missing children and, for that matter, all their life's petty woes. Some of the feckless fools even thought that the monsters were stealing jobs and attempting to overthrow their privileged white power politics. It was a menagerie of drunken fools with guns who gave chase to the dogsled carrying Dracula and Aoife.

The first to attack was the skijoring bumpkin in coveralls, spraying bullets from a mini-Uzi submachine gun with silencer. He was able to control the reins of the horse while skiing behind and splattering the scenery with a continuous *thup, thup, thup* from the barrel of the banned Israeli weapon.

The Count bared his fangs and hissed loudly with a menacing stare at the attacker's horse, which froze, startled and spooked, and reared up on its hind legs. Inertia kept the skijoring assassin sliding forward right into the horse's ass. The less than trusty steed responded to the unwanted advance by rearing its back legs and kicking the man full force in the chest, collapsing his rib cage and throwing his broken rag doll torso.

As he flew through the air, his finger spasmed reflexively on the trigger and the mini-Uzi showered the sky with lead fireworks. His body smacked into the middle of a nearby pine, crumpling around the base of the tree, bending his spine backwards in a way not conducive to survival.

Dracula had noticed that the combatant wore full body armor with neck guard, and he thought, *As if I'd even think of biting that dirty-ass neo-Nazi neck and giving him the gift of immortality.*

Another yokel rode on the back of an ice bike, a motorcycle equipped with spiked snow tires, while his partner drove recklessly toward their prey. The rear passenger aimed a compound crossbow which shot out deadly wooden projectiles at a rapid rate of speed, missing Dracula by mere inches. The thin wooden stakes made it an ideal vampire-killing weapon. For the next two weeks it was deer season. Vampire season was year-round. No limit.

Aoife got winged with a flesh wound and winced in pain, but continued mushing even faster. The Count turned around and stood up on the sleigh and launched himself over his wife and onto the oncoming ice cycle, throwing the crossbow-wielding passenger under the front of the bike. The sharp studded tires tore him to shreds while the out-of-control cycle crashed into another ice bike predator, which exploded upon impact into a black, smoking ball of flame. An instant prior to the crash, Dracula had opened his cape like a drag racer's parachute, which thrust him backwards and up into the air as if he were a drifting kite.

Just below him was a fast-approaching airboat outfitted for ice. The airboat hummed along, displaying a Confederate flag on a long pole waving in the wind like a parade float from the eighteen hundreds.

It had a smooth, flat-bottom hull, which glided effortlessly over the ice doing about sixty miles per hour. It was driven by Jeb Bronson of Jeb and Kaleb's Airboat Tours, specializing in summer and winter airboat excursions.

The machine was basically a giant fan attached to a johnboat most familiar to Louisiana swamps and alligators. His brother Kaleb rode shotgun—literally, with a twelve-gauge Bernoulli tactical assault shotgun, which he discharged in a rapid succession while their buddy Mac sat on the other side, vaping and fiddling with an African street sweeper. Both sides had elevated swivel seats that offered high visibility of potential targets while the center driver's seat was raised even more so to allow the best visibility with which to navigate. Jeb sat like a hillbilly king on his speeding throne, surveying his empire of ice. The boat's fan blades whirred loudly, sounding like a giant swarm of swamp insects echoing their call off the surface of the frozen lake.

The Count closed his cape and cannonballed swiftly straight down, landing on the very front lip of the airboat with such force that the driver lost control and the boat flipped and rolled end over end, finally coming to a stop in a heap of twisted metal wreckage. The driver and passenger were obviously dead since one of them was decapitated and the other bisected diagonally by the huge rotating blades.

The third man lost his street sweeper, but somehow managed accidently to perform his own tracheotomy with his vape pen. In the cold night air, the small cylinder exhaled his dying breaths while protruding from his neck. Dracula had jumped at the last minute to avoid harm and, with cape billowing like a hang glider, landed softly on the ice nearby.

Two snowmobiles with passengers were armed to the teeth and carried AR-15 assault rifles, because why wouldn't you? These fully converted automatic weapons were military grade and issued for servicemen and women fighting in wartimes, but they worked just fine in town. The deer never knew what hit them. Ideal for home defense.

Tad and Ricky Hafstaff were expert marksmen and well versed in their weapon systems. To them, this was a turkey shoot. The brothers served together on the weekends with the Army National Guard program, but they considered themselves soldiers of fortune. The wannabe warriors each rode on the back of the snow machines driven by their wives, Katy and Carol Hafstaff. The two soccer moms were just as adept markswomen as their husbands and would put any psychopathic Karens or MTG to shame.

By now, Aoife had turned the dogsled around and headed straight for the pursuing snowmobiles as numerous Remington .223 fifty-five-grain hollow-point bullets ricocheted all around her. These rounds were made with a high ballistic coefficient for competition match-grade performance. She was playing chicken with them and wasn't about to be the first to flinch or fry. Just as she sped past the Count on the ice, he tossed her the long Confederate flagpole from the air-boat wreckage, which she properly directed forward into a jousting position.

The two snowmobile drivers were confused and glanced at each other through tinted birefringent goggles in disbelief. Without hesitation, Aoife wedged the flagpole sideways below the front handlebars and on top of the rear stanchions, resting on the top rail. She hunched down behind the cargo bed basket onto the foot boards so as not to get knocked off by the impact. It looked as if Aoife was riding a giant crucifix led by a team of hellhounds to an inevitable fate. She then drove the sled dogs and cart directly between the two snow machines at full speed while bracing herself and leaning into the center of gravity.

The flagpole, turned sideways, struck both female drivers squarely in the chest. This knocked them and their passengers forcefully onto the hard, frozen ice lake, where they rolled in a tumbled mess of broken arms and legs. As she and her husband Dracula stood over the two broken couples, Aoife mumbled to herself, "Don't tread on me." Tad and Katy and Ricky and Carol lay scattered and broken, moaning about the ice.

"Well, what now, my dear?" asked Aoife to her groom.

"We've got work to do. Leave them and call nine-one-one for help and give them this location," said Dracula.

As he said this, Katy and Carol Hafstaff were stirring on the ice. Suddenly they were both drawing and aiming their sidearms, both SIG Sauer P229s, and opened fire. They both had extended mags with a capacity of fifteen nine-millimeter Parabellum bullets and they rapid-fired at the Count and Contessa.

Aoife was struck in the leg and Dracula in the right arm as they both pounced on their attackers. Dracula picked up Carol Hafstaff and smashed her upside-down through the ice headfirst so that only her body from her neck to her feet was visible in the cold moonlight. Her body twitched and spasmed as her head tried to breathe ice water. At the same time, Aoife tore off Katy's right hand holding her handgun and ripped open her belly. She inserted Katy's own pistol into her abdominal cavity and fired upwards, not knowing if it was empty or not. There were still three bullets left. The nine-millimeter Parabellums exploded through the top of Katy's skull like a bloody Roman candle.

Frantically concerned for each other, Dracula and Aoife checked each other's gunshot wounds. The Count had his wife sit down on the ice as he carefully excised the bullet from her inner thigh with his fangs, taking care not to turn her. With surgical precision, Dracula went to work with his mouth while Aoife winced and howled and clawed his back in pain. His bloody lips spit the bullet out onto the ice while Aoife did her best to tamponade and bandage the bleeding wound. She wrapped a scarf around her thigh and tied it tight as Dracula began excising his own bullet with his incisors.

"I hate guns. There's no honor in them," said Dracula as he spit out the bloody bit of lead from his arm. Aoife had torn a strip of cloth from inside her jacket lining and field-dressed her husband's injury.

"Where's the honor in any of this insanity? They tried to kill us for no reason," said Aoife. Dracula just shook his head and replied, "When is hate ever satiated? When does it end? Only in the demise of those who choose that foregone conclusion of never." He then proceeded to feed on the soon-to-be-dead redneck corpses until their exsanguination was complete.

The Count would satisfy his needs by feeding on the dying, not yet dead bodies. The blood. The life. Blood starts to coagulate instantly on death, and he could not drink a curdled clot any more than suck a thick milkshake through a straw. Gross. No, he preferred the fresh, free-flowing oxygenated blood of life to nourish him and propagate him into the next generation.

Occasionally, the Count would make use of a vampire straw—a reusable, titanium, eco-friendly straw with a sharp, tapered end on one side. It could be inserted directly into a blood vessel easily and was dishwasher-safe. Dracula preferred arterial to venous because of the pumping and oxygen content. His tastes had become refined over time like everyone, and he couldn't imagine feeding on the junk food that he did when younger.

The Count retrieved the vampire straw that had fallen out of his cape pocket during all of the hoopla. It was sitting on the ice next to Ricky, who was broken beyond repair. He had suffered extreme facial trauma with extensive orbital and zygomatic fractures and swelling such that only one eye was visible. As Dracula bent over to pick up the straw, Ricky mumbled, "Ahm kanna ki oo."

"My friend, I speak over one hundred languages fluently, but I'm afraid gibberish isn't one of them," said Dracula as he expertly inserted the titanium straw into Ricky's neck. A will is a way. *Vampires do make the best phlebotomists*, he thought.

Blood bonds. A more intimate framework and example of the food chain was hard to imagine. Only an erythrocyte cocktail could slake his thirst. A wretched curse no different than many modern maladies of medicine. Basically, requiring periodic transfusions that someday stem cells should replace. Darwinian reversion attested to the blood and its ever-evolving bond between genotypes and phenotypes. A cure for whatever ails ya. Anything you die from today barely misses the cure of tomorrow. Lifespan versus technological and social evolution. Potato, potato. For now, he still needed to eat. Like everyone.

He drew his lips back as the night sky had grown still and drank.

Aoife mushed the dogsled over toward her husband.

"Buurrp. Oh, excuse me, my dear. I keep forgetting that belching isn't a compliment in this day and age and country," said the Count.

Aoife replied in Romanian, "*Am fost ingrijorat.* I was getting worried. It's nice to see you eating again. Your manners and etiquette are without question. Some people today might take offense, but I know that your heart is in the right place. You even put the toilet seat down. I find you irresistible for a six-hundred-year-old man. You don't even look a day over three hundred!"

"And your sense of humor reminds me to laugh every day rather than cry or grow angry. I cherish the world around you, for I am wrapped around your heart. You taught me to like myself mostly because of the man that you have helped me become, not the monster that I was. With you, possibilities are endless. There is no hardship that we can't overcome together. You make hardship easy."

"And you, my love, are an unfinished poem waiting to be discovered. I am yours. In every way. You take me to a place that I never knew existed."

Dracula wiped his lips and chin with his monogrammed handkerchief and reposited it back into his inner jacket pocket. The blood-stained embroidered letters "VD" were sewn on several hundreds of years ago in Transylvania long before the modern medical acronym. Vlad III Draculea, the Prince of Wallachia, held the Contessa Aoife in his embrace and they shared a kiss that spoke volumes.

Husband and wife remounted their dog sleigh and continued their sojourn across the ice-covered lake which led them over the frozen river and through the woods. To the old witch's house they went. Although they wondered if this was such a good idea after all. Winter's menacing behavior was met with looming overbite as the sleigh picked up speed. The never-ending flakes of the uncompromising snow assuaged their faces and hesitation; the monsters were still out there, in the cold dark shadows of unfamiliarity and doom. They hunched over and hastened their pace as the sled sped on.

# CHAPTER 63

Frankenstein and the custodian continued their tunnel search for the maestro, which led them to one of the wings beside the stage. From there they could witness the live performance of *The Nutcracker*, which was already underway. Saul turned to see that the janitor had fled, finally succumbing to fear. A diminished chord faded just like the small, unnoticeable man escaping into the callous shadows. The toy soldiers marched to the beat of their own drum. The cadence was hauntingly familiar. The electronic language translator was rapidly flashing the sung and spoken words centered above the troupe like ticker tape. Closed caption for the living-impaired. Suddenly, the digital script changed, and the prompter just flashed, "HaHaHaHaHaHaHaHaHa."

The spotlight shone on the Rat King who performed center stage. He opened up his large, conical cloak to release the juvenile rat army underneath. But there were none. Just a glimpse of a closing trapdoor in the stage floor beneath. The group of rat tots were dropped through the hole into the waiting cage below, ensnaring them for transport.

Saul knew just who was behind this debacle of debauchery. Who else would commit a kidnapping of the theater patrons' own children before a live audience? The Phantom himself. Immediately Saul dove onto the stage, knocking aside the Rat King and other performers, and grappled with the remote-controlled, spring-loaded trapdoor.

He was finally able to trip the trap with his tactical EMT multi-tool and flung it open.

As he started into the hole below the stage, he looked up above him. There hung a gigantic prop chandelier hoisted and secured to the top of the ceiling center stage, awaiting a future performance. A small remote-controlled detonator attached to the chain securing the immense lighting structure was discharged. Its small explosive payload set free the behemoth prop from its moorings as it came crashing down in a crescendo of cascading destruction. It smashed onto center stage and burst apart into thousands of shrapnel pieces just as Frankenstein dropped through the trap door.

The Rat King wasn't so lucky. He was crushed instantly. He was the first to fall into the second act, last scene, while the remaining performers ran for cover. Frankenstein could hear the mayhem and chaos above him as his descent into hell began.

# CHAPTER 64

The man with a thousand faces and a thousand-yard stare echoed his maniacal laughter throughout the would-be catacombs and complex tunnels. Eccentricity and evil ingenuity were placed squarely on the shoulders of Erik Raeder Jr., and he bore them with confidence. The voice of the Phantom himself reverberating in and out of the confluence of tunnels and crevices reminded Saul just how mad he had become. Erik was proficient in the arts of illusion, magic, and ventriloquism such that by his design one could not discern whether these terror threats originated nearby or if the wandering pockets of air and sound waves were ricocheting off the cavern walls from a great distance. Either way it was he. The Phantom of the Opera.

Erik's voice, as sure as his talents for misdirection and acoustics, were certainly leading Saul astray. Captain Frankenstein lit his electric torch and ventured forward, making haste. He followed the path of escape and treachery through the vomitorium or "vom," making egress quickly beneath a tier of seats.

A robot vacuum cleaner entered the underground passage from the subbasement stage left. Saul thought to himself that this maze of tunnels must be really filthy … but then he then noticed that there was more than one flashing light on the rotating circular device heading his way, as well as way too many wires attached haphazardly to

237

the unit itself. As it grew closer, he saw an M18A1 Claymore anti-personnel mine with remote detonator. The robotic frisbee spun around until the small, concave rectangular block on top rotated to reveal the words "FRONT TOWARD ENEMY." Clearly Erik had some access to older military ordinance, likely thanks to his loving father.

The fine wire connected to the moving IED ran its limit and was pulled from its attachment to the mine. Saul dove into the nearest tunnel, which barely shielded him from the enormous blast. There was concrete rubble and dust everywhere, making further progress within the original passageway impossible, so he continued running in the new direction hoping it led him somewhere outside. He felt a cringe of claustrophobia and suddenly became overwhelmingly sad. Then just angry at the thought of Ralph's demise. He picked up the pace. *There is no way in hell I'm giving up hunting this bastard.*

Even though, it just so happened, that's exactly where he was headed.

# CHAPTER 65

Saul weaved his way through the system of underground walk-
ways and tunnels until finally he saw the faint change in nighttime shades of dark. It appeared that there was an opening up
ahead, and the crisp night air directed him that way. Soon there was
an immense frozen body of water with no horizon before him.

It was almost imperceptible, but he swore that he could just make
out some faint hint of illumination far, far ahead, traversing the lake
away from him and the now chaotic opera house. It was the awaiting horse-drawn prison wagon carriage filled with Christmas tykes
dressed like mice. The Phantom had hightailed them away through
the snow at breakneck speeds.

There was no time to waste, as the trail and tracks were being lost
rapidly to the gusts of wind and new falling snow. Saul refused to
give up, stepping out into the snowfield as theater revelers fled the
parking lot in droves, some of them traveling by snow chariot.

Frankenstein saw his chance and jumped onto a nearby idling snowmobile and followed the tracks left behind in the powder full throttle.
The Phantom had used the vintage tumbleweed wagon just as it was
designed. Transporting prisoners from a temporary location to a more
permanent facility. The six-horsepower paddy wagon ran at a full gal-
lop while the children were huddled together behind the bars, confused
and frightened. They didn't expect their stage debut to end like this.

The horses' snorting exhalations left visible clouds of breath like miniature steam engines. The team of six were as black as the Phantom's heart and blended into the night's horizon. Erik was manning the driver's seat, whipping the animals mercilessly into sixth gear. The Phantom's team of horses was faster than Saul thought. He noticed that his snow machine was equipped with nitrous. He thought for a second, then flipped the switch on the BoonDocker nitrous oxide injection kit attached to the engine. The Ski-Doo MXZ X 850 engine roared to life and shot out flames like a rocket as Frankenstein held on for dear life. The snow rocket shot out over and off the icy boat dock onto the frozen lake below. Flying over moguls and mounds at breakneck speeds, he dodged stumps and stones and opened up the throttle. He soon overtook the large carriage coach with its tiny screaming cargo and launched off a snowbank, crashing atop the prison carriage and thrusting himself forward into the heap. The snowmobile wreckage continued over the side and rolled over and over endlessly, as if it were dough being flattened for a holiday pie.

Erik turned around, surprised. "You again? I expected some interlopers, but you should be dead and buried in the tunnels. You've chosen the wrong side. Backing the wrong horse as it were. No matter. You'll not interfere with my reunion once I've made my delivery." The Phantom held the reins in a single hand and smiled a crooked smile as he removed a Taser gun from under his cloak.

"As I recall, you're quite a fan of electricity. You're in for a shock," said the Phantom as the double-barreled Taser points shot forth from the pistol and embedded into Frankenstein's face and neck. He discharged several thousand volts into Frankenstein's torso, creating an electric canopy. The projectile prongs were wired to the battery source, which the Phantom dispensed judiciously. The modified M26 police-issued Taser delivered voltage on a continuous cycle, zapping Frankenstein's muscles and fortitude and the behemoth's body dropped to the roof of the carriage. The Phantom turned up the juice and Saul's vision started to go black.

Frankenstein suddenly became intimate with the bottom of the Phantom's shoe just before it connected with his face. It was a Louis Vuitton with waxed alligator designs and complex zigzagged stitching, not unlike Saul's face. The kick knocked him off the roof of the racing prison carriage and he fell over the side, disconnecting from the retracting Taser prongs and hitting the ice hard. There his crumpled, limp body rolled, finally coming to rest out on the frozen snow and ice in the middle of nowhere.

As he lay there, Saul heard Erik say, "Frosty wishes you a Merry Christmas, old sod," then toss a snowball at him with very poor aim. Was it some kind of sick joke? Saul was bruised and beaten for sure, but a childish snowball couldn't hurt anyone.

Except this one had a small metal protrusion where the cotter pin used to be before it was pulled and thrown, thus allowing the internal striker to trigger the detonator igniting the fuse. A good old-fashioned relic M67 fragmentation grenade. The spherical explosive was painted white to resemble a snowball. Sick bastard.

Saul covered his head and rolled like hell, gathering snow and momentum when the grenade exploded, blowing a hole into the surrounding ice. The fractured ice and lake below absorbed much of the kinetic energy released. Bits of snow and metal shards rained down upon him as the smoke dissipated into the gusting winds.

Saul lay there on his bed of ice with the wind knocked out of him. Somehow, he could still see his frozen exhalations rise above him, temporarily obscuring the starry sky. At least his frigid, visible breath meant that he was still alive. Sporadically he could identify clearly gatherings of friendly constellations.

The Big Dipper curtsied in the sky, spilling over its contents like soup, and he thought for sure that it was half empty. Floating in the void of space, the ladle followed the star. He thought of the Star of David as he lay there looking at the infinite night sky and called for help on his smart watch.

The Phantom's mask was off. He truly was a monster. But it wasn't the physical manifestation of the man. It was what was inside. Erik's pigeonholed rationale for the genesis of his hate always gave him an out, without ever letting anyone in. His sad and pitiful existence began before he was even born. He never stood a chance. One could almost forgive such a besotted wretch because nature and nurture both combined in his creation and downfall with devilish delight. If it wasn't for all the kidnappings and murders that is.

No matter what or why or how, he simply had to be stopped, or his never-ending, unquenchable thirst for cruelty and revenge against his own birth would continue unabated. His callous soul wouldn't allow it to be otherwise. Frankenstein had met the Phantom eye to eye with sincerity and they both knew that Erik's rancid obsession needed help, which infuriated the Phantom all the more.

Saul drifted in and out of consciousness. The Phantom whipped the horses harder, and they responded in kind and hastened their pace through the barren snow-covered tundra. The antique carriage was decorated with bell-encrusted holly leaves and garland. Saul listened as the clinking of the bells faded like the path in the snow itself amidst the wind and flakes. Leaving no trace but frightened memories and frozen tears as the cage on wheels whisked the kiddies away.

Frankenstein wondered where in the hell Erik obtained a vintage prison wagon. It occurred to him that it probably came from the location handwritten on Jekyll's holiday warning. The Phantom's first stop of the night. Glastenbury. The old ghost town where Dracula and Aoife were headed.

He thought about what Erik had alluded to regarding his ultimate destination. Saul knew exactly where the Phantom would be going. It was the location that EMS had responded to in the past. The place where his true love and protégé "accidentally" fell to her death. Killington's Peak. Saul decided that it was exactly where he was going too. Right after a trip to the ER.

# CHAPTER 66

Saul was triaged in the Emergency Room, with scans of his neck and head looking for signs of closed head and neck trauma. His anatomy was unusual, but the basics were the same. *Knee bone's connected to the…* His EKG didn't reveal any long-term injuries secondary to the Taser attack. He was a little dehydrated, which was easily treated with some IV fluids. Bumped, beaten, and bruised, he was a little worse for wear but otherwise unremarkable.

The ER nurse had recognized Saul from previous encounters. They were both first responders who knew that they came last. Grace was just the other side of middle age and had seen it all. The ER was always good for someone doing some crazy shit to someone else and tonight was no different.

"Captain Frankenstein. Why are you sitting on my bed instead of filling it with one of your patients?" asked Grace.

"Hey Gracey," Saul replied. "How's it going?"

"Better than you, apparently. So tell me what happened and where it hurts," said Grace with compassion.

"You wouldn't believe me if I told you," Saul said. "But I think I'm okay."

"Yeah, some people are harder to wear down. Present company included. I'll give you that. But seriously, what's up?"

Saul went on to explain the evening's events.

"Saul, I don't know what I'm gonna do with you," Grace said. "Most of your tests look good—not sure how. But you really need to be more careful. The world is a crazy place, my friend."

"Tell me about it. Gracey, I really appreciate you," Saul replied.

"I know. Me too. Just be careful. Holler if you need anything. I'm right over at the nurse's desk all night. We'll probably just watch you tonight and, with any luck, you can go home in the morning," said Grace. Saul smiled and laid back to close his eyes.

While he waited for test results, Frankenstein drifted off for some much-needed rest and healing. His eyelids had grown so heavy that he realized that he was asleep thinking about how heavy his eyelids were. He was aware that he was lucid dreaming, the surreal seemingly real.

Saul had lucid dreams when he was younger—not littler, because he never was. Sleep had never been a comfort. Pitchforks and fire and angry mobs. The night terrors occurred during the day now. He tried to scream to wake up, but he was already awake. They were there just waiting for him to fall asleep again. They were always there. To take another piece of his mind. How much longer till the dawn? It can't come soon enough. It's always a long time away.

*I'm screaming so loud in my dream that I try to wake myself up and out of this nightmare. I cry myself awake. I'm afraid to go back to sleep, not because Santa's on his way, but because the devil is here for my soul. He's outside my open window at first. Then he's in my room. Just standing there. Staring at me. The devil's in the room when I wake up. He's just waiting. Biding his time. He has forever on his side. I try to hide under the security of my blanket, as if it were some kind of protective shield. I leave the tiniest small opening for my nose to breathe and I wait it out till morning. The night terrors aren't just at night anymore. I imagine people find peace and rest when they sleep. Hence the phrase "rest in peace." I know no solace from slumber. Just fear. It's there when I wake up too. Afraid to close my eyes, but they get so heavy. Afraid to open them and see the witch. The devil. The thing in my closet. Shadows move across the room cast by no one. He's in the room right now. Waiting for me to close my eyes. Or just blink. Are these nightmares mine or someone else's? Fractional repressed memories from a retrofitted brain and spinal cord in a glass jar.*

*Oh God, please let me just wake up.*

# CHAPTER 67

Paradoxical undressing happens in about half the cases of fatal hypothermia. A chilling ghost town in the middle of nowhere is the perfect setting for such a tragic syndrome. Dilapidated buildings in varying degrees of decay. Windblown bones in a frozen desert. People who die from these conditions are often mistakenly treated as victims of sexual assault because of the varying degrees of undress. The person becomes disoriented, confused, and combative. One of the reasons for this phenomenon is the cold-induced malfunction of the hypothalamus, which regulates body temperature.

Another explanation is that the muscles contracting peripheral blood vessels become exhausted and lose vasomotor tone, leading to a sudden surge of blood and heat to the extremities, causing the person to feel overheated. "Hide and die syndrome" or "terminal burrowing" is when the affected hypothermic patient enters small, enclosed spaces, such as under beds or behind wardrobes, and is often naked from paradoxical undressing. It is an autonomous process of the brain stem which produces a primitive, protective, burrowing-like behavior seen in hibernating animals. All that's left is the dying.

Saul had rescued and treated countless cases of hypothermia but had only seen these particular symptoms a few times. He couldn't help but ruminate about the potential tragedies that were possible should he and his friends fail in their endeavors.

As the weather grew increasingly cruel, Frankenstein become increasingly concerned for the wellbeing of the missing children. If they were in the abandoned ghost town during this weather, then they were at significant risk of developing various stages of hypothermia. He couldn't help but imagine finding a dozen or so small, naked children hiding in a cave or hole huddled together like dead baby mice. Or the Rat King's soldiers. He shuddered to think.

Saul noticed that his pulse had quickened as had his respiratory rate. He felt a bit shaky and became diaphoretic and nauseous. He couldn't catch his runaway breath, as if he were dry-drowning in air. It was a panic attack.

Frankenstein heard the ambulance sirens approaching from afar and thought of the fires. And the freezing cold. Saul was sweaty and soppy, drenched like the dunkee in a carnival dunk tank. He sat down and tried to control his breathing, then closed his eyes and prayed. There was no fire. No popsicle people. Focusing on his mantra, Saul finally came to realize that hope could never be lost. Only found. He listened as the sirens finally stopped while the ambulance pulled into the ER loading area.

The discharge nurse was removing his IVs and EKG leads and was going over his follow-up instructions and care.

Grace stuck her head in from behind the rolling curtain. "You heard what I said. I don't wanna see you again unless it's at the hospital Christmas party."

Saul gave a thumbs up while cradling his phone between his head and shoulder. He tried to call the Count and Contessa, but no go. Frankenstein heard little of the nurse's voice while he attempted to text the Count and Aoife. His message wasn't delivered. Not much Wi-Fi in their spotty service area. Not much of a signal to show precisely where they were located. Not much of anything. Except witchy folklore and legends of monsters.

Dracula and Aoife journeyed across country to search the old ghost town while Saul was headed to Killington Mountain to confront Erik Raeder Jr. Outside, the sundial shadow was ticking down to dark. Time was running out.

# CHAPTER 68

The old vintage prison wagon sped along across the ice and snow with the six jet black stallions galloping at full speed through the night. The Phantom cursed and whipped the beasts until they could go no faster as the carriage slid and slipped around bends and bumps.

Inside the rolling prison sat Emma Hawthorne, huddled up and hiding in a cold, dark corner. She missed her family terribly and couldn't stop reliving the traumatic event of which she was still in the midst.

*How could this be?* she thought.

"After what my sister Annie went through, I thought for sure that they wouldn't let me out of their sight until I was thirty. Now I'll never be that old," she mumbled, recalling how she'd thrown her biggest temper tantrum ever.

"I'll never forgive you if I can't go to my play!" she remembered saying harshly. The words bit down hard, just as she did now on her lower lip.

"I worked so hard and wanted to show off," she said now. "Everyone was all about *poor little Annie Hawthorne*. Well, I wanted some attention too. Look where that got me. Everyone thought the worst was over when that weird old woman's house burnt down. Some kids say she was a witch. When I asked Mommy and Daddy, they didn't say anything but looked just as confused as me. Annie didn't talk much about it. It's like she's different now, somehow."

She looked around the rolling cage to see who she recognized in the bouncing shadows. Emma had met most if not all of the rat soldiers at dress. Some of them went to school with her. There was Kimi, and James from class—and Piss Pants Pete? *How the hell is he here? I thought Annie said she escaped with him.* But yeah, he was in dress rehearsal as one of the rats. Maybe his parents thought it would be good therapy. Poor kid. All the luck. He was never dry. "I bet he's freezing in those wet undies," she mumbled.

Also sharing the cell on wheels were several other older kids whom she didn't know. Some she recalled from the play that now seemed so distant and was only getting farther away.

"I miss Mommy and Daddy. I wanna go home. I miss Max, and I miss Annie. I'm sorry, Annie. I wish I paid more attention to Houdini. Are these the same people that stole you from us? And terrorized the parade? I thought the worst was in the past. Weren't you saved by that fireman guy? Would he save me too? Could he?"

Sitting next to Emma were a scruffy pair of vagabonds who looked as terrified as she was. The older, a girl in her mid-twenties maybe, looked as if she had just seen a ghost. Or worse. The younger, must be her brother, just stared down the whole time.

"Hi, I'm Emma," she said as she burst into tears. And then they all three did too and cried together.

After what seemed to be forever, Ivy said, "I can't believe this is happening to us. I'm Ivy, and this is my brother Dorian. I think that you were in my class with Dorian when I was substitute teaching."

Emma just nodded and waved, barely holding her head off of her chest as her tears gushed like gutters overflowing.

"We were kidnapped by that psycho Mr. Hyde and put in this cage like the rest of you. I overheard them say that they're taking us somewhere out in the boonies, wherever that is. I'm so scared. These people are really crazy. Like dangerous crazy," said Ivy.

The horses whinnied and sped on, casting the occasional glance behind them to see if the horror was still back there. The Phantom just sneered and whipped them even harder.

# CHAPTER 69

The Phantom arrived in Glastenbury with the prison wagon full of youthful wishes and hunger pangs. The witch welcomed the new pets into their new home, and with the aid of Hyde, Erik wasted little time unhitching and unloading the wagon of its perishable cargo.

"The horses need care, good sir. Water and stable posthaste," said the Phantom to Hyde.

Hyde erupted in a rage of vitriolic splendor, "Hahaha! How 'bout I show you your own asshole? C'mere, Liberace."

Under his cape, the Phantom was sliding his sword out of its scabbard, taking care not to reveal his true intention, when Bridgett walked outside to welcome her guests and put a kibosh on their murderous inclinations. The Phantom greeted Bridgett who became otherwise preoccupied with the fresh catch of the day. Hyde sneered and retreated to his duties in the dilapidated remnants of a barn out back.

"Bravo, bravo!" the old witch said. "My maestro of malevolence! My vile and villainous virtuoso! I knew you'd come through as always. Any problems? How was the play?"

Erik replied, "Redundant, although the conductor was master class caliber. I wanted to stay and applaud but, alas, we were pressed for time. I did take great pleasure in almost killing that man-monster

Frankenstein. Almost, for now. I left him with a Christmas cracker on a frozen lakebed. How dare he defy us so."

"Oh, horseshit and hand grenades! That raggedy reanimated reject will get his comeuppance. You'll make sure of that," said Bridgett. "So, which did you enjoy more, the mayhem or the music?"

"In German, *schadenfreude* is the pleasure derived from observing another's misfortune. In answer to your query, I must say both. *Schadenfreude und kunstgenuss mussen schließlich kein widerspruch sein.* After all, *schadenfreude* and enjoyment of art do not have to be contradictory."

Hyde took the six horses to the ramshackle barn out back while Bridgett escorted Erik into her Glastenbury estate to give him the lay of the land. About that time, smoke was rising deliberately through the thatched roof out back.

The barn double doors exploded in fire and fury as Hyde rode out into the yard the fiery prison wagon heralded by six steeds totally alight in flame. The horses ran haphazardly anywhere to try and escape the inferno they had become. Hyde had dispensed the accelerant generously over all of it: horses, carriage, straps, and any godforsaken living thing that happened to be in the way. As they continued to burn, one by one the steeds fell to the ground, singeing the snowy earth with disgrace.

Entering the house, Hyde simply laughed and tossed the Phantom the bloody whip he was familiar with and said, "You're right. I believe your horses do need water after all. Hahaha."

By now, the kidnapped children were bawling and braying incessantly, which led the witch to hover above them, yelling madly in an attempt to corral their behavior. Between the cattle calls and the concerto of crying, and Hyde's madness, Erik's nerves were getting frayed, so he hastily told the witch, "*Auf wiedersehen, mein fraulein.*"

The Phantom was not amused by Hyde's antics, so he climbed

into the Polaris 4x4 UTV with snow options and cranked it up. He was surprised that it hadn't been destroyed by the lunatic's pyromania and barn-burning mayhem.

Bridgett thanked her ghoulish friend emphatically and then became engrossed and alit with the joy of cooking. The Phantom was likewise enthralled and in a hurry. After all, he had a date with an angel. His beloved Christine.

# CHAPTER 70

Count Dracula noticed that he had several missed calls and a voicemail on his phone, which had sketchy reception in the boonies. As he and Aoife crossed the top of one of the many hills, he noticed that he had a one-bar signal and retrieved the message. It was from Maria Claudia, their friend from St. Mary's Hospital. He and Aoife listened on speaker phone in earnest.

"My count, please help! We've been kidnapped! My children and I have been taken by that evil witch and her maniac friends. She found out that I was helping you two. Dear god, I'm afraid this might be my last chance to speak with you. We're being held in the old abandoned cemetery south of Glastenbury, near the natural hot springs. Go to the place which used to be Pownal, where the mountains converge. Please come at once, for I fear the worst. I can only pray that you're not too late. Please heeellllppp—nnnoooo …"

The message went dead and the Count looked at his wife and, without saying a word, they both rushed out into the night to try and save their friend and confidante. No good deed goes unpunished.

# CHAPTER 71

ownal, Vermont. About twenty miles south of Glastenbury, where the three mountain ranges came together: the Green Mountains, the Taconics, and the Berkshire Hills. Site of numerous old abandoned cemeteries, as well as a deserted horse track from days with better odds. The area was inhabited originally by the Mohicans who were later slaughtered. It was chartered after a British settlement in 1760 and named after the Massachusetts governor, Thomas Pownal. Two U.S. presidents once taught at a boy's prep academy there: James Garfield and Chester A. Arthur. The oldest house in Vermont, the Mooar-Wright House, was built there in the mid-seventeen hundreds.

Another claim to fame was the Widow Krieger. Her Dutch family immigrated to Pownal in the early seventeen hundreds. After her husband and son died, Mrs. Krieger became a ward of the town, since women weren't allowed to own land. Although the Salem witch trials had ended a century earlier, the belief in witchcraft was still widespread.

In 1765, the Widow Krieger was accused of possessing "extraordinary powers" because she predicted that it would rain and it did. She was offered a trial by water. Sink or float. In the middle of winter, a hole was cut in the river ice and after her hands and feet were bound, she was thrown into the freezing Hoosic River to see if the devil would hold her afloat.

The widow sank like a stone and was rescued by nearby bystanders, since she was then found absent of guilt. No records existed past this.

*But I know what happened,* Bridgett thought. *My great-grand-mother was one of her only friends. It turned out that the townspeople weren't happy with the verdict and didn't want to continue carrying the widow's burden. Since the Widow Krieger was alone in the world, she had no family to stand up for her. Some of the townsfolk took her and my great-grandmother up to the rocks overlooking the spot along the river where the trial had taken place and threw them both off for good measure. Because Mrs. Krieger said she thought it might rain.*

Witch or not, she was guilty of dying by a fall from a great height. But just before she was sent over the rock ledge, before her wide-eyed expression disappeared onto the sharp rocks far below, she cursed all who lived there for all time and spat in their faces. Damned if you do.

Krieger Rock overlooks the river off Route 346. To this day, some say that when it rains hard on the Hoosic River, you can see the widow's face in the stream. Others claim that she can be seen sitting on the bottom of the river underwater, just looking up at you and smiling. Most avoid fishing, hiking, trekking, or sitting in the spot below Krieger Rock.

Today, it's just a premature balding hilltop overlooking the river where the ages came to die. The witches' point. The Widow Krieger lays claim to the shame and testimony of those who would reach beyond a righteous hand to fill their palm with wrong.

Maria Claudia's iPhone location was pinned here, to these coordinates. An old cemetery in the middle of nowhere, just south of Glastenbury. Despite the winter storm, Aoife and Dracula were headed that way now. Hoping to find and rescue their friend Maria from this devilish place.

Husband and wife looked at one another, reading each other's minds like most couples. The Mohicans were right. This place was best left to the dead.

# CHAPTER 72

Witches apprehended, examined, and executed, for notable villainies by them committed both by Land and Water. With a strange and most true trial, how to know if a woman be a witch or not," stated the very old newspaper article that Bridgett had found in her new ghost house. It infuriated her all the more.

The old yellowed newspaper also displayed a sales ad for "witch windows," an architectural oddity unique to Vermont. They were installed in homes and farmhouses in the nineteenth century. The slanted little windows were tucked up under the eaves of the gable end at a cockeyed angle, installed to keep witches from flying into houses on their broomsticks. The old abandoned house in Glastenbury had these strange windows.

Hyde entered the main living room and found it empty. He looked around for his witchy benefactor, only to find her upper torso sticking in through the witch window with her back bent backwards in a most unnatural way. Both of her legs were poking through over her head like a spider as she slowly crab walked across the ceiling and down the wall.

This eerie sight caught even Hyde off-guard. She cracked and straightened her crooked bones and spine and said, "Witch window, my ass." The lost, shackled children were utterly horrified at the inhuman spectacle before them. The open floor plan that enabled them to see wasn't in the original architectural design—it just fell that way.

The old witch just sat there eerily on the wall. Up toward the ceiling, as if she were sitting in an invisible chair midair. She stared, not moving a muscle. Her hair shifted slightly with the air in the room, but nothing else. No blink. No nothing.

Hyde determined that it was time to get going, not sure if he was becoming the spider or the fly. The gusts of cold air hit him hard and almost knocked him over when he opened the door to the outside world. No matter. There were finishing preparations to be made. Graves to dig and chemicals to compound with interest. Not too many people were happy with their jobs. The poor hapless fools didn't know what they were missing, he thought as he grabbed the shovel. You just have to take pride in your work.

# CHAPTER 73

The dog sleigh helmed by Aoife with the Count situated as ballast raced through nonexistent fence lines drawn in the frosty earth. The dusting of snow powdered Aoife's nose and the north wind bristled her hair while she continued to howl straight up to the full moon above. This made the sled dogs run all that much faster, attempting to flee their fang-toothed passengers.

She noticed that the shivering Count had the tiniest of icicles forming on the tip of his regal nose. His cold countenance at first made her smile, but then she became concerned for their safety as she questioned their judgment in their actions. What the hell were they doing out in the middle of Bumfuck nowhere freezing to death and fighting for their lives?

A group of hungry buzzards circled the air up ahead looking for new carrion. Aoife and Dracula sped up in that direction and prayed they weren't too late to help their friend.

They finally arrived at the outskirts of what remained of the settlement at Pownal, just south of the ghost town of Glastenbury. Stopping to piss and get their bearings, they surveyed the snow-drenched forest all around them. By now, the hounds were wagging and licking Aoife like old family as she hugged and petted them back. "Thank you, my friends. We're not such different pups. I think we're related in more ways than one. Good boys. Good girls."

All of a sudden, the wagging stopped and the dogs' ears perked up. Their brows furrowed and they made a collective, grating growl unlike anything Aoife had heard before. "Easy guys, easy," she said calmly while still gently stroking their coats. The pervasive sense of evil was palpable, not to mention the foul smell of human decomposition that permeated the stale air surrounding them.

"Do you see what I see?" she said to the canines rhetorically. Red eyes projected through the luminescence piercing the dark. You could even say they glowed. They revealed a large, bipedal, ape-like humanoid creature covered in dark black hair and roughly ten feet tall. Its eyeshine glowed red at night and its horrible scent permeated the pines. Members of the Lummi told stories of these aggressive creatures with stone-hard skin that they called kwi-kwiyai. Their children were told not to utter its name lest they be taken at night and eaten or killed.

In 1893, U.S. President Theodore Roosevelt wrote in his book *The Wilderness Hunter* a story that included a sasquatch-type creature who stalked trappers in Idaho and broke the neck of one of them. The creatures were "foul smelling with significant strength and large feet. Nonlocals had said that it must've been a large grizzly bear walking on its hind legs but the locals feared enough to know better."

The Sasquatch sentry and soldiers stood guard over Pownal and its mysterious inhabitants. Admittance vas verboten. The forest creature was a giant—certainly a formidable foe intimidating enough to avoid if one valued one's own life.

A beautiful butcher, the gargantuan beat his chest and yowled with primeval lungs to establish dominance. The beast sprung forward while Aoife leapt back. It grabbed the leader dog by the scruff of its neck and tore it asunder, much to the werewolf's dismay. Its warm, blood-drenched beard sopped up the carnage like a crimson sponge.

The alpha male Squatch essentially scalped the second sled dog, ripping the pelt from its skull to the horror of its mates. There had been tales of humans and hikers found this way over the years, attributed to bear attacks. What was left now was the grossly disturbing truth of the attacks' carnivorous origins. Even Vlad himself was disturbed by the shocking display of savagery.

The Sasquatch grabbed Aoife by the throat and cocked his head sideways, not sure what to make of this creature that resembled a distant relative of his. Aoife bore her fangs, snarling into the monster's face, and he reciprocated in kind. Her animal instincts took over and she lashed out, tearing and biting the giant in every possible way like a tornado of teeth and claw. The big man of the woods reacted by tossing the werewolf against a tree, literally flaying aside bark and skin.

Aoife pounced back like a feral dog driving her claws into the belly of the beast and removing peritoneal lining and about twelve feet of intestine. With entrails still attached to the bewildered, screaming behemoth, she promptly fed the hungry hounds, who were ravenous with appetite. They barked and snarled and tore and ate and ate and ate, reeling in the giant brute as though it were tethered to an edible leash of tripe. They fed until full. Strands of flesh and fur complemented the crime scene. They had worked up such a frenzied hunger that all that was left were the feet. Enormous though they were.

Dracula had the ability occasionally to shape-shift into other life forms like bats, mice, and wolves, but he had never tried shifting into a Sasquatch. He wasn't sure that he could, so instead he chose the old reliable arctic wolf. This was Aoife's favorite changeling form for obvious reasons. It came in handy in their boudoir during pre-coital proclivity and foreplay.

Dracula's performance as a huge, muscular, red-eyed wolf emoted such ferocity and menace that the remaining Sasquatch retreated into the shadows. They fled back to the surrounding woods without event, not wishing to tempt the same fate as their leader.

The vampire-wolf hybrid made its way on its haunches back to his wife to rub noses while she responded by nibbling and kissing and biting his ears, making his tail wag like crazy. They licked each other's wounds while the sleigh dogs wagged and bowed their heads in support and jealousy. The werewolf and wolfbat basked and bayed in the silhouette to the silvery moon, surrounded by their canine accomplices. Soon, it became an all-out symphony of sound and warning, harmoniously announcing their presence.

Dracula exclaimed, "Listen to them, the children of the night. What music they make!"

Off in the distance replied a deep guttural howl distinctive from the rest. Suddenly, the surrounding forest became frighteningly still. Not a creature was stirring. Only death. The Grim Reaper biding his time.

# CHAPTER 74

Meanwhile, the old witch Bridgett Bishop was focusing on making one of her holiday favorite dishes. She realized that she was getting a little older and more forgetful and she couldn't quite recall how many children went into her figgy pudding. She figured to err on the side of more versus less. People would say that it was the best figgy pudding in all of London. Or at least Killington. The proof is in the pudding. Too bad the cops hadn't had a chance to try it.

The shutters askew still banged on the old house that was now her holiday homestead and penitentiary. The rat children were incarcerated and confined in the main living room, tethered to the cement floor and load-bearing beams not far from the fiery hearth. It wouldn't be right if they froze to death, she thought. Unless she was planning on doing some canning for the spring thaw.

Like most, the old witch loved to cook and sing during holiday times. With a spring in her step and a glint in her eye, she looked for one of them to die.

> One day the king invited most
> all of his subjects to a roast
> for half his wives gave up the ghost.
> The king of the Cannibal Islands.
> Of fifty wives he was bereft,
> and so he had but fifty left.

He said with them he would make shift,
so for a gorge all set off swift.
The fifty dead ones were roasted soon
and all demolished before the noon,
and a lot of chiefs vowed to have soon
the king of the Cannibal Islands.
When they had done, and the bones pick'd clean,
they all began to dance, I ween;
the fifty wives slipped out unseen
from the king of the Cannibal Islands.
He turning round soon missed them all,
so for his wives began to bawl,
but not one answered to his call.
He sprung out through the muddy wall.
Then into the woods he went with grief
and found each queen 'long with a chief
and swore he'd macadamize every thief,
the king of the Cannibal Islands.
He sent for all his guards with knives
to put an end to all their lives,
the fifty chiefs and fifty wives.
The king of the Cannibal Islands.
These cannibal slaveys then begun
carving their heads off, one by one,
and the king, he laughed to see the fun
then jumped into bed when all was done.
And every night when he's asleep,
his headless wives and chiefs all creep
and roll upon him in a heap,
the king of the Cannibal Islands.

# CHAPTER 75

The Killington Mountain Ski Resort has the largest vertical drop in New England of 3,050 feet (930 meters). It's nicknamed "the Beast of the East," which had never been more fitting than now. Killington Peak has the second highest summit in Vermont at 4,229 feet (1,289 meters) and can be accessed via K-1 gondolas. Home to numerous world-class runs incuding double black diamond challenges like Outer Limits and the appropriately named Devil's Fiddle. It averages 20.8 feet (6.4 meters) of natural snow each year, coupled with one of the most extensive snowmaking systems in the world, allowing for some of the longest ski seasons in eastern North America.

The ski resort was tricked out in an extensive array of holiday lights, music, and decorations. People came from all over the world to enjoy this winter wonderland. Trees were adorned with the sprinkling of lights and the mood in general was one of festive cheer. Spirits abounded, with mulled wine, hot toddies, and Red Bull with vodka championing the list. An eclectic mix of designer winter fashion was on display. One of the snowboarders was even wearing a diamond-encrusted holiday grille on his upper front teeth which spelled out "DAVID." The diamonds sparkled like ice in rain when he smiled, which was a lot for some reason.

Frankenstein bought a ticket and went to the gondola destined for Killington's Peak. He knew Erik would be there. The scene of the crime. No way he'd miss his annual holiday celebration with his murdered muse. Saul knew that the Count and Contessa were headed toward the abandoned ghost town of Glastenbury to follow up on Jekyll's lead regarding the witch's new home headquarters. He hoped and prayed that they were faring safely in their endeavor.

He called dispatch at nine-one-one again to tell them of their locations, but he knew that the old ghost town was inaccessible this time of year. Which is what led Dracula and his werewolf bride to choose the dogsled to continue their sleuthing, tracking, and potential rescue operation.

The mummy Nephthys was almost unrecognizable, adorned in her water-resistant boots, goggles, scarf, and Prada technical fabric snowboard outfit. She was fitted more for hot chocolate than cold killing. She stepped up to Saul like an old friend and blew him a kiss from her lips and palm. Saul received the glittery dust concoction full face. It sure as hell wasn't molly or any kind of tidings of good cheer. Glammy reflective particles interspersed with the glistening new snow that fluttered about him as he suddenly started to fall.

As he was collapsing, he thought, *How stupid of me. How did I not see it? I underestimated him again. It was a traaappp—*

And he was out. Platitudes and longitudinal goals had led him to just this place and this host: the indelible, unpredictable Phantom, or Erik Raeder Jr., non sequitur non-secretor.

Holiday parties and packed accommodations were the norm while Frankenstein was loaded into the gondola incognito, as much as was possible given his gargantuan stature. Among the well-intentioned and well-imbibed crowd, it was just another day at the beach.

# CHAPTER 76

Saul awoke to beautiful music. The drifting, waning melody accompanied quite well the cold breeze on his skin. It was *Don Juan Triumphant*, the Phantom's own opera, which he executed flawlessly on his vintage Stradivarius. The aged wood created a pitch-perfect sound with a bold clarity and richness that only the long-dead genius luthier could create.

The interior gondola lights were on and slightly offset by the twinkling Christmas lights that lined the tram car as it crept up the mountain. Saul noticed that his wrists were bound behind his back with homemade razor-wire handcuffs, leaving an inkling of trailing blood. He finally got a close-up view of the maskless, faceless Phantom. His real face was the mask—the masque of the red death, or cholera, or Covid.

A professor of prestidigitation, the bald-faced lie that he was and which lived to spread his infectious hate to innocent others—he truly did resemble the living dead. Gaunt and corpse-like, missing specific cartilage like ears and nose. Sunken eyes and cheeks with yellow parchment paper-like skin, and only a few wisps of ink-black hair and cold, dead hands. Barely concealed visible blood vessels shone through the cadaverous skin. A walking skeleton with bits of rotting flesh clinging to the past. Deformed and crooked teeth misshapen and misdirected in every way except from the lineage of first trimester maternal meth abuse.

The Phantom noticed that Saul was coming around. A groggy Frankenstein addressed him as calmly as possible. "Erik, it's not too late to stop this madness. I implore you, please let me help you. Let's end this before things get worse."

The Phantom responded as if he were in a world unto himself. "I always spend time with Christine on the holidays. We sing together just like before. I at the top of the mountain and she echoing harmonies from down below. It's magnificent! And now you can join her. You see, the witch Bishop lured her to me, to this euphoric isolated mountaintop view. Against her better judgment, I'm sure. The echoes of her screams rebounded throughout the mountains that became an orchestral luster of desperate falling cries for help. I sang with her, blending the bass brass of my voice while the woodwinds and surrounding timbre played their parts. All the way down. Her voice a dolce decrescendo due to gravity."

Saul changed the subject. "Erik, what about the innocent children? Are they going to be safe?"

"Ah, the rat children," the Phantom replied. "Like everything today, even the revised holiday tale of *The Nutcracker* had no balls. Merely a watered-down version of the truth. E. T. A. Hoffman once wrote that 'the music reveals an unknown kingdom to mankind: a world that has nothing in common with the outward, material world that surrounds it, and in which we leave behind all predetermined conceptual feelings in order to give ourselves up to the inexpressible.' Hoffman's original *The Nutcracker and the Mouse King* was, as you know, adapted by the French writer Alexandre Dumas. It's about a little girl Marie and her Christmas toys. Her godfather Drosselmeyer gives her a handmade nutcracker which, to her dismay, is broken.

"During the night, armies of mice and toy soldiers come alive to battle. Marie and her imagination are constrained and imprisoned by the regulations of the stalwart Stahlbaum family, who only follow rules in a prescribed manner. She then moves off into another world of her own choosing, thus allowing for her imagination, reality, and childhood to prevail. Marie is infinitely aware of the difference between the rule-bound hardline world of the Stahlbaums' steel trees and her choice to live in a world of imagination and innocence. They tried to control and destroy an artist's freedom and imagination by herding everyone into their same woke perspective. If chaos and anarchy be my chosen mistress, then a true love I shall be."

Having been subdued and bloodily shackled, Frankenstein fought to stay conscious while sitting in the ascending gondola lumbering its way up to the peak. The views would be stunning if only the circumstances were more pleasant. It was clear to him that he was brought here to die. He was acclimatizing his fear to the lurking presence of impending doom. He'd seen this tragic scenario countless times. He would fall from a great height, 3,050 feet or 930 meters to be exact. The coroner's report would read *accidental death* or *undetermined* and that was that. In truth he longed to be with his father again if that were even possible. He would soon find out.

Saul pointed his face skyward toward the roof of the tram and asked the Phantom, "Do you see these scars around my neck, Erik? They're not from sewing my head on. They're from evil people like you who once tried to lynch me. Just because my name is Frankenstein. But I somehow survived. Their attempt was an erroneous failure, just like their misguided animus and bigoted thirst for hate. Maybe the actual keloids that formed in my neck saved me. My scars saved me, to live another day with them. Have you ever heard of the law of *lex talionis*? An eye for an eye? It's the law of Moses and the Code of Hammurabi that an offender's punishment should fit the crime. Retributive justice."

"Save your breath and angst," Erik replied. "You're soon to have a magnificent view. While it lasts at least."

The razor-wire chains that bound his hands behind him were cutting into his wrists, and warm, dripping blood, slippery on his skin, lubricated the cut and chew of it all. He did his best to conceal his attempts at sawing his flesh with his bindings. Little by little he could tell that the sharp barbed wire bondage was amputating his hands at the wrists, the left more than the right, so he focused his efforts there. He could tell that he hit bones or, rather, the spaces in-between and quickened his efforts exponentially. Finally, his left hand had been mostly separated from the wrist and fell away, barely held by the remaining cartilaginous tissue.

"You know, it was a long time ago when my father put me together. Not all of the nerves grew back. Especially the ones for pain. But I know them by heart." Frankenstein drove forward, punching the Phantom directly in the face with his bloody stump while his severed hand went flailing through the air as if waving goodbye. In one smooth movement, he tore down a string of blinking Christmas lights and wrapped them firmly around that villainous neck and kicked him out of the open gondola door.

Saul yelled down, "Happy Hanukkah, fucker!"

The Christmas holiday light noose hung and swayed back and forth to the rhythm of the flashing blue lights like a grotesque metronome while the Phantom gasped for air, struggling against his own weight, clutching at his neck with his right hand, never letting go of the violin in his left. The lights were shorting out so that with every shock his body would dance and flail like some unholy marionette trying to come to life. His death grip spasm still clutched the Stradivarius hopelessly, like a drunken fiddler playing the devil's requiem. The programmed background music took center stage, symphonically betrothed to his death rattle.

Drunken carolers arm in arm sang and laughed along their merry way. The gondola was rimmed with lights that twinkled as it slowly defied gravity and traversed the mountain, the cables and cogs pulling it upwards toward the top.

# CHAPTER 77

B ridgett had set up her potions and notions on some shelves next to her firepit and cauldron. There were vials of blood, organs from dead and deadly night creatures, and containers of critters. She even had a mason jar full of lightning bugs, which she was always fond of. Those small, flying generators twinkled in the jar like lightbulbs not screwed in all the way. Dimming on and off. Jiminy motherfucking Cricket. She reached out and in to grab a few and crushed them in her hand. She then wrote the initials "WF" on the nearby wall and watched it glow in the dark.

Since moving into the new digs, Bridgett Bishop had acquired a new pet: an unusually large albino dire wolf that she named White Fang. Doggies make the best personal self-defense and home security systems, she thought, although "doggy" didn't seem quite fit to describe a three-foot-tall, one-hundred-and-seventy-five-pound killing machine. Dire wolves had been around since the days of wooly mammoths and saber-toothed tigers at the end of the last ice age. These apex predators could make mincemeat out of a lion and most certainly would make any human recoil in fear. They had an incredible bite force of four hundred pounds per square inch which, compared to a human's bite force of one hundred and twenty pounds per square inch, made them exceptionally deadly.

The furry four-legged fiend was all muscle. The only fat and gristle it had were from remnants of torn flesh stuck between its teeth. It stood faithfully by her side while Bridgett cast her bizarre incantations over the bubbling cauldron. She was in a ruminating trance, so the pup guarded her diligently. Even her longtime pet the black cat made the mistake of coming too close such that when the witch came out of her pensive, meditative state, she saw the gray-streaked black tail protruding from the wolf's mouth, swinging back and forth like a grandfather clock.

Bridgett knew that the Count and Contessa were getting close. She had seen as much in the black cauldron. She instructed the huge dire wolf to greet them properly and White Fang shot out of the house like a blur, running at full speed to intercept their guests. Bridgett smirked and said, "I hope they're not allergic."

# CHAPTER 78

Frankenstein bailed the gondola bucket near the top before the ride ended, just about where the Phantom's corpse hit the powder. Erik's body was still wrapped in the battery-powered blinking lights pulled loose from the car, and it rolled down the run a bit like a cartoon snowball until finally coming to rest. The moon was so full and bright it lit up the run almost like daylight.

The apres-ski party was in full force at the restaurant bar at the top of the mountain with stunning panoramic views. No one appeared to have noticed the odd goings-on between Frankenstein and the Phantom, either from being preoccupied, exhausted, blitzed, or buzzed. Glow sticks were waving to the beat along with arms and legs. Erik was partially buried in the freshie and still looked like a blinking blue mogul when some bros and Betties bonked some booters off of him. Multicolored glow sticks dangled around the necks of the night boarders who cruised by, leaving behind a palinopsia of visual trails reminiscent of a magic mushroom experience. A few had donned Garyob glow-in-the-dark face and body paint, leaving a trail of psychedelic psychodrama behind after they hotboxed in a gondola. The Phantom's swagstika lapel emblem reflected the fluorescent ROY G BIV streaming colors as they caught air off his dumb dead ass.

Saul snatched a snowboard from outside the mountaintop restaurant bar. Dick move, but he was bleeding to death. He didn't have any snowboard boots, but his feet were so big that his Air Jordans fit snugly into the bindings on the borrowed board with little ankle support. He tied a rough wilderness tourniquet around his bleeding stump with a hair ribbon he found. He had to get a proper tourniquet on his severed limb and find his friends. Time was of the essence. Saul tried calling the Count but couldn't get a signal and took it as a bad omen. He hoped that they were okay and making progress finding the kids.

The pow was perfect with big soft flakes still coming down. Too bad he couldn't enjoy it. It had been a long time since he was a park rat. The last time he was there, probably, was when he responded to the "accidental" death of Christine, the Phantom's muse. Dizzy and squirrely from blood loss, he just barely stayed upright, leaving a sketchy blood trail on the white snow blanket that became a red carpet. Frankenstein boosted some air off Erik's dead, blinking body partly down the run. *Fucking Nazi.* He freestyled his way down the gnarly fall line, bombing all the way, trying not to tomahawk the board.

Near the bottom, he saw her standing in the shadows amongst the snow-covered trees. She was beckoning him toward her. It was the same Betty that blew the faerie dust into his face to knock him out: the mummy Nephthys. Her goggles were off and he swore that he could see her emerald eyes glowing like stoplights lit green for go. He shredded his way down toward her and kicked off his board, never for a moment taking his eyes off her bewitching presence.

# CHAPTER 79

She sang to him. Like the sirens at sea. Saul's weather-lined face listened to her melodic tone and tempest, perhaps a chance to dream of something more. The sobriety of the new day's prospects hit like a slap in the face or a moment of clarity. His entire skeleton hurt. The goddess Nephthys called upon him. He had no choice but to answer.

The last of the museum mummies beckoned him over to her. She stood in the darkness between the trees by the edge of the frozen lake. She simply stared at him until his skin crept toward her. No sudden moves nor nuance of nerves. She looked through him, past all that he had become. Now it was simply death biding time. Waiting for another eternity to embrace.

Saul broke the tension like ice and called out to her as he would any potential victim, trying to deescalate the situation. "Are you okay? Do you need any assistance? I know that you didn't really mean to hurt me. The Phantom's gone. It's over now."

Saul was still a bit groggy from the drugs and trauma. He was still punching his way out of the paper bag that carried his heart and life. But there she was. A slim and slightly veiled threat which opened a cloacal kiss of conspiracy and scantily clad misinformation. Her eyes broke through the night like heaven on earth. As if God's gaze had granted him the keys to the Acropolis, Mount Olympus, or heaven itself. She reached out to him as if saying you're not that. You're not. You're not a monster to me, my darling. Come and hold me and take me away to someplace safe and full of love.

His tears crept from his face like a sad algorithm around scars and confines and suture lines irrevocably written. He took her hand willfully and welcomed her embrace.

# CHAPTER 80

White Fang had pissed and shit all over, marking his territory in the forest outside the old ghost town as a warning to trespassers that they would be prosecuted to the fullest extent of his jaw. He blended easily into the snowy backdrop as his albinotic fur camouflaged his presence. But not for long. Aoife could sense that they were being watched. No, not watched. Tracked. She realized suddenly that they were no longer the predators. They had become the prey.

Aoife smelled him before she saw him. He sprang seemingly out of nowhere from the dozens of deciduous trees and leapt onto Aoife, snarling and snapping like a mountain of rage.

Even though he had transformed back into pure vampiric form, Dracula jumped onto the back of the four-legged fury, trying to render it into submission, but to no avail. He was taken aback and thought for sure that the furry beast had rabies, or at least was mad as hell. The wolf bit down hard onto the Count's hand, drawing first blood. Dracula returned the favor by sinking his teeth into the dire wolf's neck, drawing second and third blood. Then he thought, *What have I done? I've just made this monstrosity immortal! Now we have to kill it for sure.*

In that moment of hesitation, one of the Sasquatch monsters that had been lurking and watching from the timberline took advantage and grabbed Dracula from behind, pinning his arms to his sides and attempting to squeeze the life out of him. Clearly the witch maintained some semblance of control over these enormous forest beasts through her magics and sorcery. Several more Squatch saw the way the fight was going and joined in the fray.

The forest creatures were lumbering beasts with surprising speed and agility and a long reach just outside the law, but not striking distance. They moved quickly and quietly without so much as the snap of a twig. A furious melee of blood and grit unfolded while bite-sized pieces of the Count disappeared into the hairy bellies of the beasts of the forest as he moaned in agony.

Aoife had wrestled the dire wolf down onto its back and was just about to deliver the severing blow shredding the wolf's neck and jugular when the sky suddenly changed. They had been so preoccupied lately that they weren't aware of its coming or alerted to its imminence. This particular winter solstice contained the deadly presence of a lunar eclipse. At this right time, wrong place and moment, the moon disappeared as if some cosmic magician was performing a feat of legerdemain.

Aoife changed back to full-on human, which was by no means a match for the chomping, drooling beast that had set upon her. They were dead. It was that simple. They would be torn to shreds and become dog food and a bigfoot Scooby snack. Their particular mystery had suddenly come to an end. The man in the full moon gazed on the breast of the new fallen snow watching the perverse finale. With a honeycombed heart and wandering eyes, the shroud of forever secrecy was left exposed as death and dog reared their blood-curdling heads.

# CHAPTER 81

The mummy Nephthys was the worst of the bunch. She was goddess to evil reincarnate over and over again. Time was only a plaything that she used for her immortal satisfaction, which was never satiated. Saul found himself taken aback by this other-worldly beauty whose smile and gaze were hauntingly captivating. The mummy with emerald eyes. Precious stones for orbs reflecting doubt and truth.

A perfect shade of green. Like envy. Never to be redressed. Never to be truly seen. Shades of nothingness. She was alive and absolutely beautiful. Her long, dark hair flowed about her tender, supple neck and upper back, pointing so ever gently down her body hinting of pursed lips and fruitful endeavors. With Saul hypnotized by her unique charms, she cradled his weathered face in her arms and nurturing palms to embrace his very soul.

As they both drew near for the kiss, Nephthys opened her moist, beckoning lips to reveal an adder tongue fitfully splaying its fork. Frankenstein freaked out and pushed her aside onto the ice, not sure what to believe anymore. Nephthys simply looked up from her knees and smiled, crawling toward him on all fours.

As fate would have it there was heard the faintest crack. Which grew and grew around her. The pancake ice was giving way unto the frigid lake. It sounded like a tree falling in the woods. Then the ripple effect echoed back into the Green Mountain landscape, which just breathed it in.

Nephthys disappeared below the surface tension into the cold, empty water. Floating endlessly down through the dark, green liquid, changing degrees of viscosity and color pending depth and clarity of mind. The mummy's bulging eyes stared in disbelief, gazing through the crevice between her wraparound bandages. They turned from anger to angst as she recognized her never-ending fate.

Saul grabbed for the trailing shroud of linen bandages that swirled listlessly like a kite tail in the wind. Missed by the kiss of an inch that might well have been a mile. Saul threw his arms out to grab her, but she was just beyond his reach like love so often before. Just outside of his caressing clasp, like the mummy's outstretched hands and his long gone heart. Her emerald eyes sparkled one last time for him as he watched her drop down to her liquid grave, sinking through the ice water lake to an endless bottom. Destined to be entombed forever, alive, in a sarcophagus of sea. Forever to be forgotten.

Her image was replaced by his reflection upon the water's surface. The scarred, scared, grotesque gargoyle that he himself had made. Frankenstein was lost in thought and heart.

> *Life, although it may only be an accumulation of anguish, is dear to me, and I will defend it. Nothing is so painful to the human mind as a great and sudden change. There is something at work in my soul which I do not understand. I desired it with an ardor that far exceeded moderation; but now that she's finished, the beauty of the dream has vanished, and breathless horror and disgust fills my heart. Oh, no mortal could support the horror of that countenance. A mummy again endued with animation could not be so hideous as that wretch. I gazed on her unfinished; she was ugly*

*then, but when those muscles and joints were rendered capable of motion, it became a thing such as even Dante could not have conceived. Now, I am again dependent on none and related to none. The path of my departure is free, and there is no lament to my annihilation. My person is hideous and my stature gigantic. What does this mean? Who am I? Whence did I come? What is my destination? Who is my mother? One of the many women who contributed their vital organs to deliver me life? Perhaps my heart? These questions continue, but I'm unable to solve them. I cannot describe the agony that my own reflection inflicts upon me; I try to dispel this, but sorrow only increases with knowledge.*

Frankenstein hurled bile and remnants of bygone meals onto his worn oversized Air Jordans, still encrusted with snow.

A cold sweat dripped from the tip of his nose, occasionally disrupting his already disturbing image in the reflecting pool. The ever-expanding circular ripples slowly fading to reveal his true visage. He saw his own lukewarm bated breath between beats of his abnormally enlarged heart. Neither congestive nor full of consumption. Just remorse.

"*Is love lost never to be regained?* Stop it. Get a grip. Those bullies wanna scare a bunch of poor little kids? They should try me on for size. Stand up. Beware, for I am fearless and therefore powerful. Stand up tall again, you monster. Yeah, you beautiful monster. At least I'm alive. I am fucking alive! Frankenstein lives again!"

# CHAPTER 82

The shot rang out so loud it had to have been heard around the world. It was a hell of a shot. It was by chance that Krystiyan even saw the bloody conflict unfold through his Armasight BNVD-51 dual-channel night vision binoculars. The sonic noise from the melee had traveled through the forest, alerting him to take a look. It didn't take long to see that the Count and Contessa could use a hand, and he gladly reached out and gave it. More precisely, his right index finger.

Krystiyan, the young EMT from St. Mary's, was madly in love with Maria Claudia. He was determined to come to her rescue and hadn't show up empty-handed. He had been an avid hunter in the old days, since that's how his family put meat on the table. Krystiyan brought his hunting rifle with him on his search because he knew that he'd be trekking and tracking through forest and bear country. He wasn't expecting berserker Sasquatch.

The St. Mary's EMT preferred his duties as an emergency medical technician and patient care provider, but he was a skilled mechanic as well. He was proficient in commercial driving and helped to maintain all the hospital's emergency vehicles.

Since it hadn't been in use presently but rather checked out for routine maintenance, Krystiyan took the liberty of borrowing the snowplow ambulance Combi Crawler to search for his beloved. He had filled out the requisite paperwork and informed the appropriate parties so that they could keep track of his whereabouts. He tried to contact his boss, Captain Frankenstein, but he was unavailable. Krystiyan liked and admired Saul and was pretty sure that he'd be supportive of his rescue mission.

Krystiyan grabbed his rifle, already sighted in, and set up his gear. After setting up the tripod, he lay down next to it, put his head in the box, and aligned the reticle on his target. A Bigfoot head. He inhaled and exhaled in a controlled fashion. On the last exhale he paused, focused, and gently squeezed.

His earplugs muffled the discharge explosion of the projectile seeking a home. The young hunter felt it before he saw it. Kind of like hitting a pool ball just right. Or knocking one out of the park. It just felt right. And it was. It was over in seconds. One shot was all it took from his .308 Winchester bolt-action Christensen Arms Ridgeline Scout hunting rifle. Designed to hunt and kill big game, it worked just as well on a Bigfoot. Given the size of his target's feet, it seemed to meet the criteria.

Dracula was opposed to all firearms of all kinds, for any reason whatsoever. Throughout history, the human race proved quite adept and proficient in developing more efficient ways to kill one another en masse. From guillotines to grenades, the art of war had little to do with art and more to do with self-destruction. The manmade weapons of mass destruction had no place in civilized society in any form. He would have to have a talk with Krystiyan later, if they lived.

After seeing that the Count and Aoife were out of immediate danger and gruesomely dispatching their attackers, Krystiyan gathered his spent casing to continue his search, rushing to find and save Maria Claudia. He imagined her falling into his strong arms and thanking him endlessly for rescuing her. Krystiyan hoped to set the stage for a marriage proposal and a happily-ever-after scenario.

Things don't always turn out as planned. The devil was in the details.

# CHAPTER 83

The Bigfoot had fishbowl eyes just before his head exploded from his shoulders and the rest of its corpse fell onto the blood-spattered snow, releasing Dracula from his bondage. Decompression preceding decomposition. He first jumped up and grabbed the witch's pet from off his wife and squashed its eyes into the back of its head. Then he hissed and ripped the beast's lower jaw from its skull as the rest of its remains joined the ever-expanding pool of blood at his feet. The different shades of crimson from different degrees of oxygenation all came together like an artist's palette worn with age.

The bloodlust. The Count went full on batshit crazy and grabbed the nearest solid sharp tree branch within reach and unleashed holy hell. Dracula thrust the spear into the next monster's gaping mouth and pushed until it stuck into the ground behind. The beast hung there suspended and struggling against the imparted predicament. Vlad the Impaler was back. And they sure as shit were gonna regret it.

He held the dire wolf's jaw in his hands, looking it over, thinking what a magnificent creature it had been. He then tossed it to the nearest Bigfoot, who caught it just as Dracula was bringing down the pike through the top of its skull, shish-kebabing the huge ape. The other Squatch wanted no part of this madness, so they started to retreat, but it was too late.

"An ounce of prevention..." started Dracula.

"... is worth a pound of cure, or Bigfoot flesh," said Aoife.

The Count tried his best not to relish in it.

Vlad earned his nickname by shoving a spear up his enemies' asses and having the point exit out of their mouths or chest. He would then implant the spear into the ground upright, leaving his impaled enemies hanging, leading to slow and tortuous deaths. He posed and exhibited them for all to see and to heed his warning. Lest ye who venture further also become victims of the creator of impalement.

Vlad did the same to the Sasquatch before him. Like riding a bike. The great forest apes were soon hanging on these rustic-ass pikes, slowly waiting to die. Looking at each other painfully, they conformed to the clearing, resembling some macabre lawn decor. Dracula had impaled and hung a few of them upside-down just because that's how it lined up during the fight for their lives.

A handful of the Squatch were just manually decapitated, their heads impaled together onto a single pike as if to create a totem pole. The forest of the impaled. Dracula. Son of the dragon. Son of the demon.

He lit a couple of the impaled Squatch on fire like hairy tiki torches, setting the tone for one hell of a picnic. The Count heard his wife's voice, "What's that awful smell?"

The lunar eclipse had been slowly passing, and Aoife had begun to regain her composure. Her transformation started subtly and then grew exponentially, gathering momentum like an avalanche of pain. The first thing to change were her senses. Her vision was more acute. Her abruptly improved sense of smell and hearing were almost unbearable, until she had the time to adapt to the barrage of surrounding stimuli. She fell to the ground on all fours while her body cracked and seized and shifted, shaping her musculoskeletal system and body habitus into that of a wolf. Hair grew as teeth sharpened and claws elongated to continue her body dysmorphism.

Aoife's painful scream changed in midstream, as if auto-tuned, to that of a roaring beast, never missing a note. All of her hair now stood on end, awaiting command. Her canine teeth grew more honed and edgy while she stared at the bright light in the sky to which she was bound by bloody curse. Starlight, star bright. I wish I may, I wish I might. Except it wasn't a star. It was the moon. And it was bloody red and completely full.

The next big man of the forest pounded his chest and scratched his hairy crotch, then roared to announce his presence. Aoife stared fiercely at the Squatch and snarled, "Yeah, so Bigfoot's got nards. I can do you one better by taking yours. Come at me, bro." She pounced on the great woodland ape, tearing into his femoral artery, releasing a deluge of scarlet spray. He was next in line for the title position of alpha male and Aoife just made him her bitch. She tore his leg off and threw it to Dracula, who proceeded to beat the next Bigfoot to death with its friend's grossly enormous foot. Yeah. The name fit.

Between husband and wife, they slaughtered every living thing within a twenty-yard radius, leaving not a breath to chance. Dracula thrust and impaled his tree branch spears through every Bigfoot orifice within reach while Aoife clawed, bit, and tore flesh from bone and limb from limb. Aoife's sharp talons pierced another Bigfoot's abdomen and clawed out part of its liver, adding the pastel of black blood to the erythrocytic impressionistic painting forming on the forest floor.

They were both bathed in the warm blood of their victims from head to toe such that the not-too-distant sled dogs didn't recognize them, huddled together into a small mass just outside the killing zone. They were shaking and keeping their heads down in a show of submission, daring not to meet the eyes of their new crimson masters' gaze for fear of fatal repercussions.

Aoife saw how frightened they had become, so as her blood

dropped from the boiling point to a slow simmer, she threw them an arm and a leg from one of the big men of the forest to feast upon. They must still be hungry. And they were. This time they ate every bit, including fighting over the huge foot. This little piggy went to market. This little piggy shrieked "wee, wee, wee" all the way home.

# CHAPTER 84

Krystiyan was in love with Maria Claudia. That much was clear. From the day that she first started working at St. Mary's Hospital, he was smitten. Right off the bat they hit it off and his heart was turned on ever since. They both came from the old country, even though the Ukraine had only become a formalized independent state in December 1991 when the Soviet Union collapsed.

Maria Claudia and Krystiyan felt deeply impacted by the modern horrors occurring to this very day in their homeland. Unfortunately, sometimes strife unites life. That being the case, the region in Romania known as Transylvania shares a land and maritime border with Ukraine, Ukraine itself being only 605 kilometers from Transylvania as the crow or bat flies.

Both Maria Claudia and Krystiyan came from similar backgrounds and spoke the same language. Krystiyan knew how hard it had been for her, struggling as a single mother raising two children, because that's exactly what his mother had to do when his father was killed in the war. He respected her for her strength and tenacity and dedication as a mother.

During down times when they both worked the nightshift together, they had the opportunity to talk and get to know one another. Both had fled the Ukraine after the Soviets decided to invade the sovereign nation and attempt mass genocide. Crimes against humanity without consequence lead to genocidal recidivism. *Slava Ukraini.*

Unfortunately, the Count had seen this type of madness countless times before. He himself had led the fight against power-mad despots wanting to take what didn't belong to them, including land and lives. History unfortunately repeated the worst parts of itself. Maria Claudia and Krystiyan shared a Ukrainian gypsy past fleeing from terror and had shared experiences that most others wouldn't understand.

Maria Claudia was beautiful in every way, with a hint of underlying shyness from being a stranger in an even stranger land. Krystiyan knew that she was in trouble when she didn't show up for work, uncharacteristic of her work and mom ethic. Also, she had alluded to as much during one of their last conversations. He had been texting and calling her and was finally able to narrow down her location, so he went in search of her in the snowplow ambulance. Little did he know that he would come across such a bizarre and horrific scene as had beset the Count and Aoife.

Settling back into the swivel bucket, Krystiyan turned the key and the Combi Crawler fired up easily, just like him. The gears ground together, gnashing cogs like teeth as the snow monster rumbled to life. He picked up the flimsy chain around his neck which held his St. Michael's pendant and kissed the sterling silver piece for good luck and protection. The metal symbol was tarnished and worn from good-luck rubbing, not unlike kissing the Blarney Stone or rubbing Budai's belly. This didn't seem to reduce its value, though, he thought. It sure as hell couldn't hurt.

He kissed it again and put the snow beast into gear.

# CHAPTER 85

Congealing plasma and blood spatter forensics wouldn't be needed to tell that it was an overkill slaughter. A festive battue of butchery and bloodletting. An anatomical exercise in rapid dissection and organ donation. Dracula and Aoife looked at each other soaked and covered from head to toe in bloodbath. Only the whites of their eyes weren't painted in sanguineous delight, just tinged. They looked as if they were rabid fans at a football game whose team colors were just red. Both had smeared faces covered in another's magenta sorrow.

The two lovers exchanged glances and checked each other for bodily harm. They hugged and kissed a bloody kiss and were simply amazed that they were somehow alive. As their human side pragmatically returned, they rubbed noses like an Inuit kiss and butterfly kissed the world that they loved so dearly.

Dracula couldn't bear to see Aoife suffer any bit of strife. It made him relish the days of old when the animal controlled the man instead of vice versa. It was a simpler time for justice and vengeance. That must be how the parents of the missing children felt. But not for long. No way were he and Aoife going to fail. No way in hell. If they had to confront the devil himself, then by God, that son of a bitch was dead. The Count ran his tongue across his own sharp fangs. They wanna peek inside the box? He'd give 'em a show. They'd wish they never heard of Pandora.

Checking boxes then burying them. They looked for Krystiyan, but he was long gone. They didn't fault him for not sticking around. Some things you can't unsee, and this was sure to give him nightmares for the rest of his life. They'd thank him later if he hadn't already fled the country or his mind.

The cold grip of winter tightened her hand around the throats of the frozen travelers, as they crunched their way forward through the unknowing tundra of tomorrow. Given their warm reception, they knew that they were on the right track, and they were getting warmer. So they strove onwards, toward the next task at hand. Stopping the witch Bridgett Bishop and saving their friends.

# CHAPTER 86

They trudged and traversed, following the directions on the Google maps app. It left Dracula with time to ponder these events. How can one be civil when confronted with an uncivilized situation? Should he just sheep up or go on a defiant hunger strike? Where was the sense in the nonsense of killing? It brought no joy, just sorrow. Always. To someone, somewhere, somehow. Just sorrow. But to just roll over and die would mean the same for those he swore to protect.

He thought and thought about this untenable situation and finally concluded that which he had five hundred years ago. Save yourself. Save your loved ones like the animal that you were. Just don't enjoy it. Follow the path of least resistance and if it led you down some deep, dark alley filled with danger and hate and those who would wish you harm for no reason other than their own evil enjoyment, then do what you must to protect your flock. They shouldn't have to pay for a few misguided fuck-ups. Do your job and be done and feel bad about it later. Which is exactly what he did.

Nowadays, the Count would rather use the knowledge that he'd acquired over the years to seek peaceful solutions instead of conflict. His thoughts wandered to the rhythm of the ride.

*Times were different back then. And yet, sometimes, they stay the same. Will humans ever evolve to the point of mutual civility and peaceful* coexistence? Or would that be contrary to natural selection and the necessary cycle of life and death? What if the rate of overpopulation exceeds the depletion of resources? With factual actuarial tables accounting for the worst of it, death is as important as life. And yet death is an unrequited lover, foreign to my soul. Will I ever pierce the darkness that hides behind the veiled night? Lifting curse with kiss, forever bonded and betrothed. Death be a willing bride, consummated with griefless loss and selfish lies. To finally slake the thirst from life. But not today. And not tonight, my love. My life. My wife. Aoife.

# CHAPTER 87

The stockings were hung by the chimney with care. The missing children's names were sewn onto the welts no worse for wear. As usual, the socks were empty, like their homes now seemed without them. The candles flickered and danced, casting shadows like dreams onto the walls and minds of the parents who kept them lit so that their loved ones might find their way home in the dark. The subtle scent of freshly cut noble fir wafted across the room as delicately as the joyous melody which perversely guided the tempo.

The Druids revered the hearty plant mistletoe and harvested it during the winter solstice to be used for medicinal purposes. The vividly colorful decorations set the tone and the pace for such a pose and a place as a holiday kiss. The witch Bridgett used it for other reasons: because the berries were poisonous, especially to children. Many of the families in Killington had already sent out and received photo Christmas cards mocking their children's absence in some cruel irony. Merry Christmas to all, and to all a good night.

The fir tree had been used to celebrate both pagan and Christian winter festivals for thousands of years. Another holiday tradition was the baking of mince pies filled with meat, dried fruit, and spices. It was traditional to eat one Christmas meat pie each of the twelve days before Christmas for good luck. To refuse brought bad luck, and the old witch was determined to ensure the best luck possible.

*Twelve drummers drumming, my ass*, she thought while critiquing her reflection in the mirror. "Mirror, mirror on the wall, who is the fairest one of all?" Rather than wait for a response, the witch smashed the mirror to pieces with her broom. *Seven years, huh? I'll make my own luck*, she thought.

Her clothes had gone up a size or two during recent times. Eventually she took to wearing only stretchy athleisure wear. She blamed it on that Scandinavian boy who was way too fatty and full of gristle. By midmorning some days, the Somogyi effect would kick in, making her lightheaded from a drop in blood sugar which she explained away as the chubby girl who was all sugar from eating Halloween candy well past Thanksgiving.

She gave the evil eye to her captive juvenile audience who collectively recoiled in fear, rattling their chains in some pitchy union of clinks and clanks. Bridgett had decorated her new digs with the trappings of holly, ivy, and poinsettia. It surprised even her how many natural botanical poisons were placed around people's houses during the holiday season.

*If they only knew. Oh well, Christmas only comes once a year, might as well enjoy it*, she thought as she took another bite of meat pie. This one contained a small tooth. She ate it anyway. It was time to raise the stakes. "I hope they like surprises," she mumbled, greedily licking the crumbs off her plate.

# CHAPTER 88

The fog in the old cemetery was as thick as blood, flooding the graveyard and broken tombstones and mausoleum floor. The rusted remnants of the wrought iron lichgate and fence were so decrepit that they seemed of little use in protecting the living from the spirits of the dead. The frost on the archway had settled upon the spider's web matrix, giving it the appearance of an intricate halo. The icy geometric hieroglyph was illuminated by the light of the blood red full moon, giving neither direction nor warning.

The clouds rolled across the gray-toned topography of the moon like there were heavy winds in the upper stratosphere, pushing past today quickly as if it could easily be forgotten. Deftly and dumbly, Dracula and Aoife dismounted the dog sleigh and carefully surveyed the premises. Soon they trudged and trod a path through the cement and marble headstones and markers of those travelers who had gone before. Buried in a pauper's grave. As opposed to a rich guy's hole. The weather-worn monuments to loved ones held barely decipherable names from long ago placed by family that likewise disappeared from this earthly realm decades past.

There was Maria Claudia standing in the open doorway of the chamber tomb, holding her phone light to illuminate the way. She placed her index finger to her hushed lips. They waved at Maria Claudia as they rushed to the aid of their distraught friend posthaste, as quietly as possible. The wind whipped in a forceful way as if telling them to go back.

Aoife and the Count crept their way silently around the boneyard stones and markings of those who had gone before and entered the chamber.

They could see Krystiyan in the background, but he wasn't moving. He was posed eerily in an unnatural position with his arms crossed behind his head as if he were lying back to relax and watch TV, but his arms were stretched way too far to be properly in their sockets. They had placed a soiled and bloodied dollar store Santa's hat mockingly onto his head. The cap's bobble hung down, mimicking the boy's forlorn gaze.

Upon closer inspection, they saw that he had been crucified to the back wall. His eyes were open as his head hung down, pointing left. The eyes still looked up and out as if trying to get someone's attention or ask for directions. He'd found his way, all right.

Dracula rushed forward toward the man who had saved their lives and heard a *clink* as if a metal latch had disengaged. The floor beneath him had a hollow sound.

Maria Claudia tearfully exclaimed, "I'm so sorry! Please forgive me!" With that, the trap door below the Count's feet sprung open and he disappeared into the void below. If only Saul were there, he could have told his friend that this had to be the work of Erik Raeder Jr., the Phantom. He was a maestro of many talents, and crafting traps and escape hatches was one of his specialties.

Aoife's eyes were alit and widened with shock and horror as she yowled like never before, her roar replacing the deafening chamber's cold silence. Darkness painted the rear corners of the mausoleum pitch black, with the exception of a small flickering light that bounced around in the shadows.

The werewolf went toward it, hoping it to be tunnel light or somehow an aid in reaching her husband. The creature from the black lagoon leapt from the dank darkness of the mausoleum, betraying the luminescent lure dangling from its forehead as the source of the light.

Aoife was taken off guard as the creature tore into her. The tips of the oily scales that covered its body had a strange black and blue iridescent bioluminescence to them, as did its lips and eyes. The glowing talons also were more noticeable in the dark, as it seemed to have taken on the characteristics of some deep sea occupant.

The creature snatched and deadlifted the werewolf overhead and threw her against the wall at Krystiyan's feet. It ripped into Aoife's flesh as if it were butter, leaving a subtle blue tinge behind in its wake. The werewolf snarled and jumped on top of the creature as she chose instinctively fight over flight. Repeatedly clawing at the watery devil, she inserted one of her own sharp claws forcefully into its right eye and tore it from its head.

The creature wailed and roared in pain as it reached up to cover its empty eye socket. Aoife saw her opening and tore out the creature's left eye as well. Dripping wet with disgust and black ooze, the eye remained on her fingertip until she plopped it into her mouth and swallowed it out of spite.

The creature, now blinded, lost its orientation and staggered one way then another until the werewolf tore into its neck with all of the force in her jaws and locked on. As it maneuvered across the room, its light lure exposed the floor's death trap. The creature screeched and squealed, looking up as Aoife threw the dying monster down into the hole where her husband had disappeared.

Mr. Hyde dropped down from the rafters above and landed behind the werewolf. He quickly and adeptly injected Aoife with a liquid silver and poison mixture, a special werewolf cocktail designed and mixed by none other than Hyde himself. In shock at her friend Maria Claudia's betrayal, Aoife was caught off guard. The precision of the needle's injection and immediacy of its effects were surprising.

Tetrodotoxin is the primary defense mechanism used by such animals as the puffer fish, toadfish, and blue-ringed octopus, and requires only a small amount to have the desired effect. It works by interfering with the transmission of signals from nerves to muscles, causing increasing paralysis. Unfortunately, the inflicted subject is completely awake and aware of their surroundings but cannot move a muscle—a form of "locked-in syndrome."

Aoife collapsed to the chamber floor wide awake but frozen. Not in fear, although she had plenty of that too. Aoife could not claw, kick, scream, bite, howl, or even blink. In essence, she had become a living zombie! Hyde deftly placed her paralyzed, floppy body into the waiting coffin at the back of the mausoleum.

The fancy oblong box sat on a simple altar, but was decorated ornately and made completely out of silver. Aoife looked up and out of the coffin to see the body of Krystiyan staring down at her sorrowfully as he forever rested not in peace. The dirty Santa hat pom-pom and his silver St. Michael's pendant hung down toward her parallel to his scarecrow gaze.

The horrific scene was so repulsive, she thought she'd choke on her own vomit. Aoife wanted to cry or scream or just not look at him anymore, but alas, she was helpless but to watch and imagine the living nightmare that her friend had endured at the hands of these monstrosities of nature. Nothing about them was natural though, nor super, just dead, cold evil, the result of which was looking her right in the face. *How horrible, Krystiyan. I'm so sorry. You only longed for love*, she thought. Apparently they were to be permanent roommates in the sealed-off temple of death and decomposition.

Edward Hyde felt the small medical kit inside his jacket pocket. It contained a rubber tourniquet, disposable syringes, a small cooking spoon, and pharmaceutical powder. He recalled vaguely a medical experiment exploring the human psyche through a syringe. A transformative potion studying the duality of man that was either injected or snorted. Track marks barely leaving a trace of another time and person. The little spoon was bent slightly and burnt from multiple uses of a mini torch. Hyde used it to shoot the gap between high and ruckus.

He had never noticed before, but in a moment of clarity, he realized that the tiny baby silver spoon had an inscription engraved onto it. When he wiped away the tarnish and smudge, it read, "For our baby Henry. May your world be fortuitous and always bless you with all you deserve." Hyde couldn't sync this sentiment with his deprived depravity. He instead used the little spoon to scoop out a snort-full of experiment. Just a baby bump to take the edge off and stabilize the mood.

Adding insult to injury, Hyde grossly licked the spoon clean and shoved the tarnished silver into Aoife's paralyzed mouth. He closed her lips with his index finger to signal silence. The brute abruptly slammed shut the casket lid, sealing her fate with a thud and a grunt. She was interred, and that was that. No ceremony nor mourners nor priestly blessing. The silver injection was the coup de grace, slowly poisoning Aoife's organ systems while she lay there helplessly aware of everything. Outside. He killed her in silence outside. Inside, she screamed to herself. The absence of sound heightened the smell of stale air and death filling her nostrils and palate. The putrid miasma permeated her pores, reeking of utter hopelessness.

Alas, at that moment, all she heard was the din of Hyde's maniacal laughter growing faint as he made his way out of the mausoleum back into the fresh air, padlocking the steel doors behind. Aoife had become a living zombie, encased in a shroud of death. The dark was limitless while the air was sparse. Forever entombed in a crypt of riches and silver trappings. You can't take it with you.

# CHAPTER 89

Dracula's trap had been sprung. The Count dropped through a long chute curving deeper and deeper into the cage below. The oubliette had only one entrance and exit, which was that which the Count had fallen through. The hidden chamber was lined on all sides as well as top and bottom with contiguous mirrors, leaving the Count disoriented by the 360-degree absence of his own reflection, since he had none. It was maddening. He wondered if this was similar to what his friend Dr. Ellison felt when unseen. He could imagine Ralph saying, "You know, eisoptrophobia or spectrophobia is the unhealthy fear of mirrors or what may be reflected in them, leading to avoidance behaviors and issues with body dysmorphia." Maddening indeed.

To make matters worse, the forever chamber was released from its moorings and left to sink in the bottomless hot springs that ran under the cemetery. These particular spring waters had been blessed, leaving the Count encased in a mirrored cell surrounded by scalding holy water, descending at a fairly rapid rate of speed. All the while, the holy spring water trickled and leaked into the vampire trap much to the Count's dismay.

Normally, the hot spring water itself had a smooth, tingly feel to it; the high mineral content gave medicine-seeking bathers a gentle yuzawari. That is, unless the thermal springs were superheated—like they were in that moment. Hot potting or soaking would be contraindicated since the acidity and boiling water temp would literally cook most living things.

Not far behind the Count's descent into the hellfire waters came the black lagoon creature, tumbling down the chute bleeding and blind. It dropped into the boiling hot springs and was instantly fried to a crisp. The stench from its burnt, crackling corpse sizzled its way back up through the chute, filling the mausoleum with the foulest of odors.

There was no birefringence nor prismatic display reflecting the vampire's presence in the mirrored oubliette death trap. The cleverly crafted French dungeon made escape impossible. Dracula resisted the urge to panic and assumed a comfortable meditative position in order to slow his heart and breathing, prolonging his life while concentrating on possible solutions. Long, slow, deep breaths in through the nose, slow exhale out the mouth. It now made sense. Maria Claudia's children were likely kidnapped victims of the mad witch's revenge plot for which she herself was blackmailed into compliance.

Dracula harbored no ill feelings toward her, and if he somehow survived, he would tell her so. If he survived. The sinking cell dropped through the natural spring waters in a most unnatural way.

The oubliette was meant to keep its captive prisoner away and out of sight, to be ignored and forgotten forever. In the case of the Count, this was to be taken literally. Even so, the hot water level slowly rose inside as the forever chamber sank farther into oblivion.

# CHAPTER 90

The werewolf Aoife lay there in the complete darkness of her grave vault. The tombstones and weather-worn nameplates revealed the basic stats and resting places of the travelers beneath. The desecration of decorum was unabashedly sacrilegious. Trapped miles from nowhere in a frozen grave vault in a remote tundra cemetery hundreds of years old, surrounded by death and decay. The rainbow's end.

Aoife couldn't help but think of a story that her mother told her about her grandmother. Back in those days, when people were buried, the inside of the casket contained a string which was attached to a bell hanging above the grave. Apparently, it wasn't unusual for people to be buried mistakenly while they were still alive. Whomever pronounced them deceased was sometimes wrong. The person in the casket could ring the bell from inside the grave when they became conscious. This had happened to her grandmother, who rang the bell from her coffin and was subsequently dug up. She lived for another six years. Desperate, Aoife felt for a string but found none. Given her luck, she thought, even if there had been one, she was sure the string would have broken.

Her mouth was as parched as paper. Not a drop to moisten the tongue or nourish the spirit. She so much wanted to howl, but couldn't even purse her lips, so she hid in the quiet of her alone. The silver colloidal poison diffused in her blood was coursing through her veins as she began to realize that her organs and bodily functions were slowing and starting to end. She felt like a wounded animal being put out of her misery. She had never been afraid of the dark, even as a child. There wasn't anything there in the dark that wasn't there in the light. Except death. She started to feel the air in the cramped box getting thin and stale and an overwhelming sense of claustrophobia was setting in. Poor Ralph. Calm down. Just breathe. Her telltale heartbeat grew ever louder in her head till it was almost deafening.

She then became so distraught about her beloved Count that she briefly forgot her own predicament. The pangs of absence ate away at her as her heart grew fonder. They both had been through so many obstacles and fights for the freedom to love each other in a sometimes confusing world. She refused to give up now.

Aoife remembered the first time her beloved Count had professed his love for her. He was Vlad the Impaler. But she knew his heart. As if it were her own. His gaze was vulnerable and, yes, hypnotic and fraught with fragility. Dracula had spoken directly. "I am besotted with you. My soul unclear. Loving so much I can't think clearly. I give to you my heart. Do with it as you wish. Hold it, destroy it, whatever, as long as it is yours to possess. I trust you with my life. It's a big deal for the both of us. My queen, the Contessa. I would be proud to be the husband of Aoife, if you would have me as such."

She wondered what it would be like to die. She recollected times past, but didn't really see her life flash before her eyes. *Not really*, she thought. *How strange. I was a poor peasant gypsy girl who became a wolf then a wife to a man-king who became a bat and a husband.*

Aoife tried to squirm, but could not counter the wolf poison that infiltrated her organs. *Did I merely dream of love? Only to wake into an oblivion of loneliness, a truth hidden by mortal fancy? No, my heart's love is true, and that truth will suffice. Shall what we have end as in all mortal things? Many a day and night we shared together speaking about the opportunity of a living death, rescuing myself from mortal handicap as Dracula's bride. Alas, this gift, his curse, upon which he is reminded each and every new daybreak, has never weakened his resolve to protect and shield me with his heart, not from it. Should not all love eventually succumb to loss and end in death? The belief itself seems so beyond possibility or imagination as to be ridiculous if one only knew our heartstrings so tethered to their song of us.*

The darkened space that surrounded her suddenly seemed vast, as if the night sky again welcomed her. She knew that she was dying. She could see the stars in the night sky and looked for her truant lunar companion.

*I will leave you only in space, not time nor limitless boundary that is my love for you. Keep me in your heart as you will always be in mine.*

"*Te iubesc*," she attempted to say to herself, leaving only the absence of sound.

She heard only the rhythmic clonk that she assumed were her silver-tainted heart valves beating louder and louder. She'd been in the sensory-deprived box so long that she'd begun to hallucinate. But suddenly Aoife realized that the sound wasn't coming from her own body within, but without. Someone was actively trying to free her from the silver box that was her grave.

# CHAPTER 91

Fortunately, before they took off from the hospital helipad, Saul had applied the combat tourniquet to himself as he had to others so many times before, and it seemed to be doing its job. The Combat Application Tourniquet was fairly easy and speedy to apply, especially useful in life-threatening injuries of which amputating a hand was one. The C-A-T incorporated a single routing buckle with reinforced windlass and clip and was optimal for one-armed applications. The Gen 7 C-A-T had a free-moving internal band which provided circumferential pressure to the injured extremity. Once adequate hemostasis was obtained, it was locked in place.

When he had walked into the ER, a familiar face had been up to greet him. "Are you seriously shitting me?" Grace said. "What the hell, man?"

"Hi, Gracey," Saul said. "I need your help, and I'm kinda in a rush. Can you grab me Dr. Robinson when he's free to give a quick look at this? And no, I'm not staying. Also, can you grab me a C-A-T Gen 7 and juice me up with some fluids and empiric antibiotics?"

"You're crazy."

"I know," Saul replied, "but I need to get out of here stat. Please trust me. And can you tell me if Hendrix is around?"

"Anything for you, Captain," Grace said. "And your whirlybird buddy is in the lounge. There's a storm coming, you know."

Saul headed toward the lounge. "I'll be right back. Thanks, Gracey. I owe you one," he said as he held up his stump. Grace just stood there staring for a moment, shaking her head in disbelief.

After briefly debriefing his helicopter pilot friend in the lounge, Saul returned for pit stop maintenance to the ER. Now he ran to the waiting helicopter on the helipad outside St. Mary's. It was already firing up and the pilot was performing a last-minute systems check. The red and white metal bird twirled its blades and spun the gentle snowflakes in a circular triple axel or Salchow jump. The chopper pilot's name was Hendrix and he greeted Saul with a handshake and welcomed him aboard. Saul strapped in and joined him on the headset. They again discussed the potential hazards that the weather might present and went over the equipment for the grid search. Fortunately, or not, they had done this exercise together before. Both of them hoped that this trip wouldn't make one too many.

As the flight for life lifted off, Frankenstein realized how fortunate he was to be able to mount a rescue this expeditiously. *Friends in high places,* he thought. He meant the hospital administrator and numerous others who thought they were beholden to his past actions and sense of duty.

But then he looked up into the sky. The snowflakes descended gently onto his visage, obscuring his view and disguising the distance. He just hoped and prayed that the storm didn't get worse.

# CHAPTER 92

The National Weather Service defines a blizzard as a storm with large amounts of snow or blowing snow, winds greater than thirty-five miles per hour (fifty-six kilometers per hour), and visibility of less than a quarter of a mile (zero-point-four kilometers) for at least three hours. This can lead to frostbite, hypothermia, or even a frozen death. Exposed skin can lose all sensitivity within minutes.

A Machiavellian blizzard was set to wallop the Northeastern U.S., including Vermont. Power outages and wind chill were predicted to reach record proportions. The chances of bombogenesis creating a bomb cyclone or winter hurricane seemed likelier than not. The polar vortex had been around for 4.5 billion years, and this winter was no different as it responded to the arctic blast's invitation.

Six a.m. Usually never a time for children to rise from sleep prematurely, unless of course it was a possible snow day. The cold winds and harshest temps couldn't bury the positive chain of events that could make your school one of those lottery winners to get a free day off. The radio and TV spoke the god's truth that was heeded in good faith. Ask and you shall receive.

Most schools had already cancelled. Regardless of the weather and its misgivings, a fourth or more of the students had gone missing. The next holiday was fast approaching and locals were wondering if they were ever going to have any resolution to their nightmare.

You better watch out. You better not cry. You better not pout. I'm telling you why...

The devil is coming to town. And he has his own ideas about holiday spirit.

# CHAPTER 93

The deserted graveyard. The EMS helicopter was equipped with infrared heat-seeking and night-vision technology. As a favor to Saul, Hendrix the chopper pilot had opted to fly and conduct the search despite the cautionary weather forecast. They both reconnoitered systematically in a grid pattern over the area described by the good Dr. Jekyll and came up with a hit. Smack dab in the middle of a snow-covered abandoned cemetery in what once was Pownal, just south of Glastenbury. There was some weird interference, but it was there.

The EMS pilot landed the chopper with difficulty and dropped Saul off before the treacherous weather no longer allowed him to be airborne. The wind was really picking up and the soft snowflakes were falling hard. Saul thanked him as the helicopter swayed skyward through the wind-torn backdrop of snowfall and gravity.

Frankenstein piloted the remote drone from the ground with his one good hand and the stump where his other hand used to be. The remotely piloted aerial system (RPAS) was of little use given the tumultuous weather. It was becoming a whiteout. Just before the drone crashed, the handheld flight controller image display showed an infrared hot spot not far from his location in the middle of the old cemetery.

Saul trod his way over to the spot. It was a weathered stone mausoleum, still standing in the middle of the snow-covered gravesites.

Just beyond it was a steaming geothermal spring nestled in the back. The pungent, eggy smell of sulfur was pervasive.

Saul Frankenstein was exhausted and lightheaded from blood loss but fought through the fierce wind and snow. Out of breath, he bent over and coughed and spit up on the stone statue before him. It appeared to have once represented an angel, now embittered by time, standing guard or welcoming visitors to the mausoleum.

He used his semi-frostbitten remaining hand to hold himself up as he leaned over to read the worn and barely perceptible name chiseled into the marble: Wunderwolfe. How ghastly evil were these people? No, not people. Monsters. You make your own bed to lie in. Just not this one.

Saul grabbed the Zune Lotoo tactical folding hatchet, shovel, and multi-tool from his backpack and smashed open the lock and chain on the outside door. He was breathing so hard into the white-out, he couldn't distinguish his frozen breath from the sky above or the ground below.

Unable to take another step, he fell through the door onto the floor of the tomb within. There at the back of the crypt hung the lifeless body of a young man nailed to the concrete wall with heavy spikes. Dead as grave dirt. It was Krystiyan, one of the EMT ambulance drivers. A horrific, deranged Santa crucified for someone else's sins. Captain Frankenstein had worked with him on several occasions and they held a mutual respect for each other. *Poor kid. What the hell did he ever do to deserve this?*

At first, Frankenstein thought that the drone's heat signature had come from Krystiyan, but suddenly he heard the faintest moan coming from within the oblong box at the boy's feet. On the altar before him was an ornate silver coffin etched with ancient images and dialect. He walked over for closer inspection and definitely heard something coming from the fancy burial box atop the catafalque.

Seeing that it was locked, Saul swung the Zune Lotoo hatchet blade down hard on the hinges. The shovel clashed and clanged to no effect until Saul just jumped at the metallic sarcophagus and used his enormous mitts to attack the lid. Finally he fell to the floor, panting, and leaned up against the bier, looking to Krystiyan for advice. All the while the young man on the wall just gazed on with wistful yet dismissive eyes.

# CHAPTER 94

Dirty nails scraped away the hopelessness encasing the casket. A second wind led to a third and fourth attempt to crack open the grave. Suddenly, the coffin lid flew open to reveal a most beautiful sight and face. Aoife looked up at the heavily scarred, imperfect face of an angel. It was Frankenstein! She tried in vain to smile and mouth the word *Saul*, but he was too busy lifting her out of the sepulcher.

"Hang in there, Aoife. I know you can do this," he said commandingly. His EMT instincts took over and he quickly but precisely and efficiently went about his work, all the while calmly explaining and orienting his friend to their present situation. Saul noted that she was responsive and breathing on her own but shallow, like Hyde himself. Upon opening her mouth to check her airway, he found the small child's silver spoon and removed it. What madness.

"Henry Jekyll texted me what had happened and roughly where you were. He also told me about the concoction that you were injected with. Apparently Mr. Hyde wasn't as discreet as he thought. A friend of mine choppered us over the area to search, but he had to leave 'cause of the sketch weather. I've been trying to track your phones but found your thermal signatures with a drone to get me the rest of the way here. This is somewhat risky, but we're out of time. I have O-negative blood, so I'm a universal donor. I've always signed the organ donor box on my driver's license. I just never knew if any of my organs would be used. Or who they came from for that matter. Hold still, please."

He zipped open his emergency medical backpack kit and went about inserting the lifesaving tubing into Aoife's antecubital vein. Saul had never before attempted a field transfusion, but he knew that she was dying. The silver-enriched poison circulated through her body like an unwanted party guest.

As a result of the argyria, Aoife's skin and mucous membranes had taken on a bluish-gray hyperpigmentation from the deposition of the silver granules. Silver colloidal infusions had been used by doctors in the old days to treat a variety of maladies, but this was different. Deadly different. She was going into organ failure.

He smiled and did his best to maintain sufficient poise, but his scarred forehead betrayed him with a bead of sweat, his heartbeat steady but out of sync with hers as the lifesaving blood dripped away like seconds.

Frankenstein held Aoife's hand in his. The one he had left. The monstrosity of his grip seemed to overshadow her subtle, nubile palm. But he knew better. She was the best of the bunch. The glue by which they would have never otherwise held together. She was smarter and stronger and he'd be damned if she died today. He prayed and consoled and tried to support her innate ability to survive.

Saul was monitoring the werewolf's vitals when, suddenly, she coded. He attempted to rouse her without response, then checked her carotid artery to find it pulseless. His training took over again and he started CPR. Performing proper CPR with one hand and a stump was challenging, but doable. After a few cycles without effect, he knew exactly what she needed. Electricity. Frankenstein grabbed the AED from his emergency backpack and went to work. He placed the AED pads properly and charged the unit until it gave the instruction to defibrillate. Force of habit caused Saul to shout, "Clear!," and joules flowed through Aoife, giving her more treasure than any precious gem ever could.

The human body generates more bioelectricity than a 120-volt battery and over 25,000 BTUs of body heat. Humans use redux reactions to create and store energy, just like a battery. Frankenstein was no exception. But his unique electrophysiology was somewhat different thanks to his father's ingenuity. He checked her rhythm and she was still asystole.

Frankenstein increased the energy deliverable and hit her again with the AED charge. Her chest arched forward while crackles of current coursed up and around Saul's neck and body, leaving the smell of ozone in the air. He heard it before he saw it. The faintest steady rhythmic beep of the heart monitor indicating normal sinus rhythm. She was back among the living. For the moment at least. Still not out of the woods, but she was alive. "Stay with me, Aoife. You're strong. Stronger than most. You stay alive, God damn you."

Frankenstein continued to follow Advanced Cardiac Life Support protocols and administered the appropriate meds as needed. He monitored Aoife's vitals and heart rhythm until sufficient time had passed that she became responsive and asked what was happening. Saul reassured her with confidence and kindness and continued to administer emergency medical care, the extent of which was limited by his recon field kit. Eventually he stepped out of the shelter of the mausoleum in order to attempt another sat phone call for help, to no avail. The storm was atrocious and relentless. But so was he.

He returned inside and continued to make small talk, trying to put her mind at ease while fulfilling the necessary requirements of a trained EMS paramedic. He kept both of them calm by talking in a soothing voice. "I actually have no idea what parts of me came from where. How many vital organs were male or female or black or white or otherwise. All the pieces just fit together like a jigsaw puzzle with transplantation neutrality. New stem cells allowed for minimum rejection and healthy hyperplasia. I'm basically a walking, talking transplant survivor, nothing more, nothing less. I'm forever thankful to those who donated and made my life possible. I feel compelled to pay it forward and do whatever I can to help my fellow man and woman by any means at my disposal. I can never repay their selfless gifts, but I can try my best to honor them."

Saul saw that Aoife was sleeping soundly with stable vitals, finally recuperating in the peaceful security that he maintained and guarded. He wondered who it was he was talking to. No one answered.

Frankenstein tried using the sat phone again, but he knew that the insane weather would prevent the rescue helicopter from any sort of safe flight. It was grounded. Just like the monster friends and their belief in each other. What if they were wrong? What if their reasoning was incorrect or their ideals flawed? What was the sitrep on the Count and the children? Had Saul saved Aoife just to watch her die with him? He was about to say a prayer when he remembered that it was Saturday. He grabbed the flare gun from his backpack and went back outside.

Desperate for someone to find them, he aimed the gun at the North Star and fired. The explosive projectile lit up the night sky like a Festival of Lights, and he said, "*Shabbat shalom!*" Fireworks without gunfire.

Maybe, finally, they could rest. Saul checked the werewolf's breathing and held her in his body heat and prayed. Snug as a bug. Maybe a grub or burying beetle. Huddled in the cold like little soldier rats.

# CHAPTER 95

Seconds seemed like hours seemed like no time at all when the box oubliette finally came to rest on the bottom of the blessed hot springs. The boiling water filled the oubliette slowly but surely. The Count was now standing in his death trap cage waist high in hot holy water. The pain was exquisite, even for one who had lived through many pseudo-terminal events over the long years. At the moment, he couldn't remember anything that had been quite this painful. But wasn't that how it usually was? The suffering pain of the present being worse than the past or future.

He had pushed and kicked and punched at every enclosure joint, managing only to break most of the mirrors in his attempt to escape. He thought briefly of all that he had seen and done through the course of changing civilizations, but the only thing that he could focus on was his undying love for his wife. Aoife.

"My dearest friend and truest love," he whispered, "I give myself wholly unto you. Please, dear God, be alive. Shall we be together again after death? No man knows until he experiences it what it is like to have his own lifeblood drawn away into the woman he loves. But soon I shall die, and what I now feel be no longer felt. Soon these burning miseries will be extinct."

*Vlad Tepes.* She would whisper his name in his ear, reminding him of that which came before. He remembered their early days together and the time that she informed him of what he was in for. They discussed their feelings toward one another openly and Aoife said, in no uncertain terms, "There are things that you need to be aware of. I have forty-two teeth. I have four clawed toes with a fifth vestigial wolf claw on the inside of my hind shin—some call it a dewclaw. I run on my toes and can reach thirty-eight miles per hour. I have over three hundred million scent cells and can hear up to six miles away in the forest. I have been known to eat twenty pounds of meat in one meal and swim up to eight miles. They say my howl can be heard twenty kilometers away. I don't hibernate and I am very loyal. Oh, and by the way, wolves mate for life."

The Count was completely mesmerized and unfolded his heart. Dracula, the undead, had never felt so alive as when he met her in his vulnerable embrace and dared a kiss that he knew would never end. Until now.

Dracula's beguiled, opalescent eyes longed for his betrothed. Cut to the quick by the slow, stabbing pang of death twisting his heart like Hyde's corkscrew-crooked smile. He again tried hitting the mirror-plated glass which lined and covered the interior of the steel cage behind. He pounded and pounded and pounded, weaker and weaker as his will and life force grew dim.

"At best, I am no more than a mote of dust. An inflection passing fancy upon the undead. At worst, misplaced misfortune. The past is lost. Time tells no one the truth, until it's too late. One can only cheat death for a while. Eventually, it finds you, or you find your way to meeting the last stranger," said the Count to his lack of reflection in the broken, bloody glass.

The misshapen shards of mirror discarded him. Dracula saw the blood on his hands and tasted the salty drops on his lips. "I drink to thee, my love." He gently punched the wall one last time out of spite, and the wall of the forever chamber exploded, releasing the Count into the open water surrounding the trap.

Disoriented, confused, and in shock, he swam upwards in the direction toward which his body happened to float. Burnt skin and dermis flayed off his ravaged body with every stroke till he could swim no more. He was stagnant in his motion and resilience.

His motionless, buoyant body floated aimlessly to the surface when the remnants of his cape were grasped and his blistered, charred, engorged remains thrown onto the snowy bank. His eyes were so grossly swollen and scorched that he could only form a slit and sliver of an opening to reveal his savior. It was Jekyll.

Dracula could only barely make out what the good doctor was saying as he faded in and out of consciousness. Something about mixing up an explosive in his compound pharmacy and detonating it underwater, hoping that the chemical components and ratios were correct so as not to blow up the Count.

Jekyll saw the perilous state the vampire was in and made haste to the snowplow ambulance parked nearby. He saw that Dracula was struggling to speak, so he bent over, putting ear to lips, and heard a barely audible question: "Aoife?"

# CHAPTER 96

The perfect winter storm gathered speed and fervor while forcing drifts and rifts to grow ever deeper Frankenstein continued to monitor the volatility of Aoife's medical status. Her situation was tenuous at best, but she had come around enough to slowly whisper, "My husband … trap … in danger … please help."

Saul didn't dare leave her side to continue the search, so he tried the sat phone again. Just then, they both heard the rumble of a diesel engine slowly approaching. As the sound grew louder and louder, Frankenstein recognized the unique signature noise of the Combi Crawler. This time it was driven by none other than Henry Jekyll, who parked as close as possible without destroying any of the permanent residents' headstones and solemn rest.

Jekyll ran into the tomb, exclaiming, "Dracula is gravely injured. I've loaded him onto one of the stretchers in back, but we must hurry."

Saul was surprised to see the good doctor but mainly just grateful. He lifted Henry off the floor with a huge bear hug and said, "Thank you."

They worked together quickly to load Aoife into the ambulance while Jekyll informed Saul of how he came to be there. He had left town after delivering his holiday gift and traveled in his pharmacy's delivery ATV to the ghost town to search. He continued, "I couldn't help but face him. I have to stand up for what's right, don't I? I'm lucky to have made it on time. That was close. I saw what happened to Krystiyan. I'm so very sorry. He was just a kid, really. I'll help get him down. Let's load him in the ambulance. I found it parked over behind the hot springs. It wasn't buried in snow and it was still warm, so I think Krystiyan might have driven it. And there was a picture of that Ukrainian nurse on the dash. Thankfully the keys were there. We must move quickly if we are to save the others. Make haste!"

Krystiyan was starting to exhibit some degree of lividity and post-mortem rigidity, indicating that he'd been dead for a couple hours. The muscles in his face, more specifically his eyelids and jaw, were stiff and his forelimbs were contracted as if still winning an arm-wrestling contest. His core body temperature could be misleading as to time of death given the environmental surroundings. His twisted corpse was bent into obtuse positions that were comically tragic. An inarticulate action figure that might not fit in the stretcher space. There was no dignity in a malicious death. As they took the young man's body down, the wind continued its measured breath, removing any practical hope of a happy ending. No good deed goes unpunished.

The Emergency Alert System alerted phones and media that there was a winter storm warning in effect and any means of travel was advised against except in an emergency. The snowplow ambulance had been made exactly for response to wintry search and rescue needs and transport where other vehicles were useless. It was fully equipped to provide critical care during the transport of patients to a hospital. The diesel-fueled Combi Crawler enabled high mobility operations on intense snowy and hard land conditions by its self-snow-track system. It had the ability to reach designated areas on all terrains with its front, snow-plowing shovel and traction.

In addition to the usual LED warning light bars mounted on the roof and sides, its rear had inside storage for four persons with a stretcher-loading ramp. The snow ambulance contained an external defibrillator, electronic ventilator, emergency medical kit, Trendelen-burg and reverse Trendelenburg gurneys, and stretcher trolleys. The four independent tracks could tilt up or down providing an inclined ramp for climbing over obstacles or spanning uneven terrain. The front cab had two heated swivel seats, which comfortably accommo-dated Jekyll while Saul and their three patients, two of whom were still hanging onto life, would ride in the back med bays.

Frankenstein wasted no time implementing his contingency res-cue plan with the help of Henry Jekyll. They transferred Aoife and Krystiyan to the snowplow ambulance. Once both the Count and Contessa were safely secured onto the stretchers in the Crawler, a woozy Saul hit the lights and sirens and handed the wheel over to Jekyll. The front cab of the Combi Crawler first response vehicle held the snowblade and was separated from the mobile ER medical bay mounted over the back tracks.

Saul exited the warm cab back into the biting cold and looked ahead. The white-out looked the same as behind, and all around for that matter. You couldn't see shit. Thankfully, they had the onboard navigational system, which came in a variety of languages and voices. One of the pay-per-play celebrity voices was Wanda Sykes, and he remembered that once someone had left it as the default setting. The next time that Saul used it, he heard her voice yelling at him for "going the wrong goddamn way. Dumbass."

Captain Frankenstein fumbled his way around to the back med bay and climbed aboard to tend to his friends and patients during the journey. Jekyll hauled ass over the rough tundra while Frankenstein radioed St. Mary's ER regarding the transport of the two patients, their conditions, and the timeline so that the doctors, nurses, and ancillary staff were prepared for their arrival. Saul realized that they still hadn't discovered the location of the witch and missing chil-dren, but rather than continue a blind search and rescue, he made the decision to proceed with the emergency medical treatment and transport the critically injured victims entrusted to his care. All the chips were on the table and falling as they may.

# CHAPTER 97

D r. Henry Jekyll floored the huge, weathered vehicle blindly into the onslaught of snow and freezing rain. The rapid echoes from the frozen-water projectiles pattered the metal roof like gunfire. He was hoping that he'd at least be warned of an upcoming, unseen cliff or river ahead, but then he preferred not to imagine that the last voice he would ever hear would be Wanda Sykes calling him an idiot "Ibufuckinprofen." Saul squawked over the walkie. "Henry, you doin' okay, bud?"

To which Jekyll replied, "Yeah, I guess. Not sure what all these buttons are for, though, and something keeps trying to talk to me. It sounds like some kinda K-pop."

Saul's voice broke over the walkie, "Don't worry, you're doing great. The GPS app has countless different language choices. You're a pro. How long have you been driving a Combi Crawler?"

Henry genuinely replied, "What's a combo-crawler?"

Saul laughed. "Ouch. You're hilarious."

Henry scrolled his finger across the touch screen past country, comedy, and news to land on a prerecorded message. It was from Krystiyan. From the grave. His voice sounded of desperation. He must have recorded it when he was out searching. Dr. Jekyll was hesitant at first, but thought better of it and hit play.

"Dearest Maria Claudia. I guess I'm recording this just in case something happens to me. I am frantic to find you and the children. If for some reason you do find this recording, please get help. Run away as fast as you can. I know that you can escape whatever predicament confronts you. You have before. It's crazy. Just when you thought that the worst was left behind, the evil in your rear-view mirror, then some new demons arise. I can't imagine what you're having to go through, but I promise that we can get through it together. Please help us find you. I love you. I cherish the world that you walk in. I want a future with you. With me. Please be safe. I am heartbroken without you. Please come back."

The air went silent as the digital voice recording from the corpse in the back had its final say. Henry Jekyll couldn't help but think of his own past love, lost to his own obsession. He had been engaged to be married before his experiments in medical metamorphosis consumed all his time. Neuropharmacology exploring the truest nature of man. Duality devoid of guilt.

Dr. Jekyll reached over to turn off the cab's media player. As he did so, the snow ambulance hit a bump and he accidently knocked over Captain Frankenstein's go bag, which had been tossed onto the front passenger swivel seat. Henry looked down and glimpsed a shimmer of memory. It was an infant's small spoon. A baby silver spoon to be exact. There was a name on it. Henry.

Even though he had turned off the sound, the good doctor could still hear the voice of Krystiyan resounding in his head. Saul was busy in back checking diligently his precious patient cargo while Henry Jekyll rode along with his thoughts. The snow came down even fiercer while the Crawler's lights fought through the ever-shrinking visibility.

Jekyll checked the driver's side mirror just outside his window. For just a moment, he thought he caught a glimpse of something— or rather someone—horrible. In the reflection. Just outside, in the storm. Surely not. But it was gone now. Just the storm playing tricks. Who in their right mind would be out on a hellish night like this anyway? Right mind indeed. He felt for the spoon.

# CHAPTER 98

One step at a time looked the same as any other step at a time. The snow didn't discriminate. It covered everything all the same. Until Henry and Saul both heard it: a boom-like crack that meant only one thing. Suddenly the Crawler's heavier rear end broke through the ice over some unseen lake. They were frozen briefly in space and time. No one breathed nor redistributed any weight for fear of sinking amid the ice to a watery grave.

Saul walkied Henry. "Henry, are you okay? We just broke through the ice back here. We need to evacuate the vehicle with the patients before this tank sinks all the way through. Henry, do you copy?"

Henry Jekyll thought for a moment. His head hurt so bad he couldn't think straight. He was shaking and sweaty. He grabbed the walkie and said, "Saul, I need you to grab a few items from the back and hand them to me through the back door. Just trust me, please, there's no time."

After receiving the request, Saul replied, "Copy that," and very carefully gathered the items. Henry exited the cab quickly but cautiously, the giant snow machine grumbling and shuffling as if it too were impatient.

Henry banged on the back door of the med bays and Saul carefully handed him their last-ditch attempt at survival. One shot. Henry quickly yet precisely placed the compacted, deflated emergency life raft under the sinking rear end of the Crawler and squeezed as much sodium azide powder into the inflation port as he could. He tore the wire from the left rear blinker and shoved it into the same port with a quick wrap of duct tape to seal the deal.

Henry ran back up front and jumped into the driver's seat and punched it and hit the left turn signal. The nitrous gas generated by the chemical reaction and electric current only took .3 seconds, and the impromptu airbag life raft exploded, shooting the ass end of the Crawler into the air and forward while Jekyll stared ahead and kept it floored. The metal beast lurched forward out of the ice hole and sped violently forward up and over the next hill, gaining further speed as it descended the other side.

Saul got on the walkie and said, "I'd kiss you if I hadn't just vomited."

At the same time, Wanda Sykes was saying, "What the fuck is wrong with you?" Jekyll just kept focus ahead, not behind although he could swear that he still saw something back there.

# CHAPTER 99

The night had worn on and out when an exhausted Captain Frankenstein and a white-knuckled Dr. Jekyll finally found their way to a newly plowed road. The snow ambulance crawled along steadily through crossroads leading to the main thoroughfare and St. Mary's Hospital. The inclement weather was a double-edged sword for the ER. Oftentimes, the weather would warn many of the public drunks and troubled souls to stay home. On the other hand, the wintry mix played a supporting role in admissions due to cardiac events and vehicular misfortune.

Dracula and Aoife were triaged and treated accordingly while Krystiyan's remains went to the morgue for the medical examiner's review. Fast paced efficiencies outpaced the emotionally crippled victims and their families as they succumbed to the situation.

The ER staff worked effectively and adeptly like the professional team of caregivers that they were. A busy buzzing hive of personnel surrounded the Count and Contessa and got to work. They held no bias nor prejudice toward the injured, suffering victims which the vampire and werewolf indeed were. They didn't see monsters—only dying casualties of some terrible misfortune.

Dracula was kept out of all UV light, natural or otherwise, and placed in a hyperbaric chamber for his third-degree burns. Aoife was treated with plasmapheresis and antibiotics and placed on a ventilator until the side effects of the tetrodotoxin wore off. She was quite lucky that she didn't need dialysis for her kidney damage or a lung transplant.

Saul and Jekyll stayed all night in the waiting room, pending test results and doctors' prognoses for the injured husband and wife. The waiting area was strewn with newspapers, water bottles, blankets, swaddling clothes, and a much-appreciated coffee dispenser. In the corner was one of the hospital's artificial Christmas trees, garnished with paper wishes and broken hearts. Beneath it rested several beautifully gift-wrapped presents with nothing inside except empty hope and wishful thinking. But sometimes that can be enough.

So they sat and waited … in the waiting area. A middle-aged woman sat nearby, and Saul noticed that she had been crying. He handed her a box of tissues and asked if she needed anything. She replied, "Thanks. I'm just worried about my mom. This is so crazy. We didn't think we'd be spending the holidays like this."

"Copy that," Saul said, gently. "I hope everything goes well for you and yours."

"I'm Linda, by the way," she said as she shook Saul's calloused hand.

"Saul," he said. "Pleased to meet ya. I'd wish you happy holidays, but, you know." His eyes roamed the room.

"You know, I wasn't worried until today. She's been really lucid and everything, but today she told me that she spoke with an angel. Can you believe that?"

At that precise moment, a young man in hospital scrubs wheeled a large concert grand pedal harp on a dolly past the waiting room door. The dolly wheels squeaked slowly as the six-foot freestanding instrument with forty-seven strings rolled by the open doorframe, in then out of view. As the surreal seraphic cargo crept on, the two of them looked at each other and busted out laughing. "What the hell?" said Saul, giggling.

"Don't even … no jinx!" Linda snickered, then shushed so as not to wake Henry.

It was the holiday season, and the hospital chapel wasn't far, they thought for maybe some holiday music. Henry Jekyll had been nodding off and fading in and out of sleep, finally surrendering to rest in the comfortless chair. Saul hoped that his newfound friend would be able to get forty winks at least for his sacrifice. He thought Jekyll looked haggard, as if he had been burning the candle at both ends.

"Pleasant dreams, my friend. You deserve it," he said softly to the good doctor. Little did he know what dreams awaited his friend. Nightmares to be sure. Dreams had little to do with it.

As the room of strangers waiting patiently together finally dozed off to sleep, they were given the good news. The ER doc entered the room and calmly conferred the status of their loved ones. Both Count and Contessa would pull through, and their status would be downgraded with the next day's round of orders. Soon they would all be together again. Live to fight another day.

A great sigh of relief came over Henry and Saul, quelling their worst fears. The two of them thanked the staff and each other and went to their respective homes for some much-needed rest themselves as the hesitant clock crept forward in time.

# CHAPTER 100

*I've pulled back the veil of mystery surrounding the human subconscious mind. I've looked into its eyes and seen our past. My past and, pray tell, my future. The more that we understand about human consciousness, the better the chance we give ourselves at overcoming our problems and the diseases of the human central nervous system, the nature of which we are only barely beginning to understand. The poignant truth piercing the shield protecting the psyche. Bisecting pathways converging in fight or flight decisions times two. The gross vivisection of values does not impart the potpourri of personalities comported with indifference. Hunting monsters: the most dangerous game. Kill or be killed. A one of a kind trophy taxidermied to hang in a rumpus room, or some other indignant, undignified final resting place. King of the beasts. Alpha predator. The thrill of the kill. A Freudian slip of the tongue French-kissing the ego. A threadbare balance between temperament and judgment. The never-ending battle between the id and the superego. Unpredictable at best. At worst?*

—FROM THE JOURNAL OF DR. HENRY JEKYLL

It used to be called Multiple Personality Syndrome. The DSM-5-TR 300.14 defines Dissociative Identity Disorder as the presence of at least two separate and distinct personalities within an individual.

Hyde: "Alone together on such a splendid night. It surely must be fate. It's finally time for your comeuppance, my dear, dear Dr. Jekyll. I mean to be the end of you!"

Jekyll: "You're clearly insane or faking it, you fool."

Hyde replied by biting off three of Jekyll's fingers and retorted, with garish delight, "You're right. I'm faking. And your fingers tartare were delicious. Best finger food I've had. You need to quit smoking, though. Aftertaste of nicotine. Yucky. Let's keep playing, though."

Henry Jekyll winced with pain. "Keep playing what, you psycho?"

Hyde: "Why, Hyde and seek, you silly goose. I'll count to ten. One, two, three, four..."

Jekyll: "Wait, what?"

Hyde: "...five, six..." Running to beat the band, from the unleashed id of the devil himself.

Hyde: "...seven, eight..."

Jekyll: "Someone, please help! Help!"

Hyde: "...nine, ten! Ready or not, I'm gonna kill you!"

Screams and laughter harmonized like some macabre symphony of the damned. The crimson night mist hinted of metal and wickedness. The final act played out for an audience of none. An unholy

Hyde was too busy licking his filthy Neanderthal fingers. Baying to the man in the moon, receiving neither a reply nor an answer.

Jekyll wiped the fogged glass of the bathroom mirror, suddenly seeing himself again for the first time. Yes, it was he, Jekyll, with the reflection of Hyde blurring the edges. He still had the aftertaste of Hyde in his body and being. His bloodied hands were marked up with offensive wounds and three missing fingers, which he tried to purify under the cold faucet water. He was in control again. But for how long?

"A matter of perspective, really. Beauty in the eye of the beholder. It takes all kinds. How is Hyde so different? He relies on baser instincts on a more primal level. Who's to judge one versus the other? Maybe when you see more meal than man. Gross." Dr. Jekyll proceeded to produce projectile vomitus, blowing chunks of dinner and dignity onto his expensive blood- and finger-covered shoes.

His conscious superego voiced inner shame and guilt and looked closely into the mirror, trying to get a glimpse of the other guy. Was he half of a *folie à deux*, the madness of two? But it was just him. The ego conclusion to the equation. The reality of his inner voices exalted and exhausted his morality as he himself was still playing hide and seek between Jekyll and Hyde. *Ready or not, here I come.*

*His voice inside my head. I think it's my voice. Not sure who's scratching their nails on the blackboard inside of my brain. Projection and transference toward someone else who just so happens to be me.*

He looked into the mirror yet again but didn't recognize who it was looking back at him. He started to weep. It was him all along. Hyde and Jekyll. One and the same. He grabbed one of the numerous bottles in the back of the dusty shelf. It had a red sticker with a small skull and crossbones on it and he removed the stopper. He toasted to the stranger in the mirror, who graciously toasted him back, and they both took a long swig of the poison. He collapsed, finally succumbing to its effects and into the peace and solace that was once lost to him. No longer hidden, he would seek no more.

# CHAPTER 101

No one likes being alone on the holidays. Even one as nasty and diabolical as the old woman Bridgett Bishop. The witch knew that her plans had failed, so she moped and sulked and paced around the enormous fire in the drafty remains of what once was a home in the town of Glastenbury. But a home requires love. Otherwise, it's just a grave.

Her acrimonious sentiment was like venom in her own mouth at this point. She had bit her lip in frustration and now it was so swollen that every time she chewed or uttered certain words it broke open again. She didn't even bother to wipe the blood spittle that formed in the corner of her mouth, occasionally forming a tiny blood blister bubble. At least she would still kill all of the remaining kidnapped children just to reach into the town's heart and shit on it once more. After dinner of course.

She stared into the fiery blaze past the flame and spoke out softly, to an empty room, "I knew you were still alive."

"You call this being alive? I can't change back! Ever!" said the voice.

"You should be dead, though," replied the witch calmly.

"I don't know how to live. What makes you think I'd know how to die?"

Bridgett countered, with a smirk, "Practice makes perfect."

"I didn't die that day in the hospital, not totally," said the voice from the great beyond. "I removed my sensors and monitors, leaving behind a monotonic flat line, hoping to return. I thought that the better part of valor would be to preserve my anonymous 'condition' to enable my efforts to continue unabated. Somehow I made it back to my lab. Once home, I used my office as a bedroom by day and continued my research in the lab by night, taking full advantage of the countless resources at my disposal.

"After I went away and attended to my wounds and healed little by little, I thought for sure that the effect would wear off. All of my calculations predicted it. My math is correct! But then ... I realized, slowly but surely, that the nanoparticles had permanently altered my genetic structure. Did the potion you doused me with somehow combine with the thermal energy of fire and the nanoparticles to create some unforeseen side effect? Whatever the variables, my condition is irreversible! My genetic profile is altered, permanently; I checked against my prior DNA data. I simply cannot change back to being visible."

"So why didn't you go back to your so-called friends? Or should I say *monsters*?" asked the witch sarcastically.

"At first, I just didn't have it in me to tell them," Ralph said. "Just didn't ... have me. Sometimes I'm not sure if it was the wind or myself moving things. Not sure I even existed. How could anyone love something that isn't even there? Avoiding rejection before it inevitably happens. I guess it could come down to philophobia. Intense fear of love. Or becoming emotionally connected to another person."

"You're such a pussy," the old witch said with a sneer. "Oh, and BTW, I thought you should know that one of the kiddies mentioned you by name. I think he said his name was Kwamin, or Kwamee. Born on a Saturday. I caught him snooping around, so I asked him to help me move a cabinet. I offered to pay him, but he refused to take an old woman's money, so I locked him in the cabinet. He kept muttering something about you coming to rescue him, over and over." She smiled. "He even said that as I put him in the oven. He was absolutely delicious. There was a hint of pure innocence and succulent sweetness to him. Oh well." She burped.

Ralph felt the blood rush out of his head and started to faint and woozily fell to his knees. Kwamee. Born on a Saturday.

His whole body was numb and empty. He truly was a vacant, invisible nowhere man. A nothing man. An overwhelming sense of absence filled him. As he started to crawl into a fetal position, he heard the evil witch giggle and snicker and then burst into laughter.

The see-through man reacted impulsively and grabbed the nearest thing to him and threw it at the witch. She simply ducked and the book landed in the blazing firepit. But Bridgett noticed quickly that it was her prized possession. *The Book of Shadows*. The book that she had taken from Connor and Noah's rare bookstore.

The old, yellowed parchment burst into flame, and the fire roared to life as the hysterical witch dove to retrieve the one-of-a-kind tome. Without thought, the transparent man rushed the old woman as she bent over the all-consuming inferno. He charged head on into Bridgett, shoving her surprised body into the open flames of disbelief. She lit up like a leaf ablaze and screamed and screamed and screamed and screamed, until finally there was nothing but the crackle of the flames.

The witch's broom stood defiantly in the corner, so Ralph picked it up to toss the wicked kindling into its owner's cremation.

Suddenly, the burning woman reached out all aflame and grabbed the broom handle trying to pull Ralph into the grave with her. Ralph pushed her back into the fire pit and held her in place with her own besom as the twigs ignited into a white-hot conflagration. The fire rose up to welcome the cursed gift and consumed it ravenously as if it were its last meal.

Bridgett's flesh melted like a lava lamp just starting to drip. The witch's confit carcass filled the chimney and sky above with blackened smoke and retribution that was just the tip of the tongue. After all was said and done, Dr. Ellison warmed himself by the unholy pyre fueled by evil intentions. He knew that from now on until forever, he would be a hollow, empty shell. A dry and brittle carapace covering the absence of presence of mind. An invisible man.

# CHAPTER 102

Isolophobia, also known as autophobia or monophobia, is the irrational fear of being isolated or alone. The dread of being ignored or unloved can be overwhelming and stifling, causing the affected person terrible despair, and the solitude can be debilitating. Extreme changes in behavior that can negatively impact or retard one's ability to work or have meaningful interpersonal relationships are characteristic.

Ralph was born on July 4, making his astrological sign a Cancer. The worst fear of those under this sign is being alone. They fear that they are void of love if no one is around, making perpetual invisibility particularly devastating. They can become prone to reactive attachment disorders, and their fear of abandonment forces them to sabotage significant relationships with others to counter their inevitable loss.

After his escape from the hospital, when he finally made it back home to his lab, Dr. Ellison had breathed a sigh of relief and welcomed the security which familiarity afforded. As he approached his lab he smiled at his name and titles etched in the fogged glass of his office door: "RALPH ELLISON, MD, PhD." He was almost feeling proud and comfortable when he noticed his reflection in the glass. It was that of a partial man, quickly fading. The parts that were visible were plainly grotesque and burned savagely beyond recognition, but they were disappearing like the shadow that he once cast upon the world.

The partially invisible man smashed the glass with his fists as shards of truth crashed to the floor around him. He then entered his office and went about the business of finding a cure. *But why a cure, if it wasn't a disease? No, I'm just…missing. Can you imagine being deprived of the sight of yourself? I can't remember exactly what I looked like. I stand in front of a mirror waiting for a mirage to appear like heat lightning, from a horizon never to exist.*

Once his burn injuries had healed, he was completely missing to the naked eye. Little by little he became stronger. To help expedite the process, he added daily injections of a testosterone/anabolic steroid mixture that greatly enhanced his strength and determination, with minimal side effects.

While searching for a cure, Dr. Ellison also took advantage of the adaptive light tech at his disposal. By using recent advances in metalenses and metamaterials, he was able to harness the science of transformation optics to bend light around objects. He learned that he could use a broadband achromatic metalens to render an object undetectable across the entire visible light spectrum. The metamaterial enabled electromagnetic radiation of certain wavelengths to pass freely around an object. He then adapted the same tech to develop a custom thermal biosuit to assist him in his visually challenged exploits.

The adaptive viewpoint tech worked reasonably well for inanimate camouflage. An illusion, that's all. Unlike the delusion that he could ever be normal again. The tech wasn't as proficient as the serum that ran through his veins, removing his visible existence and presence of mind.

Ralph thought aloud in the nowhere of it all.

"Some things are invisible because they're too small to notice. Microbial worlds and quark landscapes. Like specks of gold in sand. Too insignificant to notice, like at times I'm made to feel. Some mistakes can't be corrected. Ever."

His contactless existence forced him into a sologamous marriage to himself. His self-loathing blistered any hope and fostered his freedom from an unobtainable bond with anyone else. *How am I ever to fall in love or raise a family if I'm not even all there?*

No man's land.

Now, Ralph's near-death experience and inconceivable loss of his young friend cemented this cruel cascade of emotions into his very being. His soul had a hole in it that he fell into, and it swallowed him up like a dying star. An event horizon for which there was no escape nor exit. Even the light particles which he no longer reflected. Something inside of him had broken. Not all the king's horses nor all the king's men could ever modify Ralph's genetically altered quatrain of ACGT and double helices again. His disorder of the entropy of his isolated system could never be reversed.

But even so, Ralph did his best to try and console the kidnapped children who were fettered and manacled in various ways to the cement infrastructure. Hearing the boogeyman's voice from nowhere only seemed to scare them even more to the point of hysteria. Especially having been witness to the modern-day witch trial and burning. How ironic and fitting to have happened in the same place as before. History repeats itself.

Ralph knew that he didn't have the proper tools to release the children from their bondage, and even if he did, there would be no possible way for all of them to survive traveling in permafrost and subzero temperatures. So he did the next best thing and stoked the fire. He threw everything he could on it except the roof, until it was rip-roaring with red-hot tongues of flame licking their way up the chimney. You could even say it glowed. Supplies were scarce—for lack of anything else, the old witch had taken to feeding the children table scraps of each other, unbeknownst to them, to keep them plump—so for the rest of the smoke signal, he added fresh green pines, which turned resin and smoke-black like Satan's breath shouting curses across the sky.

Just as Ralph stuck his invisible face outside to examine his signal, he heard the helicopter propellers singing along with the loudspeaker announcing its presence. Off in the distance, he could faintly hear the sirens of the ground support slowly but surely making its way to his position. Thank God.

Frankenstein had debriefed his cohorts and the EMS team soon went to work. Ralph had his winter gear and vehicle stashed nearby but stayed to watch and make sure that everyone got out okay. After the house was empty again, he looked behind him one last time at the place where pain lived and shut the door.

While recuperating at the university, Dr. Ellison had "borrowed" a Hyanide multi-terrain vehicle. It was a combination dirt bike, ATV, and snowmobile using a light-flexible single continuous track that could haul ass through deep mud, sand, and snow. He sprang for the invisible cloak option, which he installed himself.

As he sped away, he looked back at the dead house with its chimney still smoldering with hate. All he left behind was a strange track in the snow and exhaust that dissipated quickly and disappeared, just like the man himself.

# CHAPTER 103

Thanks to Dr. Ellison's smoke signal, alongside Saul's debriefing info and coordinates, the police and EMS were able to converge on the exact location of the missing children in the old house in the old ghost town, and they had assembled a small army. They even called in the National Guard, which reacted with a rapid response once they were alerted where to look. Upon arrival, they found the tots chained up like animals, dirty, scared, and hungry.

They were dehydrated and somewhat malnourished, but intact. Several snowcats as well as air support were deployed to retrieve them from that god-awful place. The storm outside was clearing gradually like a tickling cough fading from a throat that had been screaming for too long.

As their irons were unlatched and warming blankets wrapped, the children were triaged appropriately. Among the kidnapped pediatric prisoners chained to the buttresses were Maria Claudia's two children. Dorian and Ivy. Somehow still alive after Hyde's procurement and subsequent imprisonment in the ghost town by the witch and her maniac cohorts. Hugs and tears and emotions were exchanged freely as the metal shackles could no longer confine them. On the outside, at least. They and the troupe of tiny rat soldiers were finally going home.

Emma, released from her restraints, ran to Ivy and Dorian and they hugged until they cried. "Not all tears are sad," said Ivy, to which they all agreed, wiping their faces. Bottled water and snacks were dispersed while numerous medical personnel went about their business and the children were eternally grateful.

"I can't believe it. I can't believe we made it," said Emma.

"I'm not kidding. Where the hell are we, sir?" Ivy asked a roving medic, who maintained his focus and just kept moving.

"Check it out," said Emma as she nodded in the direction of the boy walking over from across the room. It was Piss Pants Pete.

"He's dry as a bone," Emma said, noticing Pete's pants. "How the hell is he still alive? Doesn't he get kidnapped like every week? WTH, man."

Pete walked over to the fire where the corpse witch burned and pulled down his zipper and pissed all over her fiery grave. He then zipped up, hocked a loogie into the fire, and said, "Bitch witch."

"Badass. Note to self: Don't mess with Pete. Strong work, dude," said Emma.

As they were escorted out, Emma walked past the bloody scratches on the wall and skin scraped shackles which once held her classmates prisoner. Their cries became whispers hushed by the passing winds, lost to echoless canyons and hopeful reminders.

The old witch's remains were later identified, albeit crispy and charred, not unlike the witches who had been executed by fire long ago in the town of Glastenbury. Ralph had remained the anonymous hero, but that mattered little to the families who were just grateful to be reunited finally with their loved ones—just in time for the holidays. The spirit and fellowship of treasured days were again to be celebrated and remembered for good reasons.

# CHAPTER 104

About a week had passed and the vampire and his werewolf bride were recuperating exceptionally well. Frankenstein had been treated as well as an outpatient, receiving testing and IVs. After all, he'd been shocked, mutilated, beaten, poisoned, bloodlet, and blown up. You can't keep a good monster down.

While he was there, the ER night nurse Grace popped in to tell him that she had taken several life insurance policies out on him with herself as sole beneficiary. He laughed and said, "Gracey, you're the best."

"You better believe it, hon," Grace replied. "Good to see you, Captain. You'll haveta tell me sometime what happened."

Saul looked at her with pursed lips and shook his head as if to say, *You wouldn't believe it.*

"Nice to have you back, sir," Grace said.

Saul was also being fitted for a prosthetic hand to replace the one his father had given him, which he left somewhere on Killington Peak. He could only imagine some boarders high-fiving each other with it as they shred their way down the mountain.

The new Esper hand used intuitive self-learning technology with human-like dexterity. Electromyography-based brain-computer interfaces (BCI) gathered brain activity which, in turn, triggered robotic movement. The system collected information from over thirty

361

noninvasive sensors. Saul tried out the model, using it to attempt to contact Dr. Jekyll, but had no luck—no fault of the hand.

Aoife entered into Dracula's hospital room unannounced and uninvited and kissed his cheek. "Good morning, sunshine," she said, making sure the curtains were closed.

He winced a smile and replied, "My love." They had heard on the news of the rescue of the stolen children and their safe return home from the Glastenbury ghost town. Thankfully, law enforcement and the National Guard were able to locate and retrieve them in one piece. That is, the ones that didn't make the menu. The survivors were traumatized, but alive. Thank god.

Dracula and Aoife recalled the shocking events that they had endured and somehow survived. Thankfully it was all over. *Inshallah.* The remains of the witch Bridgett Bishop had been found in a burn pile, dead at the scene. Frankenstein had dispatched the last of the mummies, as well as the Phantom. The creature from the black lagoon was fish and chips and Hyde was MIA. Finally, the forest through the trees, the light at the end of. They both hugged and thought how easily things could have been even worse.

"No man knows till he has suffered from the night how sweet and dear to his heart and eye the morning can be. This fragile gift of life should never be forsaken or taken for granted. I sometimes think we must all be mad, and that we shall wake to sanity in straitjackets," said the Count. Still nursing their wounds, Dracula and Aoife were both just happy to be alive at all.

Aoife climbed into the ergonomic adjustable hospital bed with her husband as he groaned in pain and anticipation. While Dracula and his wife snuggled together amongst his IVs and med lines, there was a knock on the door to room 149. They both invited whomever in, and hence received a small group of unexpected visitors. It was Annie and Emma Hawthorne, and Dorian and Ivy Luminita, and Bad Ass

Pete. They all looked at each other and nodded as one, acknowledging the insanity that had become a part of their lives.

"We heard about how things went down," said Annie. "Probably not the half of it. Nobody tells us anything. Yeah, we know they're trying to protect us 'cause they love us. But we just wanted to say thanks. You guys are awesome."

"You rock my world," added Bad Ass Pete.

"Well, thanks, guys," said Aoife. "You wouldn't believe how nice it is to hear that. But you guys are the real deal. You've got our genuine respect and admiration. Not everyone would've survived."

"Not everyone did," replied Annie as the room fell silent.

Amidst the quiet, Dracula's watch alerted him to a new message from an unknown number. The Count thought, *What now?* as he reviewed the correspondence on his wrist. His heart sank just a little while he shared the news with his wife. There was more work to be done.

Jekyll had scheduled a text to be delivered at a certain time on a certain day. Which was today. And now. December 24. Christmas Eve. The cringe-worthy perma-crisis was not yet over. They had to finish what they started. Deep down in his aged bones, Dracula had had a feeling that it would come to this.

"Is everything okay?" asked Annie.

"Yes, young friends Please don't concern yourselves," Dracula said. "You've done enough already. Please, we'll take care of it."

"Are you sure we can't help?" asked Pete.

Aoife looked at the Count and then at the young'uns, and then said, "It's Christmas Eve, children. Go be with your families. That's the greatest way that you can help anyone. We're so proud of you."

They replied, collectively, "Merry Christmas."

Aoife smiled and thought, *Yeah, and say your prayers, too. Better the devil you know than the devil you don't.*

The unseen monster hid in the light, in plain sight. The second hand on the clock slowly ticked down to the bewitching hour while the mortal coil unwound over time. The true enemy had yet to be discovered. Until now.

# CHAPTER 105

Christmas Eve. Most young children were herded to bed early with the threat that Santa would be pissed and skip your house if you were still awake. Some houses just got skipped anyway. There was a light shining through the stained glass window of the upstairs church rectory while preparations were getting underway for the Christmas midnight mass.

Clearly, he was a well-respected man with numerous social duties and responsibilities. One could say that he was a man who wore many hats. Not the least of which was the miter: the two shield-shaped, stiffened halves which faced front and back with two fringed lappets that hung from behind. The mitre and crozier were commensurate liturgical tools of the Roman Catholic Bishop. Bishop Van Helsing, to be exact. The Bishop was the real puppet-master. Pulling strings and pushing buttons. The fact that his title was the same as the witch's last name was coincidental, if not fortuitous.

It was Van Helsing himself who had been complicit with the witch all along. The Bishop was descended from the vicar Van Helsing who had once saved Bridgett's life so very many moons ago. Since that time, his forebears had made a promise to God that their family would not enter the kingdom of Heaven until all monsters had been slain or vanquished from the land. He personally did not care about such verbal contracts or beliefs. He did, however, take full advantage of exploiting any and every opportunity at his disposal. His blood-line was the line in the sand that no one dared to cross. Not even the wicked witch.

Even though the vicar and his wife and children had eventually neglected Bridgett, they were still the only semblance of family that she had left. And family was everything. Overtime, the Van Hels-ings and Bridgett had forged a common bond. She was forgiven and given absolution for her sins, free to commit more at her leisure, or at the behest of her unseen benefactor. The previous encounter at St. Mary's Church between the old witch and the bishop was just a meeting of the minds. Dracula and Aoife hadn't saved the Bishop from anything other than dispensing orders to his evil first in com-mand, Bridgett Bishop herself.

Bishop Van Helsing had been gaslighting the townspeople from the start, all the while abnegating his professed basic doctrines. It was the Bishop who spoke at the town meetings. The rabble-rouser. The minister of sophistry. The good deed-doer. The symbol of parental and juvenile trust. All-around good egg. *Bless me, Father, for I have sinned.* Get in line. His unorthodox, sanctimonious, self-serving lack of virtue justified his means to other ends. He was the agent of evil doctrine graduating summa cum laude in his sect. His bitter, caus-tic speech preaching the way of misguided faith. The clickbait void of veridicality whitewashing the walls of injustice. A jigsaw puzzle of mirrored glass always with a piece missing. The piece reflecting the Bishop, auspiciously conspicuous yet hiding in plain sight.

His pocket hid a monogrammed pentagram handkerchief bearing his initials, indicating his absence of love and compassion. A man of the cloth wearing a shroud of lies with a moral compass pointing just south of down. Inciting a mob mentality, spreading fear and hatred like so many oligarchs and despots throughout history. God rest ye merry gentlemen and women.

When it came to his episcopacy, Van Helsing was a captious disciplinarian. The bishop reserved the harshest of penance for those he disliked for whatever reason. The only person that he had ever absolved of their sins was himself. He could do no wrong, he thought, in the eyes of God or Satan. He expedited cautiously the illusion of contrition, an allusion to the demon which somehow became principal. He voluntarily served the King of Lies, his dark master, under the guise of cloak and dagger and cross. How could he possibly be stopped?

He had hoped that the old witch Bridgett had kept her promise and set aside a few of the younger children for his own intimate pleasure. Their gender mattered not to him compared to the sounds of pain and terror that they could expel. The lewd and lascivious lunatic didn't consider this a sadistic fetish as much as a necessary evil to feed his ego and libido.

The Bishop was fond of flagellation and flogging the log. The flagellation of his victims of course, not himself. Do unto others and reserve self-adulation exclusively to thine own self being true. To have and to have not enough.

In truth, Van Helsing actually did enjoy his job or, rather, position of power. He was the go-between for sinners and God. The voice of reason and faith. He enjoyed participating in the sacraments when he could. Hearing the confessions and stories of the guilty who felt bad for thinking and committing sins that were far less reprehensible than the bishop's own. Pejorative pronouncements and admonishing and forgiving so that their souls were cleansed for another week at least. The bleak shall inherit the earth.

One of his favorite sacraments was that of communion. Looking down into the congregation's closed eyes and open mouths with tongues slightly protruding. Placing the wafer centrally to slowly dissolve, sometimes accidentally touching pinky to lip. Serving at marriages and deathbeds only slightly dissimilar. At least until the adultery and coveting started. A few he even followed through life, from baptism to last rites and everything in-between. The Vitruvian man with outstretched arms and legs like hour, minute, and second hands clocking away the time until the End of Days.

The Bishop was born without a birthmark, but had tattooed a small sign of his fealty to the Great Dark One, Beelzebub, onto his inner thigh. It was three 6's. He frequently touched the symbol as if rubbing a wish from a magic lamp, which always aroused him. He remembered the day that he snuck the tattoo artist into the rectory. The tattooer took a brief inventory of the equipment and supplies he had brought with him to church. The purple nurple seemed to be running low, probably because it was commonly used in so many designs. Good name for a strain of sativa. The concentrated rich, royal purple tattoo ink with blue undertones was definitely in short supply and he hoped he had enough for the Bishop's needs.

The ink-master didn't usually make house calls, but this was an exception. He thought that serving a prominent clergy member would benefit his business. Someone high up in the food chain of command. His resume reminded patrons of his trusted expertise and pseudo-celebrity endorsements. Little did he know he'd spend the rest of his life trying to forget.

The Bishop wasn't a true stigmatophile by any means; however, he did have his nipples and foreskin pierced. They were linked by a thin chain with roach-clip alligator clamps connected to a low-voltage battery source. The nipple cripple. He saw it as a kinky type of foreplay to flagellation. Van Helsing made sure to emphasize the importance of discretion to the tattooist, lest he should fear the wrath of God.

Strange enough, the ink artist packed up his supplies and equipment after he left the bishop and closed his shop that night and left town before dawn.

The bishop Van Helsing preferred wearing his ornate robes and vestments to layman's street clothes so that he could go commando in public and church without anyone being the wiser. It was his little secret and inside joke to which only he knew the punch line.

The Christmas bells of St. Mary's were ringing in the season with all of the classics. Alone in the rectory, Bishop Van Helsing was on his computer looking at sites that had little semblance to Christmas except for the red-and-white skimpy costumes. He sipped expensive whiskey and noshed on caviar and crème fraîche paid for by his victims and their families. Van Helsing smiled to himself with despicable pride and self-gratifying, carefree exuberance when he suddenly heard a voice.

"Heortophobia is the irrational fear of holidays in general. This likely is what has led you to become a despicable social curmudgeon."

The Bishop's eyes grew as wide as Christmas wreaths.

"More specifically, Christougenniatikophobia is the fear of Christmas itself, which usually comes from early childhood experience and trauma around the holidays."

"I demand to know who's there! These are private chambers between God and myself," exclaimed the bishop.

"I've got news for you, Ebenezer. You're sitting at a table for one. You of all people have betrayed the trust that love, faith, and charity has placed on you. You are definitely a few beads shy of a rosary. I dare say that you made the top of the naughty list," said no one in particular.

"Get out, demon. Be gone from these quarters!" cried the holy man as he searched the room for the source of this disturbing voice and saw nothing.

"Sorry to break it to you, pinhead, but you're all out of Christmas wishes. I'd say that if you had any good tidings at all, you've flushed them down the toilet. If you have any New Year's resolutions to make, you might consider that you'll be needing a flame-retardant smock and pointy hat, and while you're at it, bring some marshmallows. 'Cause Jacob Marley I ain't." The invisible man crept in close to within inches of the terrified Bishop's face and whispered in his ear, "Boo."

Bishop Van Helsing flew out of his oversized throne, smashing his monogrammed crystal whisky glass and decanter. His robes and ecclesiastical vestments flared haphazardly in every direction like the arms of an inflatable man at a used car lot.

It was then the Bishop noticed the wayward whisky he had flung running down Ralph's torso, evaporating quickly. "But of course. Dr. Ellison. It's a pleasure to meet you in person," Van Helsing said. "You had me startled for a second. I wasn't expecting guests. Let alone the invincible, invisible man, indistinguishable from all of your kind—monsters alike. How ironic that you lack vision and foresight. They always said you were the smartest of the bunch—a bunch of yesterday's props and pestilence. A bunch of pseudo-monsters and make-believe. You're not even real, really. Just some misunderstood freaks and knock-offs of nature having an off day. Nothing that some proper prayer and gene-splicing can't cure or console. You're just fuck-ups in costume, that's all. What's the matter? Cat got your tongue? What do you plan to do? Save Tiny Tim by convincing me to buy the Christmas goose? You're like a tiny jungle insect whose only weapon is camouflage. Compared to you, I'm the Big Bad Wolf."

Just then, the werewolf Aoife came crashing through the stained glass window behind Van Helsing, uninvited unlike the Count's usual courtesy. Hell hath no fury like a woman's scorn, especially a werewolf's. "Christ, what a fine specimen you are, my dear. Just look at those exquisite fangs of yours," said Van Helsing.

"The better to eat you with, asshole," replied Aoife.

"Charming. So you finally put all the pieces together. Big fucking deal," said the Bishop.

"How dare you even exist. You're the only real monster," Aoife said.

"Ralph was right all along. He knew there was another bad seed some-where germinating hatred. I wish he could see you now."

"Funny you should say that," the bishop replied. "Your friend, eh? How do you know how he feels at all?" Aoife looked at him curiously. He continued, "Why don't you just ask him?"

By now the whisky on Ralph had gone. She said aloud to the room, "Ralph?" She noticed his scent but couldn't believe her eyes. "Is that you?"

The tiniest golden glimmer of something shiny reflected from the firelight. There it was. Sitting on the mantle above the burning logs. It was the gold claddagh ring, with its heart, crown, and hold-ing hands. Love, loyalty, and friendship. Aoife picked it up and held it in her hand and fractured heart.

The room was deathly silent when the Bishop exited through the hid-den door, which locked behind him. "Dr. Ellison?" And she sat down, awaiting a response that never came. She didn't notice the trail of tears pooling on the hardwood floor, leading off into the future of nowhere by no one. The tiny trickle of salty droplets quickly disappeared from the glow of the fire logs' dry heat like the Ghost of Christmas past.

By now, the werewolf was saturated with sorrow and succumbed to grief. Aoife sat down by the fire and just cried. Her heart felt so heavy that she felt as though she might topple over. She cried for everyone. The children and families. For Krystiyan. She cried for all the people who had been judged cruelly and treated so inhumanely. She cried for herself and her love. She even cried for the Bishop, the broken, fallen man. And Ralph. She cried for Ralph.

The cold and snow outside whistled its way in through the bro-ken stained glass window, chilling the room and her bones. A dis-cordant wind was howling through the trees, as was Aoife, and they soon became indistinguishable from one another. Just the two howl-ing, which faded to one. It was just the wind.

# CHAPTER 106

The Bishop Van Helsing made his way from the hidden door to a secret stairwell up to the bell tower. Gambling in a game where the Bishops are wild. Doubling down on the defecation of destiny. The clanging was almost unbearable as "Silent Night" rang out at deafening decibels, piercing one of the priest's eardrums. The Bishop covered his ears firmly to little effect on the ever-so-familiar melody, running, bumping, and falling his way up the wooden staircase to the trap door above. In-between the echoes of bells, he thought he heard a voice but dismissed it.

He threw open the trap door and ran to the power shut-off switch for the preprogrammed Christmas bell app. It stopped abruptly with a deafening silence, his head throbbing with echoes of rhyme still chiming in his skull. He noticed his rapid, erratic breathing finally slowing to a normal rate and sighed in relief.

Suddenly, he saw the shadowy figure emerge from the dark corner of the open bell tower, which was exposed to the elements. The cold air and wind swished against his face along with a handful of virgin snowflakes, one of which melted on his arid, thirsty tongue. No two alike. Like people. And monsters.

Dracula himself did not abide nor condone the Draconian measures that were advanced by the Bishop despite his namesake. Van Helsing hated the Count most of all. Truth be told, he was jealous of him. He represented everything that the Bishop couldn't be. Or chose not to. It was he who had devised the vampire's oubliette and personally blessed the natural hot spring waters. It was he who spoke out at the town meetings and in church weekly, filling the air with fake truths and wicked lies. He would stop at nothing to rid the town of his greatest fear and nemesis, Count Dracula.

His bias and bigotry were cemented into his stubborn soul, regardless of religion or right or wrong. The Bishop was simply jealous of the power and control that the Count exhibited over others. He didn't realize the secret: that there was no secret other than treating others with respect, unless provoked to do otherwise.

"Of course you're here. Bats in the belfry. How droll," said the Bishop.

To which the Count replied, "You're a monster."

"It takes one to know one."

"It takes all kinds. A patchwork of people quilted together by a common thread. A belief in something better than what's left of ourselves. You're just a common criminal."

Van Helsing shouted, "How dare you preach to me! You of all people should know better. A criminal? Some of the most heinous crimes in human history have been committed under the pretense of religion. Need I remind you of the crusades, inquisitions, witch trials, and religious wars, or subjugated women, slavery, Hitler's Nazism. Hell, the thousand-year era of social stagnation which was the Dark Ages was brought on in part by Christianity. Justifiable jihads and disingenuous semantics. The countless examples of violence and tortures and abuses and corruption—do you really want me to go on? All in the name of organized religion. Why should I be any different? Why shouldn't I decide which sheep should be shorn? Who would know better than me? I am the true patriarch. They rely on me to decide for them. At least until they become civilized. It's been like that for centuries, as you well know. It's why the sheep want and need leaders like me. Not everyone can be king, or Bishop, lording over the doldrums of their daily lives. The temperance of being temperamental. Same old thing, every day, all day long, until tomorrow, when it's a brand new same old day. Why else would they put me in a position to lead them so? They don't want free will. Not really."

"Evil is simply free will run amok and gone unchecked without consequence," the Count said calmly. "Justifying and disguising evil intentions with religion doesn't have anything to do with true introspection and personal growth, anywhere. You're full of shit."

The Bishop went on, in his usual, ignominious way, "Can you even hear yourself speak? Some of the most powerful countries in the world have or have had authoritarian dictatorships. Places capable of inflicting the greatest global harm become safe havens for autocracy. Danger exists when our technological evolution outpaces our social evolution. Most people are living their lives far removed from tragedy and would rather turn a blind eye or bury their heads in the sand rather than try and tell their children that the boogeyman is real. They package and sterilize content to make it more palatable or just ignore it completely. Not until the wolf is actually at their door do they wish Red Riding Hood to get involved."

"But you're disregarding the countless millions who do care and fight however and whenever they can," the Count replied. "They strive to live in a world where people treat others as they themselves would like to be treated. You're like those you speak of: preying on those you feel are weaker by spreading shouts of fear and divisiveness. Disseminating transmissible lies like a plague across the land, forever contagious. I feel sorry for you. You don't even know love."

"Love? There's no such thing as love, or any other of that human dyslexic bullshit legalese. There is no algorithm special to apes. There is no altruistic holiday spirit. Just alternative pagan rituals inspiring more of the same. There is no Christmas. Any cloister-fucked snafus are dealt with in the confessional. Their placebo confessions of guilt are paid for in prayers and shekels, absolutely. Never to be spoken of again. I won't tell. Why should you? Half of what you believe is true today won't be tomorrow. Which shouldn't even include you, freak."

The Count listened to the man of the cloth speak, and it just broke his heart. Observance isn't the same as being observant. Our time and place apply themselves directly to now. He couldn't be more wrong, even if it felt right. The spirit of the holidays is just that. We hold onto each other's beliefs and hopes and try to make it through another cold and deadly night together. Surviving not just to survive and preserve the species, but living to be alive in all its glory, good and bad and sometimes with stupid shit in-between. He was missing the point: how you could make yourself a better tomorrow today? With a loving, caring hand along the way.

"Humans have barely staved off extinction events by the skin of their teeth," Van Helsing said confidently. "End of Days? At any given moment, an asteroid or a plague could fall into their laps. Eventually the sun burns out, or your number comes up, kinda like picking lottery numbers by birthdays. Bingo. Happenstance left to chance. People can't even believe in their own mortality, let alone the death of their species. They'll never see it coming. Or if they did, they'd close their eyes at the last second. They're already condemned, don't you see?"

"Our end will come as sure as the sun rises and sets on this very day. How you go about that day is what matters. I believe that you're wrong about the rest."

"Right or wrong? Tawdry diatribe and derelict dialect. That's hilario. A vampire taking the moral high ground," the bishop said. "How much innocent blood have you sucked today? Good and evil are meaningless ethical constructs that don't exist in nature. Culturally conceived in different places and times, developing different moral laws in order to ensure a useful social order, that's all.

"And what about AI and the future of our own evolution? Do we program those soon-to-be-sentient beings to possess a moral compass or code? If so, who writes the code? Uniquely human concepts like *time, soul,* and, yes, *love* don't exist outside of our animal Central Nervous Systems. The fallacy of the language of good and evil arises out of a certain cultural context and the fact that we are vulnerable to forgetting that the words we use are our own words."

"The limitations and relativity of language are by definition germane to the individual's expression," Dracula said. "It is that which we use to communicate with each other to hopefully increase our chances of survival. Besides, the frailties of language make strangers disappear into friends. The concept of good is the lack of self-centeredness. Evil is simply the inability to empathize with others. Peace, harmony, and balance. The way that you bow or kneel or pray, to the east or the west, leads to the same path. If you circumnavigate the globe, then east meets west and we're all brothers and sisters in-between. How can you love one neighbor and hate the next? Why not break bread together without chaos and petty, bitter disputes? Let neither table nor tract of land separate us further. Shall we not dine and grow old and die together yet apart, *como amigos*? It's the world I choose to live in. To love in. To guide my way home in this lifetime. Death has yet to cast a shadow far enough to encompass my own. Until forever, then, I will strive for peace."

"Arrogant fool!" the bishop yelled. "You seek a peaceful chaos? The symmetry of anarchy? From you I expected more—no, less. An eye for an eye and a kiss for a kiss. To the victor go the spoils and all that's left. Let death decide and have the rest. You should know. You've lived by the sword."

"But I'll die by my word," said the Count. "And I swear to you this day that I'll spend the rest of forever serving others by standing in the way of the likes of you. Apathy is food for predators. No choice is still a choice that you have to live with. I choose to stop monsters like you from harming anyone else. Karmically speaking, you're living beyond your means. Your contrition is your own but your penance is due."

The Count slowly and carefully approached the Bishop Van Helsing and offered his hand in friendship and forgiveness, despite all of the evils brought forth by this wretched poser of peace. It was Christmas Eve, after all. But the Bishop grew angry at the Count's gesture of kindness and forgiveness and his jealousy remained at full tilt. Alas, his heart knew only hate, and he despised himself for it.

Not willing to succumb to the consequences of his actions, the Bishop took three paces backwards, smiled, and said, "I'll see you in hell." Then he disappeared over the edge of the open bell tower.

The Count reached out to grab him, but it was too late. He peered over the precipitous edge to see the former man of God descend to meet his maker. He felt only sadness. What a waste. So many lives hurt and destroyed, and for what? He stood there in the dark, cool night air and took a deep breath. He missed his wife and friends and cherished the thought of reuniting with them again. Just like the families below who were rejoicing that they once again held their loved ones in their arms and hearts and homes.

Cumulous clouds covered the horizon and began to accumulate into waves. Thunder accompanied the horizontal snow and the lightning in the clouds off in the distance, as if to indicate that the storm was passing on, allowing for refuge in a new day.

# CHAPTER 107

The Count and Aoife had asked at the hospital about the whereabouts of Maria Claudia, but no one seemed to know. It was as if she had simply vanished. Her children Ivy and Dorian were physically unharmed and recovering from their traumatic experience.

There likewise was no good answer when it came to the good Dr. Jekyll. They wanted to thank him for helping to rescue them, but no one knew or would tell what had become of the talented physician. They had hoped to share with him their gratitude and express their heartfelt appreciation for risking his own life to save theirs. A stranger who became a friend. Dracula had always said that a friend is someone you can always trust to tell you the truth.

Both Maria Claudia and Henry Jekyll were added to the list of voluminous victims of the old witch's diabolical machinations.

After all that had occurred, the *broigus* between the townspeople and the Count, Aoife, and Saul seemed to have lessened, for many at least. Of course, there were some who wore their hate like a badge of honor, or disgrace, and would never exhibit some of humankind's best qualities and abilities: self-improvement and adaptation.

Others celebrated this modest group of friends as heroes, although they would never consider themselves as such. The three of them didn't see it that way. They just did what any other good-hearted person would do. Dracula was especially proud of his wife.

*You can't spell hero without her,* he thought. He didn't know how he had ever gotten along without her. A past replaced irrevocably with a better future.

And what of their dear friend Ralph? All three felt guilty for what had become of Dr. Ellison. Did the trauma and genetic and chemical changes induced by the nanoparticles somehow affect his judgment and perspective? Did it somehow twist his mind and heart?

The casualties of the witch's hate and vengeance were widespread, crossing boundaries and limits that none had considered. If Ralph had become afflicted with some form of mental illness, then they would do everything possible to help him, but he was nowhere to be found. The University and law enforcement went on to label him officially a "missing person." If they only knew how accurate they were. Even his electronic trail and social signature had become invisible.

Dracula, Aoife, and Saul talked until the words died out and there was nothing left to say. They just held each other, trying not to fall apart together.

# CHAPTER 108

New Year's Eve. Fireworks abound, illuminating the night sky in a thunderous mushroom explosion, leaving a spectral rainbow of sparks cascading back down to earth. Terror firma firmly replaced by the tranquility of tomorrow. Somewhere all over the world, someone was dropping the ball as people counted down the seconds that defined the beginning of a new year. The awkward anticipation of broken resolutions met with honest reprisals. A new start. Hopefully this year would be better than the last. At least as far as death was concerned.

*Once in a blue moon.* The cycle of the phases of the moon lasts one month, leading to twelve full moons in an average year. A lucky thirteenth full moon is called a blue moon. Many cultures and countries have different names for the full moons, twelve months and nights with twelve names. Aoife's favorite was the full wolf moon, which was the first full moon of the new year and first full moon after the winter solstice.

It happened only rarely that Aoife stared up at a full blue moon which discolored her temperament the same. Even so, it always disrupted her sleep cycle and moods, just like it did everyone else's. Blue moons only occur every three to four years. Because there are roughly 29.5 days between full moons, February can never have a blue moon. Its days are numbered, that being 28 and 29 every seventh leaping, biting, teething year. Months when February has no full moon at all are called a black moon. As rare as a hound's tooth. Or a wolf's.

That fateful orb fulfilled its mortal obligations casting moonbeams like lyrics from the songs of the earth. Tonight's forecast was for a better tomorrow. High tide washing away the residue of those would be monsters. Rest in peace. Bye, Felicia.

# CHAPTER 109

The winter weather advisory had passed, giving rise to a beautiful niveous day. The drifts had come to rest against windowsills pointing the way back home. The Count, Aoife, and Saul agreed to rendezvous at their usual place for New Year's Day. It was one of the many homeless shelters and missions and warming centers in the area.

And it truly was warm and inviting as any place on earth could be, and somehow it held the spirit of the holidays all year round. They got to meet old as well as new friends and share some holiday cheer and good tidings, toasting and laughing and rejoicing in the true fellowship of man.

The residents were just people dealt a bad hand here or there. Some were overcoming the disease of addiction or some other illness, psychiatric or otherwise. Some were fleeing dangerous and unstable domestic situations. There were any number of reasons which led them to these doors. The fact that they took that first step across the threshold is what mattered. One can never be faulted for trying to improve oneself. Truth be known, they were stronger than many simply because they had more setbacks to overcome. Sometimes walking a mile in someone else's shoes meant walking a hundred miles by comparison. One's true measure wasn't in how they got knocked down, but how they got back up.

The spirit of the holidays had nothing to do with how much money one had. It was like the wrapped Christmas presents under the tree in the hospital lobby. They were empty. Just for show. The real gift had always been love. And it was endless.

Saul carried in supplies, food, and clothing as snowflakes fell like crystals onto his face from the endless sky and great beyond. The brisk air resonated like a drum percussing against his dry, taut, scarred skin. A few cold shapes melted quickly on his tongue, reminding him that he could taste the air. He was breaking in his new bionic hand and getting used to the feel of it. The technology seemed almost magical.

Frankenstein could control his hand using brain impulses to activate specific muscle movements. It had five movable digits and was three times faster than other prosthetics. His father would have been impressed. Saul found it amusing how easily he could isolate the one robotic finger.

The daylight diminished to dusk, and Dracula was able to shed some of his protective outerwear. He hung his hat, scarf, and cape on the makeshift coatrack next to the other guests' winter garments. The Northern lights were beginning to get underway, the light show Vermont is sometimes privy to. Surface solar flares and Earthen atmospheric particulates helped create the illusion of refraction and grandiosity.

Nature's planetarium needed no Pink Floyd soundtrack to appreciate the beauty and grandeur of this amazing evening sky. The green luminescent glow bled into mesmerizing magenta, fomenting an unseen alchemy. The KP-index rising up to measure the aurora's geomagnetic activity in strokes of greens, purples, and reds. It truly was a Festival of Lights.

The three of them hugged, giving each other the gift of humanity and hospitality. A lucid and crystal clear time to embrace the love of family and friends, and even strangers who all shared in a common belief in something larger than oneself. Love. Hope. And peace on earth. Goodwill toward men and women and monsters.

They heard singing coming from the next room. The familiar song based on the Robert Burns poem about old friends sipping a cup o'kindness in remembrance of noble deeds and adventures they had long ago. Once upon a time in days of *auld lang syne*.

*Should Old Acquaintance be forgot,*
*and never thought upon;*
*The flames of Love extinguished,*
*and fully past and gone:*

*Is thy sweet Heart now grown so cold,*
*that loving Breast of thine;*
*That thou canst never once reflect*
*On old long syne.*

*On old long syne my Jo,*
*On old long syne,*
*That thou canst never once reflect,*
*On old long syne.*

With gaping hearts and gasping souls, ne'er forget the troubled times untold. A time when monsters and men and women were taught to live again.

The Count was wearing his worn, out-of-date apron while doing the dishes alongside his fellow revelers when Aoife appeared in the back porch doorway, beckoning him over. He couldn't help but notice that she was standing in the open door just beneath the mistletoe. He smiled while removing his stained apron and went to her. Her warm hair bristled as she rested her face and chin into his cold, pale skin. Though it lacked warmth, his chest comforted his true love's heart with an undying flame. Her neck was redolent and supple like a newborn day, or year.

She looked into his eyes with her green and blue heterochromic irides, which mesmerized him for a change. He said, "I love all the versions of you. Werewolf, human, it's still you. All the different idiosyncrasies. The little things that make up you. I love them all dearly. You make me want to be a better person. Vampire or not."

They kissed under the iconic red and green, leafy symbol with the full moon on full display. Their limbs entangled as the *Danse Macabre* spun them around, keeping time with the rhythm of the increasing beat of their hearts.

Aoife couldn't help but feel as if they were levitating and twirling around wrapped in each other's embrace, rising up to the stars. Bewildered, she said, curiously, "I didn't know you could fly." The Count, initially perplexed, realized that he felt exactly the same way. They simultaneously looked down to see both sets of their feet planted firmly on the ground. He kissed her ever so gently and deeply on her oh-so-familiar full lips, wishing that the moment would never end.

Manufactured by Amazon.ca
Acheson, AB